Love's Hidden Treasures

Judy Best

Copyright © 2024 by Judy Best

All rights reserved.

The content contained within this book may not be reproduced, duplicated, or transmitted without direct written permission from the author or the publisher.

Under no circumstances will any blame or legal responsibility be held against the publisher or author for any damages, reparation, or monetary loss due to the information contained within this book, either directly or indirectly.

Legal Notice: This book is copyright-protected. It is only for personal use. You cannot amend, distribute, sell, use, quote, or paraphrase any part of this book's content without the author's or publisher's consent.

Disclaimer Notice: Please note the information contained within this document is for educational and entertainment purposes only. All efforts have been executed to present accurate, up-to-date, reliable, and complete information. No warranties of any kind are declared or implied. Readers acknowledge that the author is not engaged in the rendering of legal, financial, medical, or professional advice. The content of this book has been derived from various sources. Please consult a licensed professional before attempting any techniques outlined in this book.

By reading this document, the reader agrees that the author is under no circumstances responsible for any direct or indirect losses incurred as a result of using the information contained within it, including, but not limited to, errors, omissions, or inaccuracies.

This is a work of fiction. Unless otherwise indicated, all the names, characters, businesses, places, events and incidents in this book are either the product of the author's imagination or used in a fictitious manner. Any resemblance to actual persons, living or dead, or actual events is purely coincidental.

Contents

1. New Beginnings — 1
2. Whispers of the Past — 13
3. Stories from the Past — 23
4. Echoes of the Past — 35
5. Secrets of the Old Mill — 47
6. Stronger Together — 59
7. Feast of Secrets — 77
8. Discovering True Motives — 89
9. Memories of Small Important Things — 105
10. Shadows and Reflections — 121
11. Tangled Legacies — 137
12. Family Ties and Friendships — 151
13. Mapping the Unknown — 161
14. Matters of the Heart — 171
15. Looking to the Future — 179
16. A Town's Embrace — 189

17.	Echoes of Unity	201
18.	Breaking Barriers	211
19.	A Town United	219
20.	At the Heart of It All	229
21.	A Shadowed Path	241
22.	Unlocking Secrets	249
23.	A Joyous Arrival	257
24.	Legacies Unveiled	267
25.	Love's Hidden Treasure	275
About the Author		285

Chapter One
New Beginnings

THE LATE AFTERNOON SUN cast a warm, golden hue over the peaceful outskirts of Carter's Creek. Nestled near the gently flowing waters of Carter's Creek, Emma and Luke Hunter's charming house stood as a serene retreat from the bustling town center. The annual summer cookout was in full swing, a beloved tradition symbolizing the town's resilience and unity following the tumultuous days surrounding Kevin Pollard's arrest and conviction.

Inside the spacious kitchen, the air buzzed with activity as the women of Carter's Creek gathered to prepare for the evening's festivities. The room was a flurry of movement and laughter, each woman contributing her unique touch to the array of side dishes and desserts being arranged on the long wooden table. The sweet aroma of freshly baked goods mingled with the savory scent of potato salad, creating an inviting atmosphere.

Emma Hunter, the town's dedicated mayor, moved gracefully between the counters, her hand lovingly cradling her growing belly. Her smile was radiant, reflecting the warmth she felt from her friends' presence. Hannah, Emma's best friend and a staff member at Sadie's

Sweet Rolls, was bustling around, expertly arranging bowls of fresh fruit salad.

"You're glowing, Emma," Hannah remarked, handing her a plate of Sadie's renowned sweet rolls. "We can't wait for the baby shower!"

Emma laughed softly, her cheeks tinged with a rosy hue. "Thank you, Hannah. We're so excited. It feels like just yesterday we were dreaming of living here by the creek."

Nearby, Mary Thompson, Emma's mother, was delicately placing homemade potato salad into a large serving dish. Her movements were precise, a testament to years of perfecting her recipes. She glanced up to share a tender smile with Emma.

"You've outdone yourself this year, dear," Mary said softly, placing a comforting hand on Emma's shoulder. "Everyone's going to love it."

Emma returned the smile, her eyes reflecting a deep bond with her mother. "We've worked hard to make this special, Mom. It means so much to have you here."

As the two shared this warm moment, the sound of the front gate opening signaled the arrival of the next guests. Linda, the church event coordinator, walked in carrying a tray of vibrant, colorful deviled eggs. Her practical nature shone through as she carefully arranged them on a platter.

"Hey, ladies! These are for the buffet," Linda announced cheerfully. "I hope they're a hit!"

Mary chuckled softly. "Always reliable, Linda. Thank you."

Next to arrive was Sadie, the beloved owner of Sadie's Sweet Rolls, who entered with a stack of freshly baked cookies and pies. Her presence brought an air of warmth and sweetness to the kitchen, much like her delectable treats.

"Look what I brought!" Sadie exclaimed, setting the desserts down with a flourish. "Double chocolate chip cookies and apple pie. Hope everyone has a sweet tooth tonight."

Emma clapped her hands in delight. "You're a lifesaver, Sadie. These look amazing!"

As Sadie began distributing the treats, Mary and Emma watched with pride, their smiles reflecting the strong community bonds that held Carter's Creek together.

The doorbell rang again, and Linda welcomed Ms. Beatrice and her sidekick Mabel into the kitchen. They were immediately drawn to the table, their eyes wide with excitement at the spread before them.

"Oh, look at all these wonderful dishes!" Ms. Beatrice exclaimed, her voice filled with genuine admiration. "You ladies have truly outdone yourselves."

Mabel nodded enthusiastically, her eyes scanning the offerings. "I can't wait to try them! And Emma, your fresh baked yeast rolls are incredible!"

Emma blushed slightly, feeling the warmth of the compliments. "Thank you, Mrs. Beatrice. We wanted to make this a special evening for everyone."

As more women arrived, each bringing their own contributions, the kitchen became a vibrant hub of activity. **Linda** managed the coordination, ensuring that everything was in place, while Hannah and Sadie moved effortlessly between tasks, their camaraderie evident in every shared glance and laugh.

Outside the kitchen window, Emma glanced back to see Luke manning the grill, his strong presence a comforting sight. He waved at her, giving her a reassuring smile before turning his attention back to the sizzling meats and vegetables. Though he wasn't present in the kitchen, his role was pivotal, and Emma felt a sense of pride and gratitude for his hard work.

As the sun began to set, casting a beautiful twilight over Carter's Creek, the women of Carter's Creek finished their preparations. The table was now a magnificent display of home-cooked goodness, each dish a testament to their dedication and friendship.

"Alright, everything's ready!" Emma announced, stepping back to admire their collective effort. "Let's welcome everyone and make this a night to remember."

With final touches in place, the women exchanged warm hugs and smiles, their hearts full of anticipation for the evening ahead. The cookout was not just a meal, but a celebration of community, love, and the enduring spirit of Carter's Creek.

***

As the women put the finishing touches on the side dishes in the kitchen, the backyard began to fill with the sounds of approaching footsteps and cheerful greetings. Luke Hunter emerged from the house, holding a pair of tongs in one hand and a spatula in the other. His presence exuded both charm and dedication as he expertly managed the grill, ensuring every piece of meat was perfectly cooked.

One by one, the men of Carter's Creek began to arrive, each greeted with hearty congratulations and pats on the back for Luke's recent marriage to Emma. Tommy, Luke's best friend and owner of the local hardware store, arrived first, bringing with him a cooler filled with ice-cold beers.

"Hey, Luke! You've definitely made this house into a home. Congrats, man!" Tommy exclaimed, clapping Luke on the shoulder.

Luke grinned, wiping his hands on a towel. "Thanks, Tommy. It's been an amazing journey so far."

Next came Tom Hunter, Luke's father and the owner of Southern Roots Tavern. He approached Luke with a proud smile, exchanging a warm handshake that spoke volumes of their strong bond.

"Doing a fantastic job, son," Tom said, his eyes gleaming with pride. "Emma's lucky to have you."

Luke nodded appreciatively. "Thanks, Dad. I couldn't have done it without your support."

As the men gathered around the grill, Pastor Daniel Thompson, Emma's father and the town's respected pastor, approached Luke with a friendly pat on the back. His presence added a sense of community and encouragement.

"Luke, my boy," Pastor Daniel began, his voice steady and warm. "You're doing wonderfully. Remember, serve yourself first tonight and enjoy the fruits of your labor."

Luke chuckled, feeling the weight of his responsibilities lift slightly. "Will do, Pastor. Thanks for the encouragement."

Joining them were Gabe and Mr. Jenkins, each bringing their own contributions to the cookout. Gabe, still basking in the warmth of the cookout preparations, handed out beers, water, and lemonade with ease, his demeanor friendly and approachable.

"Here you go, Tom. Enjoy a cold one," Gabe said, passing a beer to Tom Hunter.

Tom accepted it with a nod. "Thanks, Gabe. This looks great."

Mr. Jenkins, the former town councilman now running a business incubator, contributed by bringing an assortment of spicy sauces and marinades, adding a flavorful kick to the grilled offerings.

"Hope everyone likes a little heat," Jenkins remarked, setting down his sauces.

As more men arrived, the backyard filled with laughter and animated conversations. Luke glanced over to see the women gathering with Emma in the kitchen, arranging the final touches on the dessert table. A sense of gratitude washed over him as he thought about how fortunate he was to have married Emma and started a family in their dream home.

"Everything looks perfect," Luke thought to himself, feeling a surge of happiness. "We really are living our dream."

The men took their places around the grill, exchanging stories and jokes while Tom and Gabe ensured that everyone stayed hydrated and satisfied. The atmosphere was electric with camaraderie, the hard work of preparing the cookout paying off in the joyful gatherings of friends and family.

As the grill sizzled and the night sky began to twinkle with stars, Luke felt a deep sense of contentment. Surrounded by his loved ones and supported by the community, he knew that this cookout was just the beginning of many cherished memories in Carter's Creek.

***

As twilight descended upon Carter's Creek, the backyard of Emma and Luke Hunter's house became the vibrant heart of the evening's cookout. String lights cast a warm, inviting glow over the picnic tables laden with an array of side dishes and desserts. Lawn chairs, blankets, and clusters of friends and neighbors created intimate nooks for conversation and laughter.

Gabe, Tommy, Tom Hunter, Mr. Jenkins, and Pastor Daniel Thompson had already settled around one of the larger tables, plates piled high with grilled meats and fresh salads. The air was filled with the enticing aroma of Luke's expertly grilled offerings, mingling with the sweet scent of Sadie's double chocolate chip cookies and apple pie, creating an inviting atmosphere.

Nearby, Emma, Hannah, Mary Thompson, Linda, Sadie, Ms. Beatrice, and Mabel were nestled together, their voices a harmonious backdrop to the ambient sounds of the evening. Emma, her hand lovingly cradling her growing belly, shared a tender smile with her mother, Mary, as they watched the preparations unfold.

Tommy raised his beer in a toast, his voice carrying over the soft chatter. "To Luke and Emma! May your life together be as perfect as these grilled ribs."

Glasses clinked in unison, the sentiment resonating with everyone present. Tom Hunter, Luke's father, exchanged a proud glance with his son, Luke, who was expertly flipping burgers on the grill. Pastor Daniel Thompson, Emma's father, approached Luke with a warm pat on the back. "You're doing wonderfully, son. Emma and you make a great team."

Luke nodded appreciatively. "Thanks, Dad. It means a lot to have your support."

Across the yard, Gabe moved effortlessly between tables, ensuring everyone had a drink in hand. Tommy caught his eye and offered a friendly nod. "You've been a real asset around here, Gabe. You fit in so well, I'm not sure how we ever got along without you."

Gabe smiled modestly, handing a cold beer to Tom. "Glad to be of help, Tommy. Carter's Creek has been a great place to start fresh."

In another corner, Ms. Beatrice and Mabel settled into a lawn chair, their Shirley Temples in hand—Gabe had thoughtfully prepared them as a refreshing non-alcoholic option for those who preferred it. They observed the gatherings with keen interest, their eyes occasionally drifting toward Gabe as he moved about.

Ms. Beatrice leaned toward Mabel, whispering conspiratorially, "Have you noticed how Gabe has integrated so well into our community? He's such a handsome fella and single!"

Mabel nodded, her eyes never leaving Gabe. "Absolutely. And I've been watching to figure out which of our lovely town beauties might catch his eye. Haven't got a clue yet."

Meanwhile, Mr. Jenkins found himself engaged in a lively discussion with a group of men about the town's recent progress. "It's amazing how much we've accomplished since Kevin Pollard's arrest," he remarked, taking a sip of his lemonade.

Pastor Daniel joined in, "Indeed. It's a testament to the resilience and unity of Carter's Creek."

In the midst of the camaraderie, Mabel decided to bridge the conversation between the groups. She excused herself from Ms. Beatrice and made her way toward the men's table, never taking her eyes off Gabe moving between friends, refilling their drinks. Tommy noticed her approach and followed, intrigued by her intent.

"Hey, Mabel! What's on your mind?" Tommy greeted, raising his beer in a casual salute.

Mabel glanced over at Gabe, her curiosity evident. "I was just thinking about how Gabe has been such a big help around here. Don't you agree, Tommy?"

Tommy nodded, taking a thoughtful sip of his beer. "Absolutely. He's been a real asset, especially his help in gathering evidence that put Kevin away!"

Mabel leaned closer, lowering her voice. "Do you know where Gabe came from? And why he chose to settle here, in our small town?"

Tommy shrugged, his eyes still on Gabe. "Hard to say. He keeps things pretty close to the vest."

Back at the grill, Gabe sensed the underlying curiosity in Mabel and Tommy's conversation. Deciding to address it head-on, he approached them with a friendly smile, holding out a freshly poured glass of lemonade.

"Hey, Mabel, Tommy. Enjoying the cookout?"

Mabel didn't miss a beat. "Absolutely! And we were just talking about how much you've helped out around town. It's impressive."

Tommy chimed in, "Yeah, especially with everything that happened with Kevin. We couldn't have done it without you."

Gabe nodded, appreciating the acknowledgment. "I'm glad I could help. Carter's Creek has become a second home to me. I'm glad so many of you are already my friends."

Tom Hunter stepped forward, handing Gabe a cold beer. "You're part of the family now, Gabe. If you ever need anything, don't hesitate to ask."

Gabe accepted the beer gratefully. "Thanks, Tom. That means a lot."

***

As the night matured, the backyard began to empty, with guests slowly making their way home after a delightful evening. Gabe noticed Sadie gathering her empty plates, her expression a mix of satisfaction and lingering curiosity from the day's events.

"Hey, Sadie," Gabe greeted, holding out a plate filled with leftover grilled vegetables and meats. "Looks like you need some leftovers. Everyone ate all the goodies you brought!"

Sadie accepted the plate gratefully, her eyes meeting his with a hint of curiosity. "Thanks, Gabe. My sweets are always a hit, but I always try to bring plenty. It doesn't matter how much I bring, my dishes are always empty by the end of the evening."

Gabe chuckled softly. "You've definitely earned a reputation. How about I give you a ride home? It's getting a bit late."

Sadie hesitated for a moment, then nodded. "That would be great, thanks."

They made their way to Gabe's SUV, a sturdy 4-wheel drive parked near the garage. The vehicle, rugged and reliable, was perfect for the winding town roads around the creek. As they loaded the leftovers into the spacious bed, the soft glow of the fairy lights cast a warm ambiance around them.

Once everything was secured, Gabe unlocked and opened the passenger door for Sadie. She slid into the seat, and they settled in, the engine starting with a deep rumble that resonated through the quiet streets of Carter's Creek.

The drive through town was serene, the streets illuminated by the soft lights of houses and the occasional flicker from storefronts. They traveled in comfortable silence for a few moments, the sounds of the night providing a soothing backdrop.

Sadie glanced over at Gabe, her mind still buzzing with questions from the evening's conversations. "You know, Gabe," she began cautiously, "there were some lingering questions about why you moved to Carter's Creek. People are really curious, especially Mabel and Ms. Beatrice."

Gabe sighed softly, meeting her gaze in the rearview mirror. "I understand. It's natural for people to wonder, especially when you're new in town and have a bit of a mysterious past."

Sadie nodded, her curiosity piqued but respectful of his boundaries. "I just want you to know that you're welcome here. If there's anything you need or want to talk about, I'm here."

Gabe smiled, a genuine warmth in his eyes. "I appreciate that, Sadie. It means a lot."

The SUV cruised smoothly down Main Street, passing familiar landmarks like Sadie's Sweet Rolls bakery and the quaint storefronts that gave Carter's Creek its charming character. As they approached the outskirts where Sadie lived, the conversation took a more personal turn.

"You know," Sadie continued, her tone more earnest, "people have noticed how dedicated you are to helping out around town. It's really admirable."

Gabe nodded thoughtfully. "Thank you. It wasn't an easy decision to move here. My life in the Outer Banks was feeling stagnant, like I wasn't moving forward. But I have family ties to this area from way back to the Civil War. It felt like the right place to start over, to reconnect with my roots."

Sadie listened intently, sensing the depth of his words. "That sounds like a meaningful journey. It's nice to see someone putting in so much effort to rebuild their life."

Gabe glanced at her, appreciating her understanding. "It is. And meeting people like you makes the transition smoother. Carter's Creek has a way of making you feel at home."

They continued driving in comfortable silence until they reached Sadie's cozy house, nestled just a short distance from the center of Carter's Creek. Gabe pulled up to her driveway, the familiar sight of Sadie's Sweet Rolls bakery visible in the distance, its lights warmly glowing against the night sky.

"Thanks for the ride," Sadie said as she gathered her plates. "It was a great evening."

Gabe nodded, feeling a sense of gratitude for the growing connection between them. "Anytime, Sadie. It was my pleasure."

Sadie walked to her front door, pausing before entering. She turned back to Gabe with a thoughtful expression. "You know, you didn't have to do so much tonight. But I'm glad you did."

Gabe chuckled, his eyes reflecting a mixture of humility and contentment. "Well, helping out is what friends do."

Sadie smiled warmly, her eyes reflecting a sense of trust. "Gabe, before you go, could you stop by the bakery tomorrow? I promised Tom I'd prepare some fresh sweet rolls for the tavern's dinner. If you could pick them up, that would be a big help to me."

Gabe raised an eyebrow, pleasantly surprised. "That sounds great. I'd love to."

With a final wave, Sadie walked into her house, leaving Gabe to gather his things. As he drove back toward his own home, the quiet streets of Carter's Creek seemed to welcome him even more warmly. He glanced out the window, watching the town that had already started to feel like a second home.

As Gabe navigated the familiar roads toward the heart of town, he couldn't help but feel optimistic about the future. His conversation with Sadie had been a good start, a step toward sharing his past while building new connections. Carter's Creek was proving to be the perfect place to create a new life and discover new treasures.

Chapter Two
Whispers of the Past

THE MOON CAST A silvery glow through the curtains of Gabe's bedroom, illuminating the room with a tranquil, ethereal light. He lay in his bed, the soft rustle of leaves outside mingling with the distant sounds of Carter's Creek settling into the night. The bed was modest but comfortable, adorned with a few personal touches that hinted at his journey to this small town—a framed photograph of his father and mother, Lee and Julia, who still lived in the Outer Banks; a well-worn guitar leaning against the nightstand; and a stack of books on local history and folklore.

In his hands, Gabe held an old, leather-bound journal. Its pages were yellowed with age, the edges frayed from years of use. The journal had been a gift from his father, Lee Morgan, but it was written by Captain Gabriel Morgan of the Confederate Army—a tradition their family had upheld for generations by passing it on to the eldest son on his 21st birthday. Gabe had cherished it since the day he received it, as it was a significant piece of their family history, and because he had been given the same name as this distant relative.

Tonight, however, his attention was drawn to the last entry—a passage that had remained elusive, never fully explored, and which had drawn him to Carter's Creek. He had read this entry so many times that he had it memorized word for word.

> *April 18, 1865*
>
> *"The war is lost. General Lee surrendered at Appomattox just days ago, and I fear our cause has all but crumbled into dust. I write these words with a heavy heart, knowing the country I fought for will never be. But duty, even in defeat, binds me still.*
>
> *As the Union forces push deeper into the South, we are ordered to ensure that certain valuables – treasures that could fund a new Confederacy or protect our people from complete ruin – are not seized by the enemy. Today, I was commissioned with a grave responsibility: to secure a portion of the gold from the treasury, lest it fall into Northern Hands.*
>
> *I cannot entrust this mission to anyone. Only through this journal do I leave the faintest trace of its location, and even this trace is hidden inverse, so that no common thief may steal it. This burden I carry alone, though it shall be my family who decides its fate.*
>
> *If you are reading these words, then perhaps the time has come for the gold to see the light once more. Or perhaps I was wrong to ever hide it. Either way, the path to it lies within these lines:*
>
> *The Treasure's Rest*
> *Where the trees in twin formation stand,*
> *Their roots entwined in Southern land,*
> *Beyond the creek that winds and bends,*
> *Beneath the oak where daylight ends.*
> *To find the prize, in shadows deep,*
> *Dig where the weeping willows weep,*
> *But heed the stones, old moss and gray,*
> *The ones with words, now worn away.*

> *The sun at dusk will point your way,*
> *A single beam where gold does lay.*
> *But rush not forth with greed in hand,*
> *For patience guides the honest man.*
>
> *The gold awaits, buried where only those with clear hearts and sharp minds may find it. The Union may take our homes, our pride, and our future, but they will never take this.*
>
> *May God guide you in what you choose to do.*
> *Captain Gabriel Morgan*
> *4th Virginia Infantry, Army of Northern Virginia**

Gabe sighed softly, running his fingers over the inked words. Captain Morgan had always been a man of mystery, leaving behind clues and riddles that hinted at deeper secrets within Carter's Creek. This final entry had always intrigued him, a puzzle yet to be solved, and this distant relative was no help beyond this entry.

He flipped the journal open to the last written page, the handwriting familiar and comforting. The ink was slightly faded, but the message was clear. Gabe had spent countless nights pondering its meaning, trying to decipher the clues that might lead him to uncover his family's hidden legacy.

As he gazed at the words, his imaginings of Captain Morgan's life flooded his mind—the stories, the lessons, the silent encouragement to seek his own path. Gabe had always felt a connection to Carter's Creek, as his family had vacationed there periodically with the few Morgans who had lived there over the years. Once he received the journal and read the stories, he better understood the pull of this small town, the urgency to dig into his roots and learn more.

Tonight, as the weight of the journal pressed gently against his chest, Gabe felt a stirring within him—a desire to uncover the truths in the journal. It was as though this was his calling, his purpose. The room seemed to grow quieter, the stillness wrapping around him like a comforting blanket.

He closed the journal, placing it carefully beside his pillow, and turned his gaze to the ceiling. The moonlight danced across the room, casting shadows that seemed to move with a life of their own. Gabe felt his eyelids grow heavy, the day's events at the cookout blending seamlessly into the recesses of his mind.

As sleep began to claim him, Gabe's thoughts drifted away, merging reality with the vivid landscapes of his dreams.

***

In his dream, Gabe found himself standing on the banks of Carter's Creek, the water shimmering under a twilight sky. The air was crisp, carrying the scent of pine and earth. He felt a sense of familiarity, as if he had been here before, yet everything seemed slightly distorted, like a memory viewed through a fogged window.

A figure emerged from the shadows—Captain Gabriel Morgan, his distant relative, older yet unmistakably him, with the same strong jawline and kind eyes. Captain Morgan extended a hand, his presence both reassuring and commanding.

"Gabriel" he said softly, using his given name. "You're ready to discover the truth."

Gabe felt a surge of emotions—confusion, longing, determination. "Captain," he replied, his voice wavering slightly. "I've been searching for answers. What is the true treasure you spoke of?"

Captain Morgan smiled, a glimmer of pride in his eyes. "The treasure is a legacy, one that has been guarded for generations. It's not something you can hold, but something you must understand and embrace."

He gestured toward the creek, where the water seemed to glow with an otherworldly light. "Follow the path where the water meets the stone. There, you will find what you seek."

As Gabe took a step forward, the scene shifted. He was now in an ancient forest, the trees towering above him, their branches intertwining to form a natural canopy. The ground beneath his feet was soft, covered in moss and fallen leaves. He could hear the distant sound of a waterfall, its rhythm steady and hypnotic.

In the center of the forest stood an old, weathered tree, its trunk wide and gnarled, bearing the marks of time and history. At its base, nestled among the roots, was a small, intricately carved wooden box. Gabe approached it cautiously, his heart pounding with anticipation.

He reached out and lifted the lid, revealing a collection of old photographs, letters, and a key. Each item seemed to hold a story, fragments of the past waiting to be pieced together. Among them was a map, its lines and symbols hinting at hidden locations within Carter's Creek.

Gabe felt a sense of clarity wash over him. The treasure was not just a physical entity but a journey—a path to understanding his heritage and the legacy his bloodline had entrusted to him.

As he reached for the map, the dream began to fade, the forest dissolving into the morning light of his bedroom. Gabe awoke with a start, the journal lying beside him, its last pages blank as if waiting for him to write the next chapter.

***

18   LOVE'S HIDDEN TREASURES

Morning sunlight streamed through the curtains, filling Gabe Morgan's bedroom with a gentle warmth. He sat up, the remnants of his dream lingering in his mind. The old journal was open on his nightstand, the final entry a stark reminder of his father's enigmatic message.

Determined to uncover the secrets that had been passed down to him, Gabe reached for the journal, flipping back to the last entry. The words echoed in his thoughts:

"The true treasure lies not in gold or jewels, but in the heart of the one who seeks it. Follow the whispers of your soul, and let them guide you to the hidden truths of our heritage."

With newfound resolve, Gabe knew that his journey in Carter's Creek was only beginning. The connections he was forming with the community were integral to unlocking the mysteries that awaited him.

He got out of bed, the weight of responsibility and excitement settling comfortably on his shoulders. Today, he would start piecing together the clues his father had left behind, using the journal as his guide.

As he prepared for the day, Gabe felt a deep sense of purpose. Carter's Creek was more than just a place to start over—it was a tapestry of stories, memories, and secrets waiting to be discovered. And with each step he took, he moved closer to uncovering the true treasure his father had hinted at. Carter's Creek Public Library might be the perfect place to start his research.

***

The local library of Carter's Creek was a charming building with ivy crawling up its stone facade. Inside, Gabe was greeted by Ms. Jameson, the dedicated librarian known for her extensive knowledge of the town's history.

"Good morning, Gabe," Ms. Jameson said with a warm smile. "What brings you to the library today?"

Gabe took a deep breath, holding up his father's journal. "I'm researching my family history. My father gave me this journal written by a distant relative, Captain Gabriel Morgan, from the Civil War era. I'm trying to understand more about him and any connections he might have to Carter's Creek."

Ms. Jameson's eyes lit up with interest. "Ah, the Morgans. They were a prominent family in this area. Captain Morgan was indeed a figure of some renown. Let me pull up some records for you."

As Ms. Jameson sifted through old archives and photographs, Gabe glanced around the library, taking in the rows of books and the quiet atmosphere that seemed perfect for his quest.

After a few moments, Ms. Jameson returned with a stack of old documents. "Here we go. These are some of Captain Morgan's letters and records from his time here. It appears he was involved in establishing several landmarks around Carter's Creek, including the Weeping Willows Grove you might be interested in."

Gabe carefully examined the documents, his mind racing with possibilities. "This is incredible. Do you know if there are any physical remnants of his presence here?"

Ms. Jameson nodded. "Yes, indeed. There's an old monument near the grove, dedicated to the Morgans. It's not widely known, but it might hold more clues about the treasure your father mentioned."

Gabe felt a sense of excitement bubble up inside him. "Thank you, Ms. Jameson. This is exactly what I needed."

Ms. Jameson smiled warmly. "Anytime, Gabe. If you need any more assistance, don't hesitate to ask."

As Gabe left the library with the documents in hand, he felt a renewed sense of purpose. The pieces of the puzzle were slowly coming together, and with each discovery, he moved closer to uncovering the hidden treasure his father had spoken of.

***

Later that afternoon, Gabe decided to visit Mayor Emma Hunter at the Carter's Creek Town Hall to seek advice on how to further his research into his family's history. Emma Hunter was known not only for her leadership as the town's mayor but also for her deep ties to the community, being the wife of Luke Hunter, a respected local businessman, and daughter of the local pastor and his wife.

He arrived at the stately building, its facade adorned with local memorabilia and the town's seal. Inside, the halls were decorated with photographs and plaques honoring significant events and figures from the town's past.

Emma greeted him warmly in her office, a spacious room with a large desk and shelves filled with official documents.

"Hey, Gabe! I'm glad you stopped by. I wanted to thank you again for all your help at the cookout last night. Your assistance allowed me to get off my feet once in a while. What can I do for you today?" Emma asked, her voice friendly and approachable.

Gabe took a seat across from her desk, placing his father's journal and the map he received from Ms. Jameson on the table. "Hi, Emma. I'm hoping you can help me with some information about my family's history here in Carter's Creek."

Emma leaned forward, her expression attentive. "Of course, Gabe. I didn't even know you had family who had lived here. While I oversee the town's administration, the detailed historical records are managed by our town archivist, Mr. Mattison. He handles all archival research and can provide you with more in-depth information."

Gabe nodded, grateful for the direction. "Thank you, Emma. I used to visit here as a child, when some of our relatives still lived here, but they've all either moved on or passed on now, so all I have is memories of vacations. Could you connect me with him or let me know how to get in touch?"

Emma smiled. "Certainly. Mr. Mattison is very knowledgeable and passionate about our town's history. I'll introduce you via email, and you can schedule a time to meet with him at the archives. You can imagine it's not a full-time job in a town this small. And, you'll probably want to visit with Ms. Jameson at the library as well."

Gabe felt a sense of relief. "Thank you, Emma. I really appreciate your help, and I've already been to the library. Ms. Jameson was a great resource for me."

Emma waved off his gratitude. "It's my pleasure, Gabe. I'm confident between the two of them, you'll learn lots more about your family's history during their time here."

As Gabe left the Town Hall, clutching the additional records, he felt more confident than ever. With Emma's support and the upcoming meeting with Mr. Mattison, the path to uncovering the treasure was becoming clearer. The community of Carter's Creek was proving to be a valuable ally in his quest, and he was determined to honor his family's legacy by uncovering the hidden truths of their heritage.

Chapter Three
Stories from the Past

THE LATE AFTERNOON SUN cast a warm, golden hue through the expansive windows of Sadie's Sweet Rolls, bathing the bakery in a cozy, inviting light. The delightful aroma of freshly baked pastries mingled with the comforting scent of brewed tea, creating an atmosphere of homely tranquility. Gabe Morgan pushed open the door, his footsteps soft against the wooden floorboards as he approached the counter where Sadie Whitmore was meticulously arranging trays of fresh-baked, golden-brown chocolate chip cookies.

Despite the bustling energy typical of the bakery during the day, there was an unusual stillness; Gabe had arrived earlier than expected, granting him a rare moment of quiet.

"Just stopped by as I promised to pick up the order for the tavern for tonight," Gabe said, smiling as he glanced over to the cookies, "but, those cookies sure do make me think of home."

Sadie looked up from her work, her warm smile instantly putting Gabe at ease. Without hesitation, she gestured toward a cozy seating area near the window. "I know you've got some time to spare before your shift at the tavern, and I'm just wrapping up the day's baking, so let's sit a spell with a glass of sweet iced tea and some of these cookies you're eyeing."

Knowing his duties could wait a little longer, Gabe accepted, settling into a comfortable chair across from her at a small wooden table adorned with a vase of fresh wildflowers.

As Sadie approached with a tray holding two glasses of cold sweet tea and a plate of chocolate chip cookies, Gabe couldn't help but feel a pang of nostalgia. The cookies reminded him of simpler times spent with his family in the Outer Banks. The taste was a comforting reminder of his roots, grounding him amidst the swirling mysteries he was trying to unravel today.

"So, you told me a little bit about growing up in the Outer Banks," Sadie began, her eyes meeting his with genuine curiosity. "But you didn't share what drew you here to Carter's Creek."

Gabe took a moment before responding, gathering his thoughts. "It's hard to explain," he admitted, stirring his tea thoughtfully. "We had relatives who used to live here, but they've all passed on or moved away. We visited often when I was a child, so I have strong memories of this area. When I turned 21, my father gifted me with Captain Gabriel Morgan's journal, detailing his move here after the Civil war ended. I've read it countless times over the years, but something about this time and season ... something inside me felt compelled to come here. It wasn't just curiosity; it felt like a calling, a passion and purpose that I couldn't ignore. I spent this morning at the library and the Town Hall, hoping to uncover more about Captain Morgan and our family's legacy, and I feel like I'm on track to discover more about his life."

Sadie leaned back, a contemplative look crossing her features. "That journal must hold a lot of significance then."

"It does," Gabe replied, his eyes reflecting the weight of his responsibility. "Captain Morgan was a distant relative, and his final entry speaks of a hidden treasure and the legacy he wanted to protect. It's been handed down through generations of Morgans, and now it's my turn to uncover its secrets."

Sadie's expression softened with recognition. "I see. My Uncle Henry was close friends with Captain Morgan. They shared a lot of interests, especially when it came to preserving Carter's Creek's history and folklore."

Gabe felt a surge of hope mixed with intrigue. "Really? I'd love to hear more about him. Any stories or memories you can share?"

Sadie nodded, her eyes distant as she recalled the stories that had been passed on about of her uncle. "Uncle Henry was an incredible storyteller. He often spoke about Captain Morgan's dedication to the town and their joint efforts to document its rich history. In fact, Uncle Henry was instrumental in preserving some of Captain Morgan's work, ensuring that future generations would have access to these important stories."

Gabe leaned in, eager to absorb every detail. "That sounds amazing. It's like our families have been intertwined through history."

Sadie smiled softly. "They have. And speaking of stories, my Aunt Clara played a significant role in recent years as well. She believed in the power of storytelling to preserve our heritage. Clara wrote a children's book called *"The Willow's Secret: Tales of Carter's Creek."* It's filled with stories that, on the surface, seem like ordinary fairy tales, but I've always been told it holds hidden clues and symbols related to a treasure hunt started in Captain's Morgan's time."

Gabe's heart quickened at the mention of the book. "A children's book? That's fascinating. Do you still have copies of it?"

Sadie reached into a nearby shelf and carefully pulled out a well-worn copy of *"The Willow's Secret."* She handed it to Gabe, who opened it with reverence. The pages were filled with colorful illustrations and enchanting narratives, each story seemingly innocent yet imbued with subtle patterns and symbols.

"I inherited the rights to the book from Aunt Clara after she passed," Sadie explained. "I keep several copies here, both for sale and as a way to keep her legacy alive. Maybe there are some hidden messages in there that could help with your search."

Taking the book from her, Gabe began to flip through the pages, his eyes scanning the intricate drawings and whimsical stories. As he delved deeper, he started to notice recurring motifs and symbols that seemed out of place, aligning with the cryptic messages from Captain Morgan's journal.

"This is incredible, Sadie," Gabe murmured, his eyes widening with realization. "Clara really did embed clues within these stories that match up with ones in the journal I have. It's like she was guiding someone to uncover the treasure."

Sadie watched him with a mixture of surprise and anticipation. "Wow, growing up us kids always thought the treasure was just part of the tall tales told about this area. Aunt Clara told the stories, then wrote them in the book, as though they were the history of the town, so I'm sure she was telling everything she knew, but in a guarded way to protect this knowledge from falling into the wrong hands. If you're willing to work together, we might be able to piece together the clues and get closer to uncovering the truth."

Gabe felt a renewed sense of determination. "I'd like that. With your knowledge of Clara's work and the resources you have here, we might just be able to solve this mystery."

As the afternoon light began to wane, casting long shadows across the bakery, Gabe and Sadie immersed themselves in the pages of *"The Willow's Secret,"* their collaboration marking the beginning of a deeper partnership.

***

As the afternoon light gave way to the soft glow of evening, Gabe made his way to the Southern Roots, a cozy tavern nestled in the town square of Carter's Creek. Clutching the copy of *"The Willow's Secret: Tales of Carter's Creek"* that Sadie had insisted he bring along with the tray of sweets, Gabe felt a mix of anticipation and responsibility.

Entering the tavern, Gabe was greeted by the familiar sights and sounds of regular patrons enjoying their meals and conversations. He exchanged a friendly nod with the bartender he was relieving before passing through to drop off the tray in the kitchen. Gabe enjoyed his work as a bartender and often found solace in the steady rhythm of serving guests—a welcome distraction from the enigmatic mysteries he was unraveling.

As he began to clean and restock the bar for the evening service, Gabe kept one eye on the copy of the children's book, occasionally flipping through its pages to revisit the intricate illustrations and subtle symbols that seemed to hold hidden meanings. His mind buzzed with thoughts of Sadie's revelations and the potential clues embedded within the stories.

Just as Gabe was settling into his routine, the tavern door swung open, allowing a brisk autumn breeze to sweep through the room. A tall man with a thoughtful expression and an air of slight discomfort entered, and approached the bar with purposeful strides, his eyes meeting Gabe's with a mixture of curiosity and urgency.

"Hi, Gabe. We haven't met before, but I'm Grant Mattison, the town archivist," Grant began, his voice steady yet tinged with excitement. "Emma sent me an email suggesting we meet, and I was intrigued enough to pop right over, even though I don't regularly visit The Southern Roots Tavern, not being a man who imbibes in strong drink. Even so, I'd heard through the grapevine that you were the new bartender here."

Gabe smiled, gesturing to the seating area. "Join me here at the bar, Grant. I can serve you a soft drink, sweet tea, or a mocktail—whichever you prefer. We aim to please!"

Grant, unfamiliar with the term "mocktail," opted for a Coke. He glanced around the tavern before leaning in slightly, lowering his voice. "Emma Hunter reached out to me via email. She mentioned that you were seeking some insights or information related to the Morgan family legacy. I love Carter's Creek history, so I wanted to learn more about what you're seeking."

Gabe nodded, feeling the weight of his responsibilities intensify. "Yes, I visited the library and then spoke with Emma at Town Hall, who promised to connect me with you. I also wrapped up the afternoon with Sadie at Sadie's Sweet Rolls, where she shared her Aunt Clara's book, *'The Willow's Secret.'* I've only just begun my research, so I'd appreciate anything you could share with me about the Morgans who lived here, and specifically Captain Gabriel Morgan, whom I was named after."

Grant's eyes sparkled with interest. "We have a great deal in the town archives that cover Captain Morgan and that period of Carter's Creek, as well as more about the Morgan family over the years. This is actually the second time I've been contacted about this information in recent weeks. There's a lot of interest in the Morgan name, so I was curious if you could tell me what specific information you are seeking."

A sudden tension settled over Gabe. He hesitated, unsure about sharing details regarding Captain Morgan's treasure with a stranger, even though Emma had connected them. He was also aware that his search could attract unwanted rivals, which seemed to be happening already.

Gabe hesitatingly pulled out a notepad, flipping it open to a page he'd created about his search. "I'm particularly interested in the historical context surrounding Captain Gabriel Morgan's activities here in Carter's Creek. Any details about his arrival, life, collaborations with others—like Sadie's Uncle Henry Whitmore—and any information about the Morgans and Whitmores over the years. I'm just trying to learn more about the history of this branch of my family."

Grant smiled, appreciating Gabe's enthusiasm and dedication. "The town archives will have a lot of what you're looking for, plus it's already laid out. I never got it all put away after the last group who asked for the same information."

"Can you tell me who it was that asked about it?" Gabe wondered aloud. "It might be members of my own family that I'm unaware of."

Grant paused thoughtfully. "Hmm, I'm not sure if that's confidential or not. Let me discuss it with Mayor Hunter. Let's meet tomorrow morning at 9:30 in my office in the basement of Town Hall. I can show you all that I have, and perhaps also connect you with these other folks who are researching the same family."

Gabe agreed, and Grant took his leave, carrying a to-go box with one of Sadie's Sweet Rolls to enjoy later at home. Gabe was excited about the progress he'd made in just one day, but he was also concerned about others being on the same search. This realization gave him a sense of urgency to get serious about his quest before someone else could uncover the treasure ahead of him.

As Gabe watched Grant disappear into the tavern's bustling crowd, he felt a renewed determination. The pieces of the puzzle were slowly coming together, but time was of the essence. Tomorrow's meeting at the archives could be the key to unlocking the next chapter of his family's legacy—or the beginning of a race against rivals who shared his ambitions.

***

As the evening settled over Carter's Creek, the bustling energy of the tavern began to mellow into a comfortable hum of conversations and clinking glasses. Gabe had just finished restocking the sparkling glassware, his mind still abuzz with the day's revelations. The copy of *"The Willow's Secret: Tales of Carter's Creek"* rested on the bar, a constant reminder of the mystery he was determined to unravel.

Just as Gabe was preparing to take a short break, the tavern door swung open once more, letting in a gust of cool autumn air. Sadie stepped inside, her presence immediately noticeable with her warm smile and the familiar scent of freshly baked goods lingering on her. She made her way to the bar, her eyes searching for Gabe amidst the crowd.

"Hey, Gabe," Sadie called out softly, a hint of concern in her voice. "I just thought I'd check in and see how you're doing."

Gabe looked up from his tasks, a genuine smile spreading across his face as he motioned for Sadie to join him at the bar. "Sadie! It's good to see you. I'm hanging in there, thanks for asking."

Sadie settled into the chair at the bar, placing a hand on the counter. "I wanted to make sure you were okay, you were so excited about your research when you left my bakery this afternoon."

Gabe took a deep breath, his eyes briefly flicking to the book before meeting Sadie's gaze. "There's been some progress, but also some complications. Grant Mattison stopped by earlier today. He's the town archivist, and Emma had emailed him to set up a meeting with me. It turns out, I'm not the only one interested in the Morgan family legacy."

Sadie's eyes widened with interest. "Other people? Who else is searching for the treasure?"

Gabe hesitated for a moment, the weight of his discovery pressing down on him. "That's the thing. Grant mentioned this is the second time he's been contacted about this information in recent weeks. That means there are others out there—possibly even members of my own extended family—that are also looking for the treasure."

Sadie leaned in, her curiosity piqued. "Did he say who they might be?"

Gabe shook his head slightly. "Not yet. Grant seemed cautious about sharing names. But based on what Grant mentioned, it's likely related to my family or yours – the Morgan or the Whitmore family. I mentioned your Aunt Clara's book to him, and your Uncle Henry's collaboration back in the day with Captain Morgan. I have an appointment with Grant at the archive office tomorrow at 9:30. Would you like to go with me, since both our families seem involved in this?"

Sadie's face lit up with excitement. "You know, I've always wanted to dig deeper into our family history, and, to be honest, I was really hoping you'd let me be your sidekick in this search. I love a good mystery."

Gabe considered her offer, feeling a surge of relief and determination. "You know, I could use another set of eyes and ears, especially since it may be a race to see who can figure out this mystery first. It would be great to have someone with your knowledge and connection to Aunt Clara's stories on board."

Sadie smiled, her enthusiasm evident. "I'd love to help. I'm not looking for part ownership or anything like that—just a chance to solve this mystery and learn more about my own family, too."

Gabe nodded, feeling a renewed sense of purpose. "Absolutely. With your expertise and resources, we can make significant progress. Plus, having someone I trust by my side makes this whole quest feel less daunting."

Sadie reached out, giving his shoulder a reassuring squeeze. "We're in this together, Gabe. Let's meet with Grant tomorrow morning and see what we can uncover. I have a feeling this is just the beginning."

***

After their heartfelt conversation at The Southern Roots Tavern, Gabe Morgan found himself tidying up the bar as the last of the evening's patrons bid their goodbyes. With the tavern now quiet, Gabe offered to walk Sadie Whitmore home—a gesture both practical and personal, providing a chance to clear his mind and discuss their burgeoning partnership further. The crisp evening air was invigorating, and the streets of Carter's Creek were bathed in the soft glow of streetlamps that cast long shadows on the cobblestone paths.

As they strolled through the serene town, their steps eventually led them to the Gazebo in the town square—a picturesque spot framed by towering oak trees, standing as a silent witness to countless memories. The gazebo's wooden beams were weathered yet sturdy, embodying the enduring spirit of the community.

Gabe glanced around, his eyes catching the carved initials inside a heart—"ET & LH"—etched into the trunk of a nearby oak tree. "Look at that," he remarked, pointing to the initials. "Emma and Luke carved their initials in this tree when they were sixteen years old, and they just got married fifteen years later. I can't even imagine loving one person that many years."

Sadie chuckled softly, leaning against the gazebo's railing. "It's beautiful, isn't it? Their initials here have stood the test of time, much like the legacy we're trying to uncover."

Gabe nodded, a thoughtful expression crossing his features. "It's a reminder that some things are meant to last, and that our families' stories have their own kind of endurance. I guess that's part of what makes this treasure hunt so compelling—not just the mystery, but the history and the connections that come with it."

Sadie looked up at the night sky, the first stars beginning to twinkle above. "Exactly. We're not just searching for a physical treasure, but also piecing together the stories that have shaped our families and this town. It's about understanding where we come from and honoring those who came before us."

Gabe felt a renewed sense of purpose as he gazed at the stars. "With you by my side, Sadie, I feel more confident that we can navigate whatever comes our way. Tomorrow's meeting at the archives could be the key to unlocking the next chapter of our journey."

Sadie smiled, her eyes reflecting the starlight. "And who knows? Maybe we'll uncover more than just the treasure. Perhaps we'll discover new aspects of our own histories and forge connections that will last a lifetime. Sometimes history repeats itself."

As they stood together in the gazebo, the night enveloping them in its quiet embrace, Gabe and Sadie felt a deep sense of camaraderie. The path ahead was uncertain, but with their combined strengths and shared determination, they were ready to face whatever challenges awaited them in their quest to uncover the secrets of Carter's Creek.

Chapter Four
Echoes of the Past

THE EARLY MORNING MIST hovered over Carter's Creek as Gabe approached the stately facade of the Town Hall. The grand building stood as a testament to the town's rich history, its brick exterior adorned with intricate carvings and the emblem of Carter's Creek etched above the main entrance. Today marked an important step in Gabe and Sadie's quest to uncover the secrets of their intertwined family legacies.

Gabe glanced over as Sadie joined him on the steps, her expression a mix of determination and anticipation.

"Our cover story is we're just researching our family history in the area," Gabe spoke softly as they climbed the steps to the Town Hall. "That way, we'll get what we need without mentioning the treasure. I don't want to stir up any unneeded interest that could create a race to find it."

The two shared a silent understanding of the significance of the meeting ahead. Just inside the door, they headed down the stairs where Grant Mattison had said they'd find the Town Archives Office.

Grant Mattison, the town archivist, a tall man with sharp features and thoughtful eyes, extended his hand in greeting. Despite his reserved nature, there was a spark of eagerness in his demeanor today.

"Gabe, Sadie, thank you for coming," Grant began, his voice steady. "I'm glad you could come together. I have so much to show you."

Gabe nodded, gesturing for Sadie to take a seat at the sturdy wooden table set up in a larger space outside Grant's personal office. "We appreciate you making time for us so quickly. We're anxious to learn more about the Morgan and Whitmore family histories in this area, plus I was hoping we could learn about the other people on a similar search—perhaps they're family as well."

Grant settled into his chair, placing a stack of neatly organized folders and documents on the table. "Yes, Mayor Thompson ... err ... I mean Mayor Hunter – it's hard for me to remember to call her by her married name now - assured me that it was okay to share the names of others who have inquired about the same information recently."

Grant adjusted his glasses, his expression becoming more serious. "After reviewing the recent inquiries, it appears another branch of the Whitmore family has also shown significant interest. Their approach is different from yours, Gabe, but equally determined."

Sadie exchanged a glance with Gabe, both sensing the underlying tension. "Whitmore is my family on my father's side, so maybe I know them. Do you have their full names or any background information on them?"

Grant nodded, pulling out a document from the stack. "Yes, here are the names and some details I've gathered. Lily, Ethan, and Maya Adams, siblings who all have deep roots in archaeology and education, city folk from up north. They were seeking any information we had in the archives about the Morgan and Whitmore families, trying to solve a puzzle left behind in their family. Do either of you know them?"

Sadie's eyes narrowed slightly, recalling the few interactions she had with her extended family. "I met them once as a child, during a family vacation to the city. My father had two sisters, Clara, who lived here as well and remained single, and Edna, who married a Yankee, Robert Adams, and had these three kids, they were already teens then, so older than me. We were close with Aunt Clara, all living here together, but the Adams were more distant—just news in the form of letters over the years. The only other times I've seen the three of them was at my parents' funeral a few years ago and again at Aunt Clara's funeral last year. I don't remember much about their visits those times, as both were hard times for me—but I know they spent a few days in the area after my parents' funeral. Aunt Clara told me later that they'd all had a nice visit, and the kids were excited to learn more about our family here."

Grant continued, spreading out more documents. "Their goal appears to be to use whatever they find to shore up their family's status. They're not here for sentimental reasons but rather for the potential value the Morgan legacy holds. From what I can tell, they believe there's a significant advantage to be gained from uncovering some hidden family assets."

Gabe felt a chill run down his spine. "Well, it seems we're on similar paths, but each with different motives."

Sadie placed a reassuring hand on Gabe's arm. "We need to focus on understanding and recording our family histories as a legacy. No need to be concerned about them."

Gabe agreed, his resolve strengthening. "You're right, Sadie. Let's keep our focus on the history and see where that leads us."

Grant leaned back, a thoughtful expression on his face. "I have a wealth of material here that can help us piece together the Morgan/Whitmore legacy. From old letters and photographs to detailed records of Henry Whitmore and Captain Gabriel Morgan's activities in Carter's Creek. We can start by reviewing these documents and identifying any patterns or significant events that might validate information you already have."

Sadie picked up a photograph from one of the folders, examining it closely. "This one—this is my Uncle Henry. I recognize him from old family albums, and I'd bet that's Captain Morgan standing beside him. They look like they were deep in conversation."

Grant smiled softly. "Yes, that was taken during one of their many meetings to document the town's history. Their collaboration was instrumental in preserving Carter's Creek's folklore and ensuring that the town's stories were passed down through generations."

Gabe felt a surge of gratitude towards Sadie. Their collaboration was proving to be invaluable, each piece of information building a clearer picture of their shared legacy. "Thank you, Grant. I know you have other things to do, perhaps we can just review the materials you have here and jot down any questions we have for you."

Grant nodded in agreement. "I have lots of other materials to refile after other review requests, so I can knock that out while you both dig in here. I would just caution you that none of these materials can leave this office, and please handle them delicately—these historical documents and pictures are very old!"

Sadie and Gabe began to sift through the documents, their fingers gently turning the fragile pages. As they delved deeper, Sadie's eyes lit up with recognition.

"Gabe, look at this photo! In Aunt Clara's book, *'The Willow's Secret,'* there's a part where a weeping willow stands beside an old oak tree, and the description matches this photograph perfectly."

Gabe leaned in, excitement building. "You're right, Sadie, and I know that's mentioned in the Captain's journal as well. This could be one of the connections we need. I know the oak tree and weeping willows are important. And, check this one out, it looks like a picture of the two of them posed again in front of the Old Mill. I remember that from last year, when we rescued Linda there."

Sadie nodded thoughtfully. "Exactly. Since you know that location, that might be a good place to start. If we can cross-reference the book with your journal, it might lead us where we want to go."

Gabe asked if they could make copies of documents, and take snapshots of pictures, and Grant agreed with a satisfied nod. "Feel free to take pictures of any documents or photos you want to include in your own research files. Photocopies are 10 cents per page. Just make sure to return all the historical documents, so they can be properly cataloged. I'm glad you're finding some of what you need in our town archives. Did you find anything interesting I can help you with?"

Gabe took out his phone, snapping a few pictures of what they'd found, and the pictures of Sadie's Uncle Henry with Captain Morgan. "Thanks, Grant. We aren't even sure what we're looking for yet, so who know what really matters yet."

Sadie added, "We're really grateful for your help and your time this morning, Grant. We may be back as we learn more!"

After a productive morning at the archives, Gabe and Sadie knew they had to get on with their day, so headed up the stairs of the Town Hall, where they unexpectedly ran into Mayor Emma and Luke Hunter, who were just leaving Emma's office headed for lunch.

"Emma! Luke!" Sadie greeted them with a warm smile. "What a surprise. How are you two doing?"

Emma returned the smile, adjusting her bag strap. "Hey, Sadie! Gabe! It's been a busy morning, hasn't it?"

Luke nodded, offering a friendly nod. "Definitely. We're off to grab some lunch at Dew Drop Inn. Care to join us?"

Gabe exchanged a glance with Sadie, who nodded enthusiastically. "We'd love to. A good lunch with friends sounds perfect."

***

The Dew Drop Inn was a beloved local diner known for its hearty meals and welcoming atmosphere. As the four friends pushed open the door, the doorbell jingled, drawing the attention of two of the town's most well-known gossips—Ms. Beatriz Lopez, the high school history teacher, and Mabel Henderson, the retired resident with deep knowledge of local lore.

Ms. Beatriz, with her ever-present shopping bag and a curious gleam in her eye spotted the group and waved enthusiastically. Mabel, carrying a basket of groceries, joined in the greeting, her warm smile lighting up her face.

"Look who's here!" Ms. Beatriz exclaimed as they approached the counter. "Sadie and Gabe, Emma and Luke! It's so wonderful to see you all together. What are you lovely couples doing here today?"

Mabel chuckled softly. "Yes, I heard through the grapevine that you're diving deep into some family history."

Emma laughed, pulling up two chairs for Sadie and Gabe. "We're just four friends having lunch at the moment!"

Shea added softly to just their table, "Gabe, you need to be aware that being seen with Sadie, an attractive single woman of Carter's Creek, you will now be the hottest topic of gossip for the next 24 hours at least."

Gabe blushed, and stammered, "Sadie and I are just friends, working on family research together, it doesn't mean anything more than that."

Ms. Beatriz and Mabel settled into their own nearby tables continuing their lively conversation and keeping an eye on the group. As they ordered their meals, the friends exchanged knowing glances. They understood that any significant activities in Carter's Creek would soon become the talk of the town, thanks to Ms. Beatriz and Mabel.

Emma leaned back in her seat, looking curious. "So, how did your meeting with Grant go, Gabe? Any interesting findings?"

Gabe took a sip of his coffee before responding. "It went well. Grant has a lot of valuable documents and photographs that can help us piece together the Morgan legacy. Yesterday, Sadie shared her Aunt Clara's book with me. Apparently her Uncle Henry Whitmore was a close friend of Captain Morgan's, so we've teamed up to learn more about both our families together. Sadie and I found some interesting connections between Aunt Clara's book and Captain Morgan's journal. It's promising."

Sadie nodded, adding, "Yes, and Grant was kind enough to let us take pictures of the documents for our research files. We're starting to see some patterns that might help us learn more about both families."

Gabe shot Sadie a questioning glance, considering sharing more with Luke and Emma. They already were good friends, who had shared mysteries and secrets together before, and Emma silently nodded.

"This is more than just a genealogy search on our families. Captain Morgan's journal suggests he hid some of the Confederate treasury near Carter's Creek. That's what drew me to the area, I felt like his journal was urging me to take action. That solidified even more when Sadie shared similar stories about hidden treasure shared as children's stories in her own family. The information is too similar to be a coincidence, even though up to now, Sadie has considered those stories fiction."

Emma's eyes sparkled with interest. "That's fascinating. I knew there was more to your quest than just uncovering family histories and preserving legacies. While that's important, your passion seemed more intense, and a mystery surrounding a hidden treasure explains it completely."

Luke chimed in, "And it sounds like you two are making a great team. Let us know if we can help, because both Emma and my families have lived here for a long time, too."

Gabe smiled appreciatively. "Thanks, Luke. It means a lot. We're trying to approach this carefully to avoid attracting too much attention from others who might have their own agendas."

Emma nodded thoughtfully. "Speaking of which, Grant mentioned there are others interested in the Morgan legacy, possibly even from your own extended family, Sadie. It's good that you're aware and taking steps to manage the situation."

Sadie took a moment before responding. "Yes, Grant provided us with names, thanks to your approval—Lily, Ethan, and Maya Adams. My father's oldest sister's kids, cousins who are older than me, and from the city, so I didn't know them well. Grant said they seemed focused on the potential value of the legacy. We just learned that, so Gabe and I haven't even discussed our next steps yet."

Luke looked intrigued. "It sounds like there's a lot of history and mystery wrapped up in this. If there's anything we can do to help, just let us know. You were both a big help when we were dealing with Kevin and his projects last year. Thankfully, he's now serving time in prison."

Emma smiled warmly. "Absolutely. We're all connected in some way, and supporting each other can only help us all uncover the truth."

Gabe felt a surge of gratitude for the unexpected camaraderie. "Thank you, Emma and Luke. Your support means a lot." Glancing at Sadie, he continued, "We are taking this one step at a time. This may be nothing, but I feel like I have to follow the clues to see where they lead. Since we all worked together so well last year, perhaps we can all get together with Tommy and Hannah as well, to team up again!"

As they continued their conversation over lunch, the bonds between the friends and allies strengthened. The journey to uncover the secrets of Carter's Creek was taking shape, with each step bringing them closer to understanding their shared legacy and the treasures hidden within their family histories.

***

The mid-afternoon sun streamed through the large windows of Sadie's Sweet Rolls, casting a warm, golden glow over the bustling bakery. The air was thick with the enticing aroma of freshly baked bread, sweet pastries, and rich coffee. Sadie moved gracefully behind the counter, her hands expertly icing cupcakes and arranging croissants in the display case. The gentle hum of conversation and the clinking of cups created a comforting backdrop.

As Sadie placed the final cupcake into the display, the bell above the door jingled softly. She looked up to see Grant Mattison stepping inside, his expression friendly yet purposeful. He offered a polite smile as he approached the counter.

"Afternoon, Sadie," Grant greeted, his voice steady. "Do you have a moment?"

Sadie wiped her hands on her apron and returned his smile. "Grant! Of course. What brings you by today?"

Grant leaned slightly forward, lowering his voice as if sharing a private concern. "I thought you might be interested to know that your cousins—Lily, Ethan, and Maya Adams—have called to make another appointment at the town archives. They're planning to come by two days from now."

Sadie paused, a flicker of curiosity crossing her face. She stirred her coffee absentmindedly, the spoon clinking against the mug. "That's interesting. Did they mention what they're looking for?"

Grant shook his head. "Not specifically. I didn't mention your visit with Gabe to the archives, since they aren't from around here. But I thought it was important you knew they'd be back in town soon, especially since you're related."

Sadie nodded thoughtfully, her mind already racing with possibilities. "Thanks for letting me know, Grant. I'd definitely be interested to learn more about their search. Could you do us a favor, and leave out what they look at again. We could come back the day after to take a look again."

Grant gave a reassuring nod. "No problem. If you need any assistance or have questions about the archives, feel free to reach out."

"I will," Sadie replied, offering a grateful smile. "Thanks again, Grant. And, here's one of my carrot cake cupcakes you love, don't want you to leave without a treat. My treat for all your help!"

With a final nod, Grant turned to leave, cupcake in hand, the door closing softly behind him. Sadie watched him go, her thoughts swirling with the new information. She returned to her work, but the weight of the news lingered, adding another layer of complexity to their quest.

***

As dusk settled over Carter's Creek, The Southern Roots Tavern buzzed with the lively chatter of evening patrons. The warm glow of lanterns and the soft melodies from the old jukebox created a welcoming ambiance. Gabe Morgan leaned against the bar, sipping his drink while watching the steady flow of customers enjoying their meals and conversations.

The door swung open, and Sadie walked in, her cheeks flushed from the day's work and determination evident in her eyes. She spotted Gabe and made her way over, pulling up a stool beside him.

"Gabe, do you have a minute?" Sadie asked, her voice tinged with urgency.

Gabe turned to her, a smile playing on his lips. "Always for you. What's up?"

They found a quieter corner near the back of the tavern, away from the main hustle and bustle. Sadie sat down, pulling out her phone and tapping on it thoughtfully before meeting Gabe's gaze.

"Grant stopped in the bakery this afternoon," she began. "He mentioned that Lily, Ethan, and Maya Adams have scheduled another visit to the archives in two days. And, he didn't tell them about us, since we are town residents, and they are not."

Gabe raised an eyebrow, his interest piqued. "Wow, that's big. Did he say anything else?"

Sadie shook her head slightly. "Not much, but it got me thinking. Maybe it's time I reached out to them directly. They might have insights or resources that could help us in our search."

Gabe nodded, his expression serious. "That could be a good move. But remember, they've been visiting Carter's Creek without reaching out to you. I'm not sure why, but we need to be careful about what we reveal."

"I know," Sadie replied, determination hardening her features. "I was thinking of approaching it delicately—just offering help without pushing too hard. See if they're willing to collaborate or share any information they have."

Gabe considered her words for a moment before responding. "I agree. It's worth a try. We need all the help we can get, but we can't afford to let our guard down either."

Sadie smiled, a spark of hope lighting her eyes. "I'll call them tomorrow, just to reconnect. Maybe we can set up a meeting with them, just as family when they're here next, so we can see what they'll tell us."

"Sounds like a plan," Gabe said, raising his glass in a silent toast. "In the meantime, I'll keep digging on my end. There might be connections between the clues we've found and something the Adams siblings are looking into."

Sadie clinked her glass against his. "It's a partnership, right? Together, we might just crack this mystery wide open."

"Exactly," Gabe affirmed. "Let's stay focused and support each other through this. We're in this together."

They sat in comfortable silence for a moment, the weight of their mission pressing down on them but also strengthening their resolve. The tavern's lively chatter continued around them, but in their secluded corner, Gabe and Sadie were united in their quest to uncover the hidden treasures and truths that had long been concealed in Carter's Creek.

Chapter Five

Secrets of the Old Mill

THE EARLY MORNING SUN cast a golden hue over Carter's Creek as Gabe Morgan pulled up in front of Sadie's Sweet Rolls. The bakery stood as a beacon of warmth and community, its inviting windows showcasing an array of freshly baked goods. Sadie waved as Gabe pulled up in his SUV.

Sadie opened the car door, her face lighting up with a welcoming smile. "Morning, Gabe! Ready for another day of treasure hunting?"

Gabe returned her smile. "Absolutely. Thanks for agreeing to meet so early."

Sadie glanced back the bustling bakery, where Hannah was already busy serving customers. "Hannah's covering today, so I'm free for the whole day. We can focus entirely on the Old Mill without any interruptions, and I can't remember having a day off in recent months, except Sundays, of course. This is going to be a great day, I can feel it."

Gabe nodded, driving through the town square, waving at Ms. Beatriz as they passed. "Perfect, you guys are making me paranoid about the grapevine in this town! Let's talk through what we're going to need, and make sure we have everything we need before we get to far out of town. I brought the flashlights, extra batteries, and battery-operated lantern you mentioned."

"I brought food and water, as usual, things I consider essential!" Sadie glancing back at the picnic basket and thermos that she's dropped in the back. "Plus I tucked in a copy of Aunt Clara's book."

"I brought along the maps we've been studying, never know when we may need them suddenly, cameras and notebooks." Gabe added, making the next turn to head out of town smoothly, as he continued, "I've also printed out the additional journal entries we found yesterday. They might have more clues about the mill's exact location and what we're looking for. Plus I snapped copies of the Captain's Journal – it's too old to risk damaging during field work."

"Alright, here's the plan," Gabe said, pointing to a specific spot on the map, which Sadie had spread out on her lap. "We'll head straight to the Old Mill, avoid the main paths to stay unnoticed, and start our search from there. We need to document everything thoroughly."

The rest of the drive to the Old Mill was quiet, the road winding through dense woods and open fields. As they approached their destination, the atmosphere shifted from serene to foreboding. The once-grand structure of the mill loomed ahead, its windows shattered and walls crumbling, overtaken by nature's relentless embrace.

Gabe slowed the SUV to a stop near the creek, the sound of rushing water adding to the mill's eerie ambiance. Sadie stepped out, taking a deep breath as she surveyed the dilapidated building. "This place hasn't been operational in decades. It's going to be tough to navigate, but it seems Captain Morgan's telling us it holds the key to the next part of his legacy."

Gabe grabbed his flashlight, the beam piercing the shadows around them. "Let's proceed with caution. We don't know what we might encounter inside."

They approached the mill's heavy wooden door, its hinges squeaking ominously as Gabe pushed it open. The interior was dark and silent, the air thick with the scent of damp wood and decay. Sunlight streamed through gaps in the walls, casting long, ominous shadows across the expansive space.

The historical significance of the mill was evident in the remnants of old machinery and tools scattered throughout. Every corner seemed to hold a story, a piece of Carter's Creek's rich past waiting to be uncovered. And, clearly some intruders had left their marks as well, as walls carried marks of graffiti and trash from consumed snacks were scattered around.

Inside the mill, Gabe and Sadie began their search methodically, moving from room to room and examining every nook and cranny. Their flashlights illuminated faded signs and old photographs that hinted at the mill's bustling days long gone.

"Hey, check this out, " Gabe said, pointing out one of the symbols they had found carved into a decorative piece on the wall. "Sadie, look at this symbol carved on this piece. It matches the one we saw earlier."

Sadie examined it closely, her fingers tracing the intricate carvings, and suddenly she felt something like a button built into the carving. "There's something here," she said, as she pressed the button hard, and the wall moved slightly.

"Wow, a hidden door!" Gabe gasped, as he came over to add his weight to Sadie's to open door.

Working together, they got the door moving more freely, and the wall swung open slowly, and a cloud of dust poured out into the main hall. They both recoiled slightly, coughing as they adjusted their flashlights to penetrate the darkness beyond. Initially, they just saw lots of dust and spiderwebs covering the interior of the newly revealed space.

Gabe's breath hitched, his fear of spiders evident in his tense posture. "Uh, Sadie, I..."

Sadie stepped forward, taking the lead, laughing. "Don't worry, Gabe. I'll handle the spiders." She began to carefully clear out the webs with her flashlight, sweeping the beam across the room to expose any lurking arachnids. Gabe took a deep breath, he had hated spiders since his childhood.

As the web-covered area began to clear, they could see the outlines of old furniture covered in cloths and storage containers. Gabe turned on a battery-operated lantern, and the room filled with a dim light. After finding a wall that was a door, they felt confident their forefathers had gone to great lengths to secure their treasure.

Sadie felt an indention in another wall, pressed it hard, and to her surprise, a hidden compartment sprang open, "Gabe, check this out, another hidden panel!"

Inside the hidden compartment, they found a dusty, weathered box nestled within the concealed space. Gabe carefully lifted the lid, revealing a collection of aged documents, black-and-white photographs, and a beautifully bound journal. The air was thick with the scent of old paper and ink, a testament to the compartment's long-forgotten existence.

Gabe reached for the journal, his fingers trembling with excitement. "This must be it—the founding journal Captain Morgan mentioned."

Sadie carefully picked up a stack of photographs, blowing off layers of dust to reveal images that had clearly been preserved with care. The photos depicted the groundbreaking ceremony of the Old Mill, showing Captain Gabriel Morgan and Uncle Henry Whitmore standing proudly beside the construction site, surrounded by a multitude of workers. The camaraderie and collaboration between the two men were evident, their smiles reflecting the hope and determination that built Carter's Creek.

"Look at these," Sadie said, pointing to a photo where Captain Morgan is handing a blueprint to Uncle Henry. "They seem to be working on something significant."

Gabe flipped open the journal, revealing handwritten entries that detailed the founding and operations of the Old Mill. The pages were filled with meticulous notes, sketches of machinery, and references to secret symbols—mirroring the ones they had discovered in the mill. As they began to read, it became clear that the seemingly confusing collaborations between Captain Morgan and Uncle Henry were strategic efforts to protect a hidden treasure.

"This entry here," Gabe read aloud, "mentions the importance of unity and the symbols we've encountered. It's as if they were guiding someone to the treasure at the right time."

Sadie nodded, her eyes scanning the pages. "And these symbols... they're consistent with what we've found so far. It all fits together, but it's still unclear where we should go next."

Among the journal entries, they found a riddle that stood out:

> *"Beneath the watchful gaze of the ancient tree,*
> *Where light meets shadow, the path shall be.*
> *Seek the place where brothers convene,*
> *There lies the legacy unseen."*

Gabe and Sadie exchanged puzzled glances, the pieces of the puzzle now spinning in their heads. "Another riddle to solve, this really is beginning to feel like a treasure hunt," Gabe mused, shaking his head.

Sadie smiled, feeling a surge of determination. "It seems the Old Mill was just the beginning. We need to keep following the clues. We didn't expect this to be easy, did we?"

As they carefully organized the contents of the box, Sadie noticed several additional photographs and documents that seemed to hint at deeper connections. "Gabe, these documents ... they provide more context, but it's still a bit confusing. We need to keep digging."

Gabe examined the photographs, noticing the collaborative efforts between Captain Morgan and Uncle Henry, along with images of workers and various symbols. "We're definitely on the right track, but we still have a lot to research to fully understand these clues. Let's gather this all up and get out of here."

***

As they headed out of the Old Mill, carrying their stuffed backpacks on their backs, Sadie was startled to see two familiar figures approaching from the front. Maya and Ethan, her cousins, were walking toward them, their expressions guarded and intense.

Sadie froze, her heart pounding. "Maya? Ethan?" she whispered, her eyes wide with surprise.

Gabe glanced over, confused. "Do I know you two?"

Maya stopped a few feet away, her gaze fixed on Gabe and Sadie. "We don't know you, but we know Sadie." Her tone was cold, her eyes sharp with suspicion.

Ethan stepped forward, his posture stiff and confrontational. "We've been keeping an eye on things around here. Saw the car, figured we'd stick around to see what was here and what was found. Since, it's you, dear cousin, what have you been up to in the Old Mill?"

Sadie took a deep breath, trying to steady her nerves. "I've been so rude, Gabe, let me introduce you to my cousins, Maya and Ethan Adams. They have another sister as well, Lily. Maya is an expert in technology, specifically in cryptology, and Ethan is an entrepreneur, expanding their family's assets worldwide. And, this is Gabe Morgan, new resident in Carter's Creek, descendent of Captain Gabriel Morgan who lived here after the Civil War."

Gabe nodded politely, still trying to process the sudden appearance. "Nice to meet you both. So, what brings you to the Old Mill?"

Ethan stepped closer, his voice taking on a more authoritative tone. "Our family has deep roots in Carter's Creek, especially tied to Henry Whitmore's legacy. We have a legal right to whatever is uncovered here."

Sadie interjected smoothly, attempting to defuse the tension. "Henry Whitmore's contributions are indeed significant, but we're here to ensure that Carter's Creek's history is preserved properly. There's no need for disputes."

Gabe sensed the underlying tension but now was beginning to understand the family connections. "Legal rights will be determined by what's found, especially since it all seems to surround the history of Carter's Creek. What exactly have you discovered?"

Maya smirked slightly, her attempt to hide her true intentions evident. "Seriously, you're both leaving historic ruins with stuffed backpacks, and you want to know what we've discovered?"

Ethan's gaze softened for a moment, but his tone remained firm. "We're not here to cause trouble. We just want to make sure that whatever is found here aligns with our family's interests and the town's best interests."

Sadie felt the pressure mounting, realizing that Maya and Ethan were more involved than she initially thought. "We understand the importance of your family's legacy, Ethan. But our goal is to protect and preserve the town's history, which includes the Old Mill."

Gabe smiled tentatively, trying to appease, "I don't think our search is at odds with yours. We're happy to share what we've found when we understand it fully, and it's time to take it public."

Maya's expression hardened, and she took a step back, clearly not satisfied with Gabe's response. "Collaboration would require transparency, which doesn't seem to be happening here."

Ethan crossed his arms, his frustration evident. "Sounds like you are you just protecting your own interests. We need to ensure that the legacy tied to Henry Whitmore isn't overshadowed by the agendas of others."

Before the situation could escalate further, another car drove up, and Tom Hunter stepped out of the driver's side, "Hey, Gabe, I've been trying to reach you, I need you at the tavern this evening. Are you guys ready to head back?"

"Sure, Tom, we'll head that way now. We were just wrapping up this conversation," With that, Gabe and Sadie headed to his SUV, dropping their backpacks in the back, before driving away with Maya and Ethan just watching in silence.

"Weren't you already on the schedule for at the Tavern tonight?" Sadie asked.

Gabe nodded, smiling, "Yep, I'm sure Tom was just driving by and decided to rescue us from those two! I'm so thankful for good friends. I'll drop you off at the bakery, then head on over to the tavern to thank him for that!"

***

SECRETS OF THE OLD MILL 55

Gabe pulled into the familiar parking spot of Southern Roots Tavern, the warm glow from its windows a comforting sight after the harrowing events at the Old Mill. As he stepped out of the SUV, he took a moment to steady himself, the weight of the day's discoveries pressing on his mind. The riddle from the journal buzzed incessantly in his thoughts, its cryptic verses intertwining with the tension from the confrontation.

Inside, the tavern was bustling with patrons winding down their evenings. Gabe greeted Tom with a nod. "Evening, Tom. Ready for another busy night?"

Tom clapped him on the shoulder, his face breaking into a hearty smile. "Always, Gabe. Grab a seat and take a minute to unwind. Looks like you've had quite the day."

Gabe dropped down on one of the bar stools, and smiled, "Thanks for that save back there, Tom. Those are Sadie's cousins – on the Adams side apparently, and they seem to think they have some claim on ... whatever we're trying to find, saying it's their family legacy. I really appreciate Sadie, but these cousins are definitely becoming a problem."

Tom laughed, "No problem, Gabe. I recognized the look on your face from the road, and I thought you might need some help extricating yourself without resorting to violence. You know what they say, keep your friends close, and keep your enemies even closer. The bar is yours, I'm headed home!"

The doors swung open, and Ms. Beatrice, the town's beloved gossip, strode in with her usual flair, and Mabel right behind her. "Gabe, darling! I hearing about sightings of you and Sadie? Is there something you can tell me ... you know I'd never tell a soul!"

Gabe chuckled, pouring their usual Shirley Temples. "No big announcements pending, we've just teamed up for a mutual project that affects both our families."

"Let's find a table by the window, Beatrice. Need to be able to see the action outside and in. Thanks, Gabe, you make the best drinks," as Mabel settled in at their usual front table.

As the evening progressed, Gabe found himself juggling orders, serving drinks, and engaging in light-hearted conversations with the patrons. Yet, his mind kept drifting back to the riddle and the encounter with Maya and Ethan. Every time he handed someone a glass or took an order, he pondered the lines:

> *"Beneath the watchful gaze of the ancient tree,*
> *Where light meets shadow, the path shall be.*
> *Seek the place where brothers convene,*
> *There lies the legacy unseen."*

For the first time, he wondered about this family back home. The Captain's journal had been passed down from generation to generation until his own dad has given it to him. Maybe it was time to connect with his roots again. It was too late to call now, so he'd have to remember to do that tomorrow, and tomorrow was another good day for researching the Captain's words.

***

As closing time approached, the tavern began to empty, patrons bidding their goodnights and leaving the cozy establishment. Gabe wiped down the bar, the day's exhaustion evident in his movements. Just then, the door swung open again, and Sadie stepped in, her eyes weary yet determined.

"Hey, Gabe," she greeted softly, taking a seat beside him. "Mind if I join you for a bit?"

Gabe smiled, pouring her a glass of wine. "Of course not. Come on, let's figure this riddle out together."

Sadie sighed, sipping her wine. "I just can't shake the feeling that we're missing something obvious. The clues seem scattered, but there has to be a connection."

Gabe nodded, his mind racing through the possibilities, as he locked the front door. "Beneath the watchful gaze of the ancient tree... there are so many trees around here, where do we start? And where do brothers usually convene around here?"

Gabe glanced at Sadie, a playful idea forming in his mind. "You know what? Maybe we need to take a break and clear our heads."

He reached down and dropped a few coins into the jukebox, selecting the song. As the familiar melody of Rascal Flatts singing "Bless the Broken Road" filled the tavern, Gabe reached toward Sadie. "Care to dance?"

Sadie hesitated for a moment, then smiled and placed her hand in his. They moved to the small dance floor, swaying gently to the heartfelt lyrics. The rest of the world seemed to fade away as they lost themselves in the moment, the riddle temporarily set aside.

As the song reached its chorus, Gabe leaned in, singing a line softly into Sadie's ear, "Every long lost dream led me to where you are." His voice was warm, filled with genuine emotion.

Sadie blushed, feeling a flutter in her chest. The connection between them felt deeper amidst the uncertainty of their quest. As the song drew to a close, Gabe gently kissed the top of Sadie's head. "Let me drive you home," he whispered, a promise lingering in his eyes. "We'll start fresh tomorrow and tackle this treasure hunt together."

Sadie nodded, her smile radiant. "I'd like that."

"Maybe we do need to take a break," Gabe admitted, his hand finding Sadie's, as they headed for the parking lot.

Sadie squeezed his hand gently. "Yeah, but tomorrow's another day. We'll figure this out, Gabe. Together."

As they shared a quiet moment, the bond between them solidified, setting the foundation for the challenges and discoveries that awaited in the days to come.

Chapter Six

Stronger Together

THE FIRST LIGHT OF dawn filtered through the thin curtains of Gabe Morgan's modest bedroom in Carter's Creek. Exhausted yet restless, he sat on the edge of his bed, the events of the previous day swirling in his mind. The confrontation with Maya and Ethan Adams still lingered, and the riddle from Captain Morgan's journal gnawed at his thoughts. Determined to seek some clarity, Gabe reached for his phone, his fingers trembling slightly as he dialed his parents' number back in the Outer Banks.

After a few rings, his mother's warm voice greeted him. "Gabe! Is that you? ... Lee, come in the living room, Gabe's on the phone!"

Gabe smiled, relief washing over him. "Hey, Mom. It's me."

"Sweetie, it's so good to hear your voice! How are you settling into Carter's Creek?"

Lee spoke as he entered the room, the phone on speaker, "Hi, son, how are you?"

Gabe took a deep breath, feeling the comfort of his parents' love. "I'm happy, and I feel like I'm exactly where I'm supposed to be. I've started researching the Captain's Journal, and it's really interesting. One of my friends, Sadie ... she owns the local bakery here ... is related to Henry Whitmore, apparently one of the Captain's close friends, so she's helping me figure this out."

There was a brief pause before Rachel replied, her curiosity piqued. "Sadie? Tell me more about her. What's she like?"

Gabe leaned back, considering how much to share. "She's smart, determined, and really passionate about preserving our town's legacy. We're having fun trying to figure all this out. And, she bakes the best treats!"

His father, Lee, chimed in from the other end of the line. "Hmm, I love treats! I had the Captain's Journal all those years, but it never had a pull on me, like it has on you. I'm so proud of you, for taking a risk to move and figure this out. I can't wait to hear what you find."

Gabe's heart skipped a beat. "Actually, Dad, I was just thinking about all our visits here when I was a kid. Do you remember meeting any kin of Henry Whitmore?"

Lee chuckled softly. "Oh, I had so many cousins in that area. Family cookouts were massive—everyone from miles around would come. There were always stories about Captain Gabriel Morgan and Henry Whitmore founding the town right after the Civil War. They were the backbone of Carter's Creek, bringing everyone together and laying the foundation for what it is today."

Rachel added, her voice tinged with nostalgia, "The Whitmores were remarkable. According to stories we heard, Henry was always passionate about building and preserving, much like what you and Sadie are doing now."

Gabe felt a surge of connection to his heritage. "It's fascinating how their legacy still influences things today. I have the Captain's Journal, and Sadie has a book her Aunt Clara wrote, publishing all the stories she'd heard passed down over the generations. We've already seen a few pictures of the two of them together – the Captain and Henry."

Lee's tone became more serious. "You know, Carter's Creek has a way of keeping its secrets close. If you're delving into the Whitmore legacy, be prepared for some surprises. Those old families had layers of history that even we might not fully understand, and secrets are there for a reason."

Gabe nodded, even though his parents couldn't see him. "I will, Dad. Hey, yesterday we found a hidden compartment, and inside there was a riddle we're trying to figure out. Perhaps it will ring a bell with you."

"Sure, son, what was it?" his Dad asked.

> "Beneath the watchful gaze of the ancient tree,
> Where light meets shadow, the path shall be.
> Seek the place where brothers convene,
> There lies the legacy unseen."

Lee was quiet for a moment, then said, "It doesn't immediately bring anything to mind. Text that to me, and I'll keep thinking about it. ... where brothers convene – all I can think of is fishing. The guys always got together to go fishing down at the creek when we visited."

Gabe paused to text the riddle to his Dad, "No worries, if either of you think of something from the past that might help, let me know. I'm just working my shifts at the tavern, and spending my time figuring out where the Captain is leading me. That's exactly how I feel, that he's leading me."

Rachel's voice softened. "Just remember to take care of yourself, Gabe. We're proud of you for pursuing this, but don't let it overwhelm you. Take time to enjoy life, perhaps ask out Sadie."

Gabe smiled, feeling the warmth of his family's support despite the distance. "Thanks, Mom. We're just friends, working together, don't want to mess that up. How are things back home?"

Lee laughed, the sound echoing through the phone. "Busy as always. The fishermen are prepping for the season, and Grandma Ruth's been experimenting with new recipes for the cookouts. You know how she is—always trying to outdo herself."

Gabe chuckled. "Sounds like classic Grandma. Send her my best."

As the conversation wound down, Gabe felt a renewed sense of purpose. His parents' stories about the Whitmores provided historical context and a personal connection to the mysteries he and Sadie were unraveling. The weight of responsibility settled on his shoulders, but so did the strength of his resolve.

"Thanks for chatting, I love you," Gabe said, his voice steady. "Talk to you again soon."

"Love you, Gabe. We're always here for you," Rachel replied warmly before the call ended.

Gabe placed the phone down, the room now silent except for the distant sounds of the tavern beginning to stir. He stood up, stretching his arms, and glanced out the window. The morning sun cast long shadows over Carter's Creek, the town already waking up to another day of secrets and stories waiting to be discovered.

With a deep breath, Gabe grabbed his backpack and headed out the door, ready to face whatever challenges the day would bring. The legacy of the Whitmores was intertwined with his own journey, and he was determined to uncover the truth, no matter where it led.

As he walked briskly out the door, Gabe thought about the riddle and the lingering confrontation. He knew he needed more perspectives to make sense of it. Pulling out his phone, he quickly typed a message to his friends, Tommy and Luke:

"Hey guys, up for lunch at Dew Drop Inn today? Need to pick your brains about a riddle I found. Might help us figure out the next step."

Within minutes, he received responses:

Tommy: "Sounds good! Count me in. Could use a guys' lunch."

Luke: "I'm in too. Let's meet at noon? Maybe discuss over some sweet tea."

Gabe smiled, feeling grateful for their support. "Perfect, see you both at noon."

***

Later that morning, Sadie's Sweet Rolls was alive with the comforting scents of freshly baked bread, cinnamon, and vanilla. The warm, inviting aroma enveloped the cozy bakery, drawing in passersby with its irresistible allure. Inside, Sadie was busy kneading dough and arranging an array of pastries on the display counter, her hands deftly working the flour-covered surfaces.

The door jingled melodiously as Hannah walked in, her face lighting up with a bright smile. "Hey, Sadie," she called out cheerfully.

Sadie turned, her face breaking into a warm smile. "Hannah, you're early! Come get us both a cup of tea, and let's catch up."

Hannah dropped her bag behind the counter and moved to make the tea. "I woke up early this morning, so thought I'd head on in to see if I could help you with the morning baking."

"I'm ahead of schedule myself. I had trouble sleeping last night, thinking about this project with Gabe—so much we don't understand yet," Sadie shared.

Before Hannah could respond, the door swung open again, and the bell above it rang as Emma walked in, smiling brightly. "Hey, ladies! It smells great in here. I'm putting on weight just smelling it. Ohh ... I think baby just moved."

She dropped down on a chair, holding her belly. "That's a first. Oh, there she goes again—come feel this."

Hannah immediately stepped over to touch Emma softly. "Wow, he's going to be a kicker for the football team. Let me get you a cup of tea—we were just going to visit, join us."

Sadie rushed over, not wanting to miss out. Sure enough, the baby kicked again when Sadie laid her hand on Emma. "Wow, this makes all this really real. I'm so happy for you. Luke is going to be so sad he missed this."

"I'm sure baby will kick for him later too!" Emma laughed. "I'd love a cup of tea and some girl talk. It's been too long since we've had girls time!"

Right then, the bell above the door jingled again as Linda and Mary arrived, laughing and smiling. "Look, everyone's here ... and, wow, Sadie, this place smells wonderful!"

"Mom, the baby just kicked ... first time!" Emma glowed. Mary came over to hug her daughter's neck.

Sadie smiled warmly. "I hope you all buy something before you leave, but let's all have a cup of tea on the house to celebrate Emma's active baby."

Hannah was the first to respond to Sadie's offer. "Honestly, I don't know how you don't eat every last thing you bake, Sadie. I love working here!"

Sadie chuckled as she wiped her hands on her apron, settling into a chair beside the others. "Trust me, I get my fill when I'm baking. But something about working with the dough keeps me on track."

Hannah leaned in, teasing, "So, speaking of Gabe... he's been around a lot lately, hasn't he?"

Sadie blushed slightly, waving her hand dismissively. "It's just the project we're working on. You know, trying to figure out this whole treasure thing. Just teamwork."

Linda, who had been quietly stirring her tea, smiled knowingly. "Nothing, huh? Funny how he's always hanging around here, though. Researching history with a beautiful baker—sounds like a romance novel to me."

Emma burst out laughing, her hand still on her belly. "Linda's right. And trust me, I've known Luke for years. Men don't spend that much time on 'research' unless there's more to it."

Sadie felt her cheeks heat up even more but couldn't help the small smile tugging at her lips. "Okay, maybe there's a little more to it, but we've got bigger things to focus on right now. Like figuring out what these riddles mean and what we're supposed to be uncovering."

Mary nodded in agreement. "Well, honey, I'm sure the mystery will reveal itself in time, but don't let that boy slip away while you're busy looking for clues." Her words were warm, encouraging, and full of motherly wisdom.

As they sipped their tea, the conversation drifted back to the riddle and the mystery Gabe and Sadie were trying to solve. The air in the bakery became charged with the excitement of the unknown.

"So," Linda leaned in, her voice curious, "what exactly did you two find at the Old Mill?"

Sadie glanced around, realizing the circle of women would keep this conversation close. "We found a journal," she began, her voice soft but steady. "It's from Captain Gabriel Morgan. He and Henry Whitmore worked together on so many projects around town—things I never realized were connected. There are symbols, riddles... and I think they've left a trail leading us to something important. The problem is, we don't fully understand the clues yet."

Hannah raised an eyebrow. "Well, you've got a lot of brilliant minds right here. Maybe we can help?"

Emma set her teacup down, her excitement bubbling up. "I love solving puzzles. Tell us the clue. Maybe a fresh set of eyes will help piece things together."

Sadie recited it from memory, her voice dropping to a more serious tone as she spoke:

> *"Beneath the watchful gaze of the ancient tree,*
> *Where light meets shadow, the path shall be.*
> *Seek the place where brothers convene,*
> *There lies the legacy unseen."*

The room fell silent for a moment as each woman mulled over the words. Finally, Linda broke the silence. "Where brothers convene? Sounds like the tavern to me. That's where I used to always go to meet men. Glad those days are past!"

Mary nodded thoughtfully, then chimed in. "Or maybe it's the men's prayer breakfast at church. That's where a lot of the men gather every Saturday morning."

Sadie nodded, considering the suggestions. "Those are both great ideas. The tavern is definitely a hub for the men in town, and the prayer breakfast is another place where they come together regularly. But there's also the local diner—so many men gather there to shoot the bull in the morning."

Hannah tapped her chin, thinking aloud. "The diner could be a key location. It's central, and there's always a lot of activity. How do we figure out what it has to do with the riddle?"

Emma leaned forward, her eyes sparkling with determination. "Or maybe it's not just about the location, but the time. 'Where light meets shadow' could imply a specific time of day—like sunrise or sunset—when the lighting changes. We should consider when these gatherings happen and what might be hidden during those times."

Linda nodded in agreement. "Good point. Perhaps there's a specific event or ritual they do at the tavern or the church that ties into the legacy. We should look into the history of those gatherings."

Sadie felt a surge of excitement as the ideas flowed. "This is perfect. With all of us brainstorming, I'm confident we can make some progress. Here's a thought—Mary, could you talk to Pastor Daniel about this, since he is your husband? Perhaps he'll see a connection if it's the prayer breakfast at church. I'll talk to Gabe about the tavern."

Hannah grinned. "I love that idea. It's like our own little investigative team. Girl power!"

Emma nodded enthusiastically. "Absolutely. And who knows, we might uncover something amazing for Carter's Creek. It's about time we honored the legacy our families built."

Linda placed her hand on Sadie's shoulder. "Count me in. The more perspectives we have, the better our chances of solving this mystery."

Mary smiled warmly. "And it's always more fun doing it together. And, don't forget, ladies—especially you, Sadie—sometimes we miss what's right in front of us every day!"

Sadie felt a deep sense of gratitude and camaraderie. "Thank you all. This means so much to me and Gabe. Now, who needs what from my bakery."

Hannah rose, wrapping her apron around her waist, joining Sadie behind the counter.

Emma said, "I came in to get a box of treats for the workers at the Town Hall. Throw in a pie for dinner tonight – Luke may need some consoling if the baby doesn't kick for him, too."

Linda put her arm around Mary in a side hug, "And, we just wanted a box of cookies for a women's gathering at the church later today. You are all welcome, but I know you're working at that time"

Sadie felt a surge of optimism, as she and Hannah started boxing up their products. "You guys are the best, and this is a great start to the day. Thanks for being my friends!."

The women nodded in agreement, their unified purpose evident in their determined expressions. As they finished their tea and began to gather their things, the sense of camaraderie and shared mission filled **Sadie's Sweet Rolls** with an electric energy. They were ready to delve deeper into the mysteries of Carter's Creek, supporting Gabe and Sadie every step of the way.

***

The late morning sun cast a warm glow over Dew Drop Inn, a beloved local spot where Carter's Creek town folks gathered often for hearty meals and good conversation. Inside, the rustic decor and the inviting smell of sizzling bacon and brewed coffee made it the perfect place for Gabe, Tommy, and Luke to meet.

Gabe sat at their usual corner table, scanning the room while waiting for his friends to arrive. The place was bustling with activity, but the trio always found a quiet spot amidst the lively crowd.

A few minutes later, Tommy and Luke walked in, waving as they approached. "Hey, Gabe! Sorry we're late," Tommy greeted, taking a seat beside him.

"No worries, guys. Thanks for meeting up today," Gabe replied, glancing at the menu. "We need to talk about what we found yesterday, it's a riddle and I can't figure out what it means."

Luke nodded, leaning forward with a serious expression. "We've got three good heads on us. Let's see if we can make some sense of it."

They ordered their meals—Tommy opting for pancakes, Luke choosing a hearty omelette, and Gabe going for the classic breakfast sandwich. As they waited for their food, the conversation naturally turned to the riddle:

Tommy prompted, "Alright, let's break this down. 'Beneath the watchful gaze of the ancient tree'—what could that refer to?"

Gabe sighed, rubbing his temples. "Yeah, that part is pretty vague. We know there are a few old trees around town, but none stand out as particularly 'watchful.'"

Luke added, "Well, 'where light meets shadow' might hint at a specific time of day—maybe dawn or dusk when shadows are long and the lighting changes."

Tommy pulled out his notepad, jotting down notes. "Right. And 'seek the place where brothers convene'—that could mean a spot where men gather regularly. The tavern, the prayer breakfast at church, or even this diner doing exactly what we're doing now."

Gabe leaned back, considering their options. "The tavern is a possibility. We have a lot of regulars there. But so is the church's prayer breakfast. And the diner is a central spot for morning conversations."

"Maybe the 'ancient tree' is near the creek where the men fish. Fishing and telling tall tales, that's all part of men bonding in slow motion!" Tommy said, laughing.

Luke pondered on it thoughtfully, adding, "That makes sense. The creek has those old trees that have been there forever. 'Beneath the watchful gaze' could refer to the large, old oak trees by the water. We probably need to put out eyes on that landscape out by the creek."

Gabe felt a surge of clarity. "Exactly. The creek is a central part of the town's history. Maybe the riddle is pointing us to something hidden there, possibly something connected to the Whitmore legacy.

Tommy suggested, "Why don't we head down to the creek late this afternoon and throw a line out. It may clear our minds, it may give us an idea, and maybe we can have fish for dinner."

Gabe felt a sense of relief and determination. "Agreed. Let's meet at the creek around 4 PM. We can bring some gear and see what comes up."

Tommy raised his coffee cup in a toast. "To solving mysteries and making new memories."

Luke leaned forward, his expression serious. "Alright, so we've narrowed it down to the creek. But there's something else bothering me—Gabe, how are things between you and Sadie? You seem a bit... tense lately."

Gabe hesitated, his fork paused midway to his mouth. The question struck a chord deep within him. "What do you mean?"

Luke exchanged a knowing glance with Tommy before responding. "You've been working closely with her on this project. It's great, but sometimes it feels like there's more going on beneath the surface."

Gabe sighed, his gaze dropping to his coffee. "It's complicated. Sadie is amazing—her dedication, her passion. But sometimes I wonder if this whole mystery is stirring up an attraction, just because working together is exciting."

Tommy nodded sympathetically. "I get it. When you're deeply involved in something, especially something like this, it can blur the lines between friendship and something more."

Gabe looked up, meeting his friends' concerned eyes. "I don't want to jeopardize what we have, but I can't deny that there's something there. Every time we're working together, I feel this tension—like we're on the brink of something, but I don't know how to navigate it."

Luke placed a reassuring hand on Gabe's shoulder. "Have you talked to her about it?"

Gabe shook his head. "Not yet. Full story – we danced together last night. We were tense trying to figure out this riddle, so ... we danced. It really cleared the chaos in my brain for the moment, and now I'm feeling tense again."

Luke leaned back, offering a thoughtful smile. "You know, when I first got back to town and the same feelings I'd had forever stirred up again for Emma, I was terrified of messing things up. But here's what helped me: communication. It might be scary, but talking to Sadie could clear the air. Whether it's just about the project or something more, honesty is the best way to move forward. They can tell when we're struggling with something, and it's better for them to know what it is, than to guess and come to the wrong conclusion."

Tommy nodded in agreement. "Luke's right. Plus, Sadie respects you, Gabe. She might be feeling something too, which would be great to know."

Gabe took a deep breath, absorbing his friends' advice. "You're both right. Maybe I need to find the right moment to talk to her. Not during a rush or when we're distracted by the mystery."

Tommy clapped him on the back. "Exactly. Take it one step at a time. Focus on solving the riddle, and let things unfold naturally. We'll here for you no matter what."

Gabe smiled, feeling a bit lighter. "Thanks, guys. I appreciate it. Let's go knock out our day, and I'll meet you later at the creek. The fish are waiting with baited breath."

***

The afternoon sun began its descent, casting long shadows across Carter's Creek as Gabe drove toward the creek. The hum of the engine and the rhythm of passing scenery provided a temporary distraction from his swirling thoughts about Sadie. His phone buzzed, reminding him of Sadie's earlier message: "The ladies ended up at the bakery today, and we put our heads together. Can't wait to tell you our thoughts. - Sadie."

As Gabe navigated the familiar roads, he glanced in his rearview mirror and noticed Mr. Mattison, the town archivist, driving ahead of him. Gabe slowed down slightly to keep pace, remembering the strange vibes he'd felt the last time they visited the Town Archives.

They reached a fork in the road. Mr. Mattison took the right path toward the outskirts of town, an area seldom frequented. Gabe opted for the left path, leading directly to the creek.

When Gabe arrived at the creek, he saw Tommy and Luke already unloading their gear. The familiar sound of water flowing and birds chirping filled the air. They studied the landscape, searching for anything that might relate to the riddle. Nothing obvious stood out—just the serene beauty of the creek with its towering ancient oaks and gently rippling water. However, they did notice another truck parked nearby—Luke's dad's truck.

"Dad must be fishing, too," Luke remarked, shrugging. "Shall we join him?"

"Yeah," Tommy agreed, heading down the path to the creek. "The more, the merrier."

As they stepped onto the banks, they saw Tom Hunter and Pastor Daniel Thompson fishing side by side and laughing. It was a surprise to see these two sharing such friendly moments after years of avoiding one another. Their newfound friendship had blossomed in the weeks leading up to Luke and Emma's wedding.

"Wow, Daniel, look who's here! Luke, Gabe, and Tommy—pull up a seat and help us catch supper," Tom invited with a warm smile.

They cast their lines into the water, the rhythmic splash of bait creating a soothing backdrop for their conversation.

"We've been trying to figure out a riddle we found in a journal at the Old Mill," Gabe began. "One of the lines says, 'Seek the place where brothers convene.' We thought it might point us here, to the creek, especially since all of us ended up here today."

Daniel nodded thoughtfully. "Mary mentioned the riddle too. The ladies think it might be related to the Men's Prayer Breakfast at church, but I don't see anything related to that here. If there had been, I think I'd have found it already. But things are exciting at your house—she mentioned the baby kicked this morning."

"Seriously?" Luke asked, his eyes wide. "That's the first I've heard of it. I'm so jealous."

Tom smiled warmly. "You'll have plenty of opportunities to feel those kicks in the months to come. The girls were lucky to share that experience together today."

Throughout the conversation, the guys were pulling in fish, one after another. They threw back the small ones and kept the larger fish for a meal. Luke decided there would be enough for a cookout, so he called Emma to see if she and the ladies were up for dinner. She thought it was a great idea and began rounding up the girls to join them.

"Let's catch a few more fish, then head to my house for a cookout. The ladies are already gathering," Luke said, casting his line once more. "I don't think the riddle will lead to an obvious answer. It's meant to be hard to find."

"All I know is I feel drawn to this journey, so I believe we'll know when the time is right," agreed Gabe. "What's bothering me right now is that I ended up following Mr. Mattison while driving out here. He took the right path at the fork, but I can't remember anything out that way but open land."

Tommy pondered, "He lives in town, right? There's not much out that way. Maybe he's just taking a quiet drive or checking on something."

Luke nodded thoughtfully. "It's odd, though. He's not the type to go off on solitary drives without a reason. Maybe he's onto something or has his own mystery to solve."

Tommy glanced at Gabe, sensing his unease. "Do you think he's connected to this riddle somehow?"

Gabe shrugged, trying to shake off the lingering tension. "I don't know. Maybe. Sadie and I got some weird vibes from him during our last visit to the Town Archives, and now this. It just doesn't feel right."

Tom stood up suddenly. "Daniel, are you ready to head back? I'd like to make a stop along the way."

Daniel gathered their gear and paused. "Men, follow your instincts—they're often right. And, Gabe, it feels like you're on a path meant for you. Keep moving forward and trust others to help you stay focused on what matters."

Tom and Daniel headed toward their truck, leaving the rest of the guys to continue fishing. Their conversation drifted back to the riddle and the clues they were uncovering. The tranquil setting provided a perfect environment for their thoughts to flow freely.

Suddenly, Gabe's phone buzzed with a message from Sadie: "Thanks for today, guys. Looking forward to our next steps. - Sadie."

He showed the message to Tommy and Luke, feeling a pang in his chest. "She's keeping everything so together. I don't want to mess things up between us."

Tommy placed a hand on Gabe's shoulder. "You've got this, man. Just take it one step at a time."

Luke smiled, saying, "Come on, men, it's time to provide the fish for the meal. Let's head home—I need to feel my baby kick."

Gabe loved the sound of that. "Let's head home."

Chapter Seven

Feast of Secrets

THE LARGE WINDOWS OF Luke and Emma's kitchen framed the brilliant colors of the sunset, casting a warm glow on the bustling activity within. The kitchen was the heart of their home, with its wooden countertops, mismatched chairs, and the lingering scent of freshly brewed coffee. Pots and pans hung neatly from a rack above the island, and vibrant vegetables lay scattered across the cutting board, waiting to be transformed into a delicious salad.

The door swung open, and Mary Thompson stepped inside, a cheerful smile lighting up her face. In her arms, she carried a large pan of baked beans, the rich aroma promising comfort and warmth.

"Evening, Emma!" Mary called out as she approached the kitchen island. "I brought some baked beans for the cookout. Why don't you sit down and let me handle the veggies for the salad?"

Emma glanced up from her chopping, her face brightening at the sight of her mother. "Thanks, Mom! That sounds perfect. I was just about to start on the lettuce."

Mary set the pan down and handed Emma a basket filled with colorful bell peppers, cucumbers, and cherry tomatoes. "Here you go. Let's make this salad something special."

As Emma began to chop the vegetables with practiced ease, a brief knock preceded Sadie Walker's entrance. She walked in, balancing a perfectly golden pie on a plate. Her presence brought a sense of calm and determination to the room.

"Hey, everyone," Sadie greeted, setting the pie down on the countertop. "Emma, I know you bought one for Luke this morning, but I figured we'd need a few more servings for the gang."

Emma beamed, wiping her hands on her apron. "Thanks, Sadie! You're too kind."

Mary glanced over, a hint of amusement in her eyes. "Emma, I have to warn you. I told your dad about the baby kicking, and he apparently ran into Luke and told him. We may have messed up, sorry!"

Emma smiled, her eyes twinkling. "No worries, Mom. Luke will understand. It was too exciting not to share with you when it happened. And the baby is still moving, so he'll have his chance too."

Just as the kitchen settled into a comfortable rhythm, the door opened again, and Linda and Hannah entered together. Linda carried a large bowl of creamy potato salad, while Hannah held a tray of meticulously arranged deviled eggs.

"Good morning, ladies!" Linda announced, setting down her bowl. "I brought the potato salad. Thought it'd pair well with everything else."

Hannah nodded, her eyes twinkling with excitement. "And I have the deviled eggs. They're always a hit."

With all the main dishes accounted for, the kitchen buzzed with activity. Conversations flowed effortlessly as the women shared stories and laughter, the bond between them evident in every interaction. The preparation was a testament to their unity and the shared purpose that had brought them together.

"Alright, everyone, everything's ready," Emma declared, glancing around the room. "Let's head out to the backyard with our glasses of tea and wait on the men with the fish."

The patio was adorned with string lights that twinkled as the day progressed, and a large table was set with plates, utensils, and pitchers of sweet tea. The backyard was already a welcoming place, with large tables arranged for the meal, ensuring everyone had a place to gather and enjoy the feast.

As they settled into their seats, the women began to engage in the anticipated baby talk. Emma's eyes sparkled as she shared that the first ultrasound would occur at their next appointment.

"I think we want to know the baby's sex if they can see clearly on the ultrasound," Emma shared. "I've been calling the baby a 'she,' and Luke has been saying 'he,' but I know we'll both be happy either way. We're just so excited."

"We're going to plan a baby shower for you," Linda said, smiling warmly. "We can plan it without knowing the sex if that's what you decide, but it will be so fun to choose a theme and buy gifts for a specific gender."

"Planning a shower for our friend's first baby is just what we need while working on this confusing mystery," Sadie added thoughtfully. "And, ladies, I have to admit to you first, I'm definitely feeling something for Gabe. It's all entangled with this mystery, and I really want to help him on this path because it's driving him."

Mary smiled, gently touching Sadie's arm. "All those feelings will come together over time. Gabe has shared that he moved here with a strong sense of purpose to figure this out, and the two of you together discovered that both your families are part of that. I think you'll find your way together as you find your way to solving this mystery!"

Right then, Luke, Tommy, and Gabe came through the gate with their cleaned fish, striding like conquering heroes. The women rose in laughter to gather the sides inside, as Luke slid over to kiss Emma, touching her belly gently just as the baby kicked.

"Wow," Luke whispered, "that was worth the wait. I understand the excitement you felt today. I think we need to let the doctor tell us the gender at the appointment, if he can tell, right?"

"Oh, yes," Emma agreed, "This is turning into the best day ever!"

***

Tom and Daniel rolled in last, laughing as they walked into the backyard together. Mary smiled as Daniel hugged her, saying, "I was about to send out the search parties for the two of you. The fish are grilled and the table is set. We were about to sit down for the meal. Sit down, you two, and join us!"

The table of friends and family filled their plates, passing the food around family style as everyone dug in. The atmosphere was lively, filled with the sounds of laughter, clinking glasses, and the occasional splash of fish being served.

"Luke, you have to tell us again how strong that baby is kicking," Hannah urged, leaning in with genuine curiosity.

Luke chuckled, ruffling Emma's hair affectionately. "It was incredible. I felt a strong kick while I was fixing the grill. It was like a little reminder of the life growing inside."

Mary nodded, her eyes softening. "There's nothing quite like it. It makes all the preparations worth it."

The conversation naturally shifted to the joys and challenges of parenthood. Laughter and heartfelt stories filled the air, creating an atmosphere of warmth and camaraderie.

"Where'd you guys go, Dad? We were growing concerned when the fish were done, and you still weren't here," Luke asked, a hint of worry in his voice.

Tom shrugged and spoke, "I'm sorry, I'm afraid this was my fault. When you mentioned Mr. Mattison heading off to the right at the fork, it reminded me of something, and I wanted to check it out before saying more about it."

"There's so much history in Carter's Creek," explained Pastor Daniel, "so many people and places have come and gone over the years, and there aren't many records for some of those years, especially those when town soldiers were coming and going from wars. Tom and I have lived here all our lives, so we remember much of the stories that were passed on, and this is one of those."

"Carter's Creek has had a Masonic Lodge for years. Many of the guys we had been in school with were drafted for the Vietnam War. It was such a divisive war, and some of them never returned—died or were missing in action, while the ones that did return weren't quite the same. Those families started moving to the city to find a new start, and we heard as young men that only a handful of men still gathered at the Masonic Lodge, so it closed."

"What does that have to do with what we're doing?" Gabe asked, clearly confused.

Tom shared, "It was your comment about Mr. Mattison turning right at the fork... that's where the Masonic Lodge used to be. It's abandoned now, like the Old Mill, and it's not visible from the road, as the vegetation has grown up around it. I wanted to drive by just to see what we could see."

Daniel jumped in, "And guess whose truck was parked there? Mr. Mattison, and there were others with him, a Jeep with out-of-state plates. We turned around and high-tailed it back here, but he was there, and he had company."

Gabe felt a chill run down his spine. "So, Mr. Mattison was checking out the old Masonic Lodge? There's a twist if I ever heard one."

Sadie took a deep breath and added, "Ethan and Maya were driving a Jeep when we ran into them at the Old Mill. I thought Mr. Mattison dismissed them as outsiders. What are they doing together at the Masonic Lodge?"

"I'll tell you what, let's finish this meal and enjoy the company. Doing so will clear our minds, then let's sleep on it. When we push too hard, things just don't come together well. But when we relax and allow it to happen naturally, everything seems to just slip into place," Luke encouraged.

They all nodded in agreement, and Sadie rose, saying, "I think that means it's time for pie. Nothing like dessert to clear a mind!"

They all laughed as they wrapped up the meal. As everyone headed their own way, Gabe walked Sadie to her car and opened the car door for her. "Thanks for being part of this adventure with me. I don't know where it's leading, I just know I'm glad it's you by my side."

As she slid into the car seat, glancing up at him, Sadie spoke softly, "Me, too. I feel like I've been living my whole life to reach this place at this time. Good night, sleep well!"

Gabe watched her drive away, a mix of relief and lingering tension settling in his chest. As he turned to head back to his own home, his mind buzzed with the day's revelations and the mysterious connections unfolding in Carter's Creek.

***

Later that night, Gabe lay in bed, the events of the day replaying in his mind. Exhausted yet restless, he drifted into a deep sleep, his subconscious pulling him into a vivid dream.

He found himself standing in the Old Mill, the same dismal setting where he and Sadie had uncovered the journal. The moon hung high in the sky, a gentle breeze flowing through the abandoned building, and the towering ancient oaks surrounding the building whispered secrets in the gentle breeze.

From the shadows emerged a figure dressed in old-fashioned attire, a captain's uniform that seemed to belong to another era. It was Captain Gabriel Morgan, the very name that had been etched into the journal they found.

"Gabe," Captain Morgan greeted, his voice both commanding and reassuring. "You've come a long way to seek the legacy of Carter's Creek."

Gabe felt a surge of recognition and awe. "Captain Morgan? How is this possible?"

Captain Morgan smiled, gesturing towards the creek. "This place holds many secrets, and you're part of unveiling them. The riddle you're trying to solve is more than just words; it's a guide to the truth that lies beneath the surface."

Gabe approached, feeling a mixture of fear and determination. "What do I need to do? How can we solve this mystery?"

"The answers you seek are intertwined with the history of this town and the bonds you've formed," Captain Morgan explained. "Trust in your friends, for they are your strength. And remember, the past is never truly gone; it lives on through those who seek understanding."

Gabe nodded, feeling a newfound clarity. "I understand. We need to stay united and keep pushing forward together."

Captain Morgan placed a hand on Gabe's shoulder. "Indeed. Stronger together, just as you've learned. Now, go forth with courage, and let the legacy of Carter's Creek guide you."

With those final words, Captain Morgan began to fade into the mist, leaving Gabe standing alone by the Old Mill, the moonlight reflecting in his eyes. He woke up with a start, the message from the captain lingering in his mind.

Gabe sat up, his heart pounding. The dream felt so real, as if Captain Morgan had handed him a piece of the puzzle they were trying to solve. He reached for his phone, contemplating sharing this with Sadie or keeping it to himself for now.

Shaking off the remnants of sleep, Gabe knew what he had to do. Tomorrow would bring another day of investigation, and the dream had given him a renewed sense of purpose. With determination, he prepared for the challenges ahead, knowing that his friends were truly stronger together.

***

The heavy wooden door of the Town Archives basement office creaked open as Mr. Mattison entered the dimly lit room. The space was cluttered with stacks of old records, shelves filled with worn books, and a large, worn-out desk that bore the marks of countless years of diligent work. The lighting was designed for daylight, not for the deep of night, so the dim bulbs hanging from the ceiling cast long shadows, heightening the room's austere atmosphere.

Behind Mr. Mattison, the Adams siblings—Ethan, Maya, and Lily—entered cautiously. Their expressions were a mix of frustration, suspicion, and determination. The tension in the air was palpable, thick enough to be sliced with a knife.

Ethan, the eldest of the trio, took a step forward, his hands clenched into fists at his sides. "Mr. Mattison, we need to talk," he said, his voice firm yet controlled.

Mattison gestured toward the chairs scattered around the desk. "Please, have a seat. Let's discuss this calmly."

Maya exchanged a glance with her brother before nodding and moving to sit in one of the chairs. Lily followed suit, her eyes darting around the room as if searching for any sign of deception.

Ethan remained standing, unable to quell the storm of emotions brewing within him. "We saw you at the old Masonic Lodge, rummaging through their records. Why were you there? You promised if you found anything during this search, you'd tell us first, but now it seems you're seeking for yourself!"

Mattison sighed, leaning back in his chair and rubbing his temples. "Ethan, Maya, Lily, I understand why you're upset. The Masonic Lodge holds many secrets, plus more of the history of Carter's Creek, and I've been trying to uncover that history for this office alone. I will not be accused unjustly."

Maya frowned, crossing her arms over her chest. "Secrets? Mr. Mattison, we've been coming to you for weeks, trusting you to lead us. Instead, you're sneaking around at night, alone. It feels like you're hiding something."

Mattison leaned forward, his gaze earnest. "I'm not hiding anything. The Masonic Lodge was a significant part of Carter's Creek's history, especially during the wars. Many of the town's records were lost or destroyed over the years. I'm trying to piece together the events that took place there to better understand this town's history."

Lily, the youngest, looked skeptical. "And why haven't you shared anything about the Masonic Lodge with us during our visits to your office? Are you helping us, our competitors, or yourself?"

"I have a job to do for this town, that's all," Mattison snapped. "I simply wanted to secure the historical records before all of you started tearing them apart on a treasure hunt."

Ethan took a deep breath, his frustration evident. "I don't believe you for a minute. You are sneaking around doing this on your own, not for the city. I'd suggest you get out of town before we report you to the authorities for using your position to gain personal reward."

Mattison felt the weight of their accusations pressing down on him. He knew he needed to regain their trust quickly to prevent the situation from escalating further. Taking a steadying breath, he reached into a drawer and pulled out a weathered, leather-bound notebook. "Ethan, Maya, Lily, before you make any hasty decisions, let me show you something."

Ethan's eyes narrowed, suspicion still lingering. "What is that?"

Mattison placed the notebook on the desk, sliding it towards them. "This is photocopies of Captain Gabriel Morgan's journal. He was a key figure during the Civil War and played a pivotal role in founding the Masonic Lodge here in Carter's Creek with my uncle, Henry. His writings contain references to the very riddle you're trying to solve."

Maya exchanged a glance with her siblings, curiosity momentarily overriding their frustration. "Why are you showing us this now?"

Mattison nodded slowly, understanding their need for evidence. "Captain Morgan was a Confederate officer who, along with Uncle Henry, founded this town, many of it's establishments, including the Masonic Lodge to preserve the town's heritage and support the community during tumultuous times. His journal details meetings, events, and significant contributions he made to Carter's Creek. More importantly, it hints at a hidden legacy that is intertwined with the riddle we're all trying to solve."

Lily, flipping through the pages, looked up with a mixture of awe and skepticism. "Captain Morgan's contributions are impressive, but how does this help us solve the riddle?"

Mattison leaned forward, pointing to a specific entry. "Here, Captain Morgan writes about a ceremony held at the Masonic Lodge on the night the riddle was created. I strongly suspect that something was hidden or exchanged hands to protect the legacy. These artifacts are not just valuable; they hold the key to solving the riddle by providing context and uncovering connections that have been long forgotten."

Ethan's posture softened slightly as he absorbed the information. "So, the riddle is less about finding physical treasure and more about uncovering historical truths?"

"Exactly," Mattison replied. "The legacy of Carter's Creek isn't just in its landmarks or hidden treasures, but in the stories and sacrifices of its people. By understanding these, we can interpret the riddle correctly and preserve the town's true heritage."

Maya nodded thoughtfully. "If that's the case, then accessing these artifacts could provide us with the answers we need. But why keep this a secret?"

Mattison sighed, his earlier defensiveness giving way to vulnerability. "Because some of these artifacts contain sensitive information about the town's involvement in the Civil War and the Vietnam War. If this information were to become public, it could tarnish the town's reputation and lead to unnecessary conflict. I wanted to handle this discreetly to protect everyone involved."

Lily leaned in, her skepticism fading as she considered Mattison' words. "Alright, Mr. Mattison. We'll trust you for now. But from here on out, we need full transparency. No more solo missions."

Mattison nodded appreciatively. "Agreed. I should have communicated better from the start. I didn't want to burden you all with the complexities of the town's history, but I see now that collaboration is essential."

The siblings exchanged glances, affirming their decision to move forward with trust, "We'll expect better communication going forward. We're going to get out of here, in case someone else wonders in. Let's regroup soon!"

Mattison stood, his confidence restored by their renewed trust. "Excellent. Together, we'll uncover the truth behind Captain Morgan's legacy and solve the riddle once and for all."

As the siblings left, Mr. Mattison breathed a sigh of relief. He'd dodged a bullet by sharing more, but it may have been to much. It was long past the time he should have been recognized for his work on historical documents, so he was going to take care of his legacy on his own. If there is a treasure to find, he planned to find it first. Time to expedite his schedule to do so.

Chapter Eight
Discovering True Motives

The first lights of dawn filtered through the curtains of Emma's office at the Town Hall, casting soft rays across the neatly organized desk. Emma Thompson stretched, the remnants of a restless night still tugging at her eyelids. She glanced at the clock—8:00 AM. Time to start another day at the Town Hall, where mysteries seemed to find her at every turn.

As she approached her mailbox in the hallway, Emma felt a strange mix of anticipation and unease. Today felt different, the air thick with unspoken tension. She opened the mailbox, expecting the usual stack of letters and notices, but instead found a single envelope addressed to her in Mr. Mattison' handwriting.

Curiosity piqued, Emma carefully opened the envelope, revealing a neatly typed resignation letter. Alongside it, she found a set of old-fashioned keys, likely those to the Town Archives basement office. Her heart skipped a beat as she read the words penned by Mr. Mattison.

> **Resignation Letter:**
>
> *Dear Mayor Hunter,*
>
> *I regret to inform you that I must resign from my position as Town Archivist effective immediately due to a family emergency that requires my presence out of state. Unfortunately, I do not know if or when I will be able to return. I apologize for any inconvenience this may cause and trust that you and the council will manage in my absence.*
>
> *Thank you for your understanding.*
> *—Mr. Mattison*

Emma sat back, the implications of the letter sinking in. Mr. Mattison had been a pivotal figure in their ongoing investigation, his knowledge and dedication invaluable. His sudden departure left a void that felt both unexpected and unsettling.

Determined to address the situation promptly, Emma reached for her phone and dialed the number for the Carter's Creek Town Council. Within minutes, she had arranged an emergency meeting to discuss Mr. Mattison' resignation and the immediate steps forward.

***

The Town Hall was abuzz with anticipation as council members and key community figures gathered in the main meeting room. Emma stood at the front, the resignation letter and keys in hand, her expression a mix of concern and resolve.

DISCOVERING TRUE MOTIVES 91

"Thank you all for coming on such short notice," Emma began, her voice steady despite the turmoil she felt inside. "As you can see, Mr. Mattison has submitted his resignation due to a family emergency. His departure comes at a critical time for our ongoing investigations into Carter's Creek's history and some mystery as to his involvement in the same."

Councilwoman Parker, a seasoned member with graying hair and sharp eyes, leaned forward. "This is indeed concerning. Mr. Mattison was instrumental in our efforts. Do we have any indication of how long he might be away?"

Emma shook her head. "He mentioned that he doesn't know if or when he will return. Given the nature of his work and his sudden departure, we need to act quickly to ensure continuity."

Councilman Harris, a practical man known for his level-headedness, cleared his throat. "In light of this, I suggest we consider appointing Mr. Jenkins as the interim Town Archivist until we can find a suitable replacement. Mr. Jenkins has experience with the archives and has worked closely with Mr. Mattison in the past."

Emma nodded thoughtfully. "Mr. Jenkins understands the needs of the office, and since his resignation from the town council, has assisted the city in attracting new business with the new business incubator he designed. However, considering the sensitive nature of our current investigations, particularly the recent findings related to Carter's Creek history, we should also take this opportunity to review our current findings and ensure everyone is up to speed. With Mr. Mattison gone, it's crucial that we all have a clear understanding of where things stand."

Daniel, the town's pastor, added, "And perhaps we should reach out to Mr. Mattison, if possible, to see if he can provide any guidance remotely. Even a few insights could be invaluable at this stage."

Emma smiled, grateful for the council's proactive stance. "Great suggestions. I'll reach out to Mr. Jenkins immediately and arrange for him to meet with the team if he's willing to accept this temporary assignment. We'll also organize a session to review our findings and ensure everyone is aligned moving forward."

As the meeting progressed, the council members discussed the logistics of the transition, ensuring that the sudden departure of Mr. Mattison wouldn't derail their mission. The consensus was clear: unity and swift action were essential to maintaining their momentum.

Emma returned to her office, the weight of the meeting still heavy on her shoulders. She placed the keys on her desk and took a deep breath, trying to steady her nerves. Just then, her phone buzzed with a message notification. It was from Luke.

Text Message: *"Hey Emma, I'm with Gabe, we just heard about Mr. Mattison sudden resignation through the town grapevine. Let me know if you need any help with the transition. See you later!"*

Emma typed a quick response. "Thanks, Luke. Appreciate it. See you soon."

She leaned back in her chair, contemplating the next steps. Mr. Mattison' resignation had thrown a wrench into their plans, but the council's swift response offered a glimmer of hope. The investigation was far from over, and now more than ever, their unity would be crucial.

***

The town grapevine had spread the news quickly, igniting whispers and speculations among the residents. Everyone seemed to be talking about Mr. Mattison' sudden departure and the strange events sur-

DISCOVERING TRUE MOTIVES 93

rounding the Masonic Lodge. As a result, the trio found themselves the focus of both support and suspicion.

Gabe leaned forward, his elbows resting on the table, eyes narrowing thoughtfully. "I don't believe in coincidences. So, the fact that Mr. Mattison was searching the Masonic Lodge last night, at almost exactly the same time as your cousins, Sadie, is more than a coincidence. Either one of them, or together, found what they were looking for, or Mr. Mattison is taking off on his own for some reason we don't know, but whatever is happening here has to do with the treasure hunt and the four of them."

Sadie sighed, running a hand through her hair, her gaze drifting to the bustling crowd outside. "Agreed, but I think the Masonic Lodge is our next destination. Apparently, we're not the only ones working with the riddle, so shall we go there to see what we can find ... if there's still anything there to find?"

Luke nodded, tapping his fingers on the table in contemplation. "There's something off about all of this. Mr. Mattison had so much knowledge about the town's history, especially with Captain Morgan and the Masonic Lodge. If he's leaving town so abruptly, it might mean he's stumbled onto something significant."

Gabe frowned, pulling out his notebook filled with scribbled notes and maps. "Look here," he said, pointing to a series of interconnected symbols drawn around the riddle they had been trying to solve. "These symbols match the ones we found in Captain Morgan's journal. It's like they're guiding us to specific locations within the lodge."

Sadie leaned in closer, tracing her finger over the symbols. "That makes sense. Captain Morgan was a Confederate officer and founded the Masonic Lodge with Uncle Henry. Their legacy is deeply embedded in the town's history. If we follow these symbols, we might uncover the hidden compartment Captain Morgan mentioned."

Luke's expression hardened with resolve. "Then we don't have much choice. We need to go to the Masonic Lodge, thoroughly search it, and see if we can find any clues left behind. If others are involved, we need to be prepared for whatever they might be."

Gabe looked between his friends, seeing the determination mirrored in their eyes. "Alright, but we need to plan this carefully. If Mr. Mattison has taken off to another state, we can't rely on his expertise. We need to work together and use everything we've learned so far."

Sadie nodded. "Let's gather all our resources and maybe even reach out to Mr. Jenkins. If he's stepping in as the new Archivist, he might have some insights or additional documents that could help us."

As they strategized, a server approached their table with fresh coffee, interrupting their discussion. "Coffee, anyone?" she asked with a friendly smile.

"Yes, please," Gabe replied, grateful for the brief respite. "Thank you, Marge."

As the server left, the trio exchanged glances, their resolve solidifying. They knew the path ahead was fraught with challenges, but the bonds of friendship and their shared mission gave them the strength to press on.

"Let's meet here after lunch," Luke suggested. "We can go over everything we've gathered and decide our next moves."

"Sounds like a plan," Sadie agreed. "I'll coordinate with Ethan, Maya, and Lily to make sure we're all on the same page."

Gabe stood, pushing his chair back. "Alright, let's get to it. We have a town to save and a legacy to uncover."

As they stepped out of the bakery, they saw Lily, Ethan, and Maya approaching the bakery. Lily asked, "Could we have a minute of your time, Sadie?"

Sadie shook her head, saying, "Anything you have to say to me, you can say in front of these two guys. I trust them with my life."

"We wanted to warn you about Mr. Mattison," Lily said, sighing. "We learned last night he's searching for the treasure himself, when we thought he was helping us, but he was really milking us for information. We didn't know if he was doing the same with you, so we wanted to warn you."

"Why would you warn us now?" Gabe asked. "What do you have to gain doing so?"

"A rat behaves badly, as Mr. Mattison has," answered Ethan, snidely. "I don't know where he really is, but I feel our interests, divided as they are, are better served if we all known what kind of man we're dealing with. And, I'll further put you on notice, that I intend to obtain this treasure to enhance our family's legacy. And, that's all I have to say on this matter, it was a waste of time to come here. Have a good day!" And, he strode away to their car down the block.

Lily glanced at Maya, who nodded encouragingly, and she spoke softly and quickly, "We aren't in total agreement with Ethan, so don't lump us in with him. We believe what we're searching for will have historical impact for this area, and we're very concerned if either Ethan or Mr. Mattison gets his hands on whatever this is first. We've got to go before he comes back, just know, Maya and I are not the bad guys, we're trying to do the right thing."

With that, they took off down the street quickly, headed for their car where Ethan waited.

"Wow, another twist ... do we believe her?" asked Luke. "None of that made sense to me!"

Sadie seemed to reflect on it, as she answered slowly, "I think she's warning us, and she has no reason to do so, but ethically as a purveyor of history, as an archaeologist, doing so makes sense. And, I think they were trying to tell us they were double crossed by Mr. Mattison. Luke, I think you have to go tell Emma what just happened. It may have bearing on protecting the Town Archives, plus whatever we find from both Mr. Mattison and Ethan, which both have personal agendas that are not aligned with the town's best interests."

"Gabe, what do you say? Let's go check out the Masonic Lodge on our own, if you think you can find it," she asked.

Gabe nodded, "That's exactly what I want to do. Last night, while we were cleaning up, I asked Tom lots of questions about it's location, so I'm pretty sure I can get us there. Our gear is still in my car, so let's go!'

Even though the friends were headed in opposite directions, they felt as though they were moving in unison.

***

Gabe glanced over at Sadie, seeing the determination in her eyes. They had faced numerous challenges together, but the current situation felt more complicated than ever. The conflicting motives of Mr. Mattison and Ethan added a layer of danger that couldn't be ignored.

As Gabe and Sadie made their way to the parking lot, Luke lingered behind, pulling out his phone to call Emma. The bakery's warm interior buzzed with life, oblivious to the storm brewing outside.

Inside the car, Sadie turned to Gabe, her expression serious. "We need to be cautious. If Mr. Mattison and Ethan are both after the same thing, we might be walking into a trap. We should come up with a backup plan."

Gabe nodded, starting the engine. "Agreed. First, we need to secure our gear and make sure we have everything we need for the search.

DISCOVERING TRUE MOTIVES

Flashlights, maps, and any tools that might help us uncover hidden compartments."

Sadie reached over to the passenger seat, grabbing her backpack. "I have copies of the documents we agreed are important and of Captain Morgan's journal. We might find more clues there."

As they drove towards the Masonic Lodge, the town's streets were still waking up, the early morning sun casting long shadows across the historic buildings. The lodge itself stood at the edge of town, its once grand facade now showing signs of neglect and decay. Vines crept up the walls, and the windows were dusty, the glass barely reflecting the light.

Gabe parked the car and turned to Sadie. "Alright, let's do a final check before we head in. We don't know what to expect, so being prepared is key."

They meticulously went through their checklist, ensuring they had all necessary equipment. Satisfied, they approached the lodge, the air thick with anticipation and a hint of foreboding.

"Remember, we stick to the plan," Sadie reminded Gabe as they pushed open the heavy door. It creaked loudly, echoing through the empty halls. The interior was dimly lit, shadows dancing on the walls as they navigated through the maze of corridors and rooms.

Gabe led the way, pointing out the symbols from the journal etched into the walls. "Captain Morgan was very specific about the locations. We need to find the oak tree with three acorns symbol."

As they moved deeper into the lodge, their flashlights illuminated old photographs and memorabilia lining the walls. The scent of aged wood and dust filled their senses, adding to the eerie atmosphere.

Suddenly, Gabe stopped, shining his light on a particular area. "Look here. This symbol matches the one in the journal."

Sadie knelt down, examining the symbol closely. "It's a hidden mechanism. Captain Morgan must have designed it to conceal the compartment."

With careful precision, they pressed the symbol, and a section of the wall began to move, revealing a narrow passageway. Excitement and tension surged through them as they stepped into the hidden corridor, unsure of what awaited them.

"Stay close and keep your eyes open," Gabe whispered, leading the way.

The passageway led them to a small, dimly lit room filled with artifacts and documents. Captain Morgan's journal was spread out on a table, along with various items that seemed untouched by time.

Sadie picked up a faded photograph of Captain Morgan and Uncle Henry standing proudly in front of the lodge. "This is incredible. We're really here, uncovering their legacy."

Gabe scanned the room, his eyes landing on a locked chest in the corner. "There's something here. It might be what we're looking for."

Before they could approach the chest, a noise echoed through the corridor—a soft, deliberate footstep. They froze, hearts pounding, as a shadowy figure emerged from the darkness.

"Looking for something?" the figure asked, stepping into the light. It was Mr. Jenkins, the new Town Archivist, his expression unreadable.

"We didn't know you were here," Gabe replied cautiously. "We could ask you the same thing."

Jenkins raised his hands in a gesture of peace. "I came to help. I heard about Mr. Mattison' departure and wanted to assist with the investigation. The treasure hunt isn't just about finding wealth; it's about preserving our town's history."

DISCOVERING TRUE MOTIVES

Sadie exchanged a glance with Gabe before stepping forward. "Then let's work together. There's no time to waste."

Jenkins nodded, moving closer to the chest. "This chest contains artifacts Captain Morgan deemed essential for understanding our past. Let's open it together."

As they worked to unlock the chest, the room seemed to hold its breath, the weight of history pressing down on them. With a satisfying click, the lock released, and the chest opened to reveal a collection of journals, letters, and small artifacts.

"Here we go," Gabe said, relief evident in his voice. "Now, let's see what secrets they hold."

Within the chest, among the journals and letters, they found an old, ornate key adorned with the same oak tree and three acorns symbol found in the Town Hall. Additionally, there was a small, intricately carved stone with a map etched into it, highlighting both the Masonic Lodge and the Town Hall.

Sadie picked up the stone, her eyes lighting up with realization. "This map shows both locations with connecting pathways marked by our symbols. It must be the key to unlocking the secrets in the Town Hall."

Gabe nodded, carefully handling the key. "And these rings... they might be part of a coded system that grants access to different parts of the town's hidden legacy."

Luke examined the letters, finding references to joint ceremonies held at both the Masonic Lodge and the Town Hall. "Captain Morgan and Uncle Henry were clearly working together to safeguard the town's history. This chest holds the clues we need to connect everything back to the Town Hall."

Jenkins smiled, a sense of purpose rekindling in his eyes. "With this key and map, we can uncover the true legacy of Carter's Creek and ensure that its history is preserved for generations to come."

As the weight of their discoveries settled, Gabe felt a surge of concern. If Mr. Mattison and Ethan were both after the same secrets, they needed to protect the real artifacts from falling into the wrong hands.

Gabe turned to Mr. Jenkins, an idea forming in his mind. "We need to leave something behind for other searchers to find that will lead them away from the truth. A decoy to mislead them."

Mr. Jenkins pondered the suggestion for a moment before nodding thoughtfully. "I think I know just the thing."

He reached into the chest and pulled out an old, faded ledger and a set of seemingly unrelated documents. "These items are convincing enough to throw them off our trail. Captain Morgan kept meticulous records, and these should appear valuable to anyone searching for historical artifacts."

Sadie looked intrigued. "What do you propose we do with them?"

Jenkins carefully arranged the ledger and documents on the table, creating an illusion of importance. "We'll place these in a more accessible part of the lodge, maybe even in the library where others might think to look first. They contain minor details and fake clues that point to non-existent artifacts in different locations around town. It should buy us the time we need to secure the real relics in the Town Hall."

Gabe nodded, appreciating the plan. "That way, anyone else who comes looking will be chasing shadows instead of the truth."

Luke chimed in, "And we can monitor any activity around those decoy clues to ensure no one uncovers our actual hiding spots."

Sadie smiled, her confidence bolstered by the collaborative effort. "It's a solid strategy. We'll need to ensure the decoy is convincing enough to keep them occupied."

Jenkins added, "I'll handle the placement of the decoy items. Meanwhile, you three focus on securing the key and mapping out the Town Hall's secret compartments. Time is of the essence."

Gabe felt a sense of relief. "Thank you, Mr. Jenkins. With your help, we can protect our town's true legacy and stay one step ahead of anyone who might want to exploit it."

As they finalized their plan, the atmosphere in the hidden chamber shifted from discovery to strategic action. The team worked together seamlessly, each member playing to their strengths to ensure the protection of Carter's Creek's most valuable secrets.

***

With the decoy strategy in place, Gabe, Sadie, and Mr. Jenkins exited the Masonic Lodge, the weight of their responsibilities pressing upon them. They made their way to the nearby parking lot, where Gabe loaded their findings into the car. Mr. Jenkins gave them a reassuring nod before departing to handle the decoy placements.

As they drove back to their base, the quiet hum of the engine provided a momentary lull from the intense activities of the day. Gabe glanced over at Sadie, his expression softening.

"You know, Sadie," Gabe began, his tone earnest, "I really trust you. You've been incredible through all of this."

Sadie offered a warm smile. "Thanks, Gabe. I couldn't have asked for better partners."

Gabe took a deep breath, feeling the importance of the moment. "I think it would be good for you to call Lily and Maya. Thank them for coming to us and let them know that we'll include them when the time comes to do so."

Sadie nodded thoughtfully. "That's a good idea. They deserve to know how much their help means to us."

Gabe continued, his voice dropping slightly to emphasize the seriousness of his warning. "But we have to be very careful. Ethan may try to follow us or interfere. We need to stay vigilant and make sure they don't join Ethan in any actions against Carter's Creek."

Sadie reached out, placing a reassuring hand on Gabe's arm. "I understand. I'll make sure Lily and Maya are aware of the risks. We can't let Ethan's actions jeopardize everything we've worked for."

Luke glanced in the rearview mirror, sensing the gravity of the conversation. "We need to stay one step ahead. Ethan won't give up easily."

Gabe nodded. "Exactly. Our priority is to protect the town and its legacy. We'll keep our circle tight and only involve those we can fully trust."

Sadie pulled out her phone, her fingers moving swiftly across the screen. "I'll call them right now."

The phone rang twice before Lily picked up, her voice tinged with curiosity. "Lily, are you and Maya alone. It's Sadie."

"Sadie! Yes, it's just the two of us, " Lily's voice was filled with relief and warmth.

Sadie smiled, feeling the weight lift slightly. "Can you put in on speaker, so I can talk to you both. I'm good. I just wanted to thank you both for coming out and helping us today. Your support means a lot."

Lily chimed in, "Of course. We're in this together."

DISCOVERING TRUE MOTIVES

Sadie continued, "I promise we'll include you both when the time comes. But we need to be very careful. Ethan may try to follow us or interfere with our plans. Please, don't join him in any actions against Carter's Creek. Our priority is to protect the town and its legacy."

Maya responded firmly, "We understand. We'll stay vigilant and keep our distance from Ethan's activities. We're here to support you, not to add any complications."

Lily added, "If Ethan tries anything, we'll handle it together. Just let us know how we can assist without getting too involved."

Sadie nodded, feeling a sense of reassurance. "Thank you. We'll need all the help we can get. Let's stay in close contact and keep each other informed of any developments."

With the calls concluded, Sadie returned to the main group, sharing the updates. "Lily and Maya are on board. They've agreed to help us while staying clear of Ethan's actions."

Gabe smiled, a sense of unity strengthening their resolve. "Perfect. The more we work together, the better chance we have of uncovering the truth and protecting Carter's Creek."

Sadie smile back. "Let's stay focused and keep our guard up. We're getting closer to the answers we need."

Gabe exhaled, feeling a renewed sense of purpose. "Good. With their support, we'll have a stronger team moving forward."

The car continued its journey back, the friends united by trust and a shared mission. Despite the looming threats and hidden agendas, their bond provided the strength needed to face the challenges ahead.

Chapter Nine

Memories of Small Important Things

GABE LEANED BACK IN his chair, sipping his coffee as the morning sun streamed through the bakery windows. Sensing a moment of calm, he turned to Sadie with a curious smile.

"Do you like to fish?" Gabe asked, breaking the silence. It was an unusual question to start the day, but he felt a strong urge to understand Sadie's connection to fishing.

Sadie laughed softly, a hint of nostalgia in her eyes. "My parents shared a love of fishing, so I was practically raised with a fishing pole in my hand."

The simple question unleashed a torrent of bittersweet memories for Sadie. Since their passing, she cherished the happy days spent with her family but longed for their presence.

"Even Aunt Clara joined us sometimes. We always made a day of it—Mom and Clara would pack a picnic basket, and Dad would build a fire by the creek to grill the fish we caught. So many great memories. Yes, I love fishing, but I haven't been since they died."

Gabe felt a surge of emotion and reached out, pulling Sadie into a tight hug. "Let's go this Saturday. I had so much fun fishing with the guys the other day, and I'd love nothing more than to spend the day fishing with you. Let's do it like your parents did. If you pack the basket, I'll build the fire and grill the fish. In fact, let's call it our first date. What do you say?"

Sadie gently pushed him away, her laughter ringing out. "I'd love nothing more than spending the day fishing with you. Let me arrange for Hannah to cover the bakery, and I'll get ready for my customers today. Get out of here for now—and take a cinnamon roll with you!"

Gabe couldn't tear his eyes away from her joyful face as he handed her the small box holding the cinnamon roll. He reached out, their fingers briefly touching—a deliberate, tender gesture. She laughed as she headed back into the kitchen, and Gabe followed her direction, stopping only at a bench a short distance down the street.

Sitting there, he realized just how deeply he felt for her. He had never experienced such a whirlwind of emotions before, feeling that his entire life was intertwined with hers. Without her, his world felt incomplete.

As Gabe drove away, his mind drifted back to the last entry of Captain Morgan's journal, the words echoing in his thoughts:

> *"The true treasure lies not in gold or jewels, but in the heart of the one who seeks it. Follow the whispers of your soul, and let them guide you to the hidden truths of our heritage."*

He felt his heart shifting, making room for another emotion—an empty space yearning to be filled by the love of another. This feeling was so uncomfortable, yet so perfect. Was this what love felt like? And how could he be sure if it was a love that would last a lifetime? He'd never felt like this before, and for some reason, Gabe felt that the phrase from Captain Morgan's journal was speaking directly to his current state of mind.

As the car hummed along the quiet streets of Carter's Creek, a familiar melody began to play on the radio. "Landslide" by Fleetwood Mac floated through the speakers, its gentle guitar and reflective lyrics perfectly mirroring Gabe's tumultuous emotions.

"Can I sail through the changing ocean tides?
Can I handle the seasons of my life?"

The song's lyrics resonated deeply with Gabe, intertwining his personal journey with the quest for the town's hidden truths. The metaphor of navigating changing tides mirrored his feelings for Sadie and the uncertain path they were on together.

He glanced at the key and map they had discovered in the Masonic Lodge, symbols that now seemed to echo the sentiments of the song. The journal's message was no longer just about the physical treasure but also about the intangible connections and emotions guiding him.

"Well, I've been afraid of changing
'Cause I built my life around you."

Gabe sighed, feeling the weight of his responsibilities and the newfound depth of his feelings for Sadie, but he wasn't afraid. He'd never been scared of taking risks, he just always wanted to be sure the risk was worth the reward. Balancing the mission to protect Carter's Creek with his personal emotions felt like navigating treacherous waters, but he was determined to find harmony between the two.

The road stretched out before him, winding through familiar landscapes that now felt charged with hidden significance. The intertwining of his personal journey with the town's legacy created a tapestry of emotions and purpose, driving him forward with renewed resolve.

As the final chords of "Landslide" faded, Gabe made a silent promise to himself. He would protect both the town's secrets and the burgeoning love he felt for Sadie. The journey ahead was fraught with challenges and uncertainties, but with Sadie by his side, he felt ready to face whatever came their way.

***

Gabe wasn't even surprised when he found himself in the library parking lot again. He made his way inside, hoping to find Ms. Jameson on duty. The last time he had visited, his search was vague—seeking any information related to Captain Gabriel Morgan. Now, armed with a deeper understanding of Carter's Creek's people and connections, he hoped Ms. Jameson might hold the key to the next piece of the puzzle.

As he approached the front desk, Ms. Jameson looked up and smiled warmly.

"Hey, Gabe, I was wondering when you'd come back to see me again. Welcome back," she cooed. "I've been hearing rumors about some of what you've been up to. It's quiet today—come sit with me and tell me what you've been working on. How can I help you today?"

Gabe pulled up a chair, feeling a mix of relief and concern. He was pleased that Ms. Jameson remembered him, but uneasy knowing that gossip about his activities was circulating.

"Thanks, Ms. Jameson," Gabe began, settling into the chair. "I've been digging deeper into Captain Morgan's connections here in Carter's Creek. There are more layers to this mystery than I initially thought."

Ms. Jameson's eyes sparkled with interest. "Ah, Captain Morgan was quite the man. His involvement with the town's early days is significant. What exactly are you looking to uncover?"

Gabe pulled out a notebook, flipping to a page filled with notes and sketches. "I've mapped out some of the key connections and locations tied to him. I'm particularly interested in anything you can tell me about the Masonic Lodge. Do you have any additional records or personal accounts that might shed light on his intentions?"

Ms. Jameson leaned forward, her expression thoughtful. "Captain Morgan was always very secretive about his projects. However, I recall he mentioned something about preserving the town's heritage in a way that went beyond mere documentation. There might be old correspondences or unpublished journals that could provide more insight. I'll need to check the restricted section of the archives. I can give you a call when I have something for you?"

Gabe nodded appreciatively. "That would be incredibly helpful. Any information you can provide could be crucial to understanding the full scope of his legacy."

"I have something else I'd like to show you though, if you have a few minutes, I'll set you up to read this on our microfilm readers in the next room," she said, pointing toward the adjacent room. "If you'll come with me, I think I can pull that up for you pretty quickly."

Gabe followed Ms. Jameson to another room nearby, a quiet space with a long wooden table filled with microfilm readers and chairs lined up in front. He settled into a chair in front of one of the machines.

"Here you go," Ms. Jameson said, placing a folder on the table between them. "These are some of Captain Morgan's personal correspondences and a few unpublished journal entries. I think you'll find these particularly interesting."

As Gabe glanced through what looked like a table of contents labeled "Captain Gabriel Morgan: Private Correspondence," he noticed a letter addressed to Eleanor Whitaker of the Outer Banks.

"Ms. Jameson, can you tell me who Eleanor Whitaker is?" Gabe asked, looking up from the letter he'd opened on the machine.

Ms. Jameson took a seat opposite him, her demeanor softening. "Eleanor Whitaker was Captain Morgan's lost love. The story goes that they grew up together in the Outer Banks, and their relationship was intense but brief. Gabriel Morgan left to fight in the Civil War, and Eleanor waited for him. Unfortunately, she succumbed to a fatal illness—pneumonia— was suspected at the time. He received the sad news shortly after the Battle of Gettysburg, where Captain Morgan was engaged."

Gabe's eyes widened with empathy. "So, Captain Morgan never married?"

Ms. Jameson shook her head. "No, he never did. Their separation was tragic, and her untimely death deeply affected him. After receiving news of her passing, Captain Morgan threw himself into his work, dedicating his life to preserving Carter's Creek's heritage. It was as if he was trying to honor both the town and the memory of the love he lost."

Gabe carefully picked up the letter, reading a passage aloud:

> *"Eleanor, my heart mourns your absence, yet my soul remains tethered to the legacy we both cherished. In preserving our town's heritage, I strive to keep a piece of us alive, ensuring that our shared dreams endure through the generations."*

"It's clear that Eleanor's death had a profound impact on him," Gabe remarked, looking back at Ms. Jameson.

"Absolutely," she agreed. "Captain Morgan never sought companionship again, choosing a life of solitude instead. His dedication to the town was, in many ways, a tribute to the love he lost and the life they might have had together."

Gabe closed the folder, a mixture of sympathy and determination in his expression. "Thank you for sharing that, Ms. Jameson. It adds a deeper layer to our investigation."

Ms. Jameson smiled gently. "You're welcome, Gabe. Understanding the personal motivations behind someone's actions can provide valuable insights. If you need more personal accounts or any other information, don't hesitate to ask."

Gabe felt a renewed sense of purpose. "I appreciate your help more than you know."

As he left the library, the story of Captain Morgan's lost love added a poignant dimension to the mystery he was unraveling. It wasn't just about hidden relics and town secrets anymore; it was also about understanding the human emotions that shaped the legacy he was now tasked to protect.

***

The sun was slowly dropping below the horizon, casting a warm, golden glow over Carter's Creek. In the heart of the town stood the stately Town Hall, its white facade gleaming against the twilight sky. Inside, Mayor Emma Hunter sat behind her large oak desk, meticulously organizing papers and reviewing town proposals. Her office, adorned with historic photographs and plaques commemorating

Carter's Creek's heritage, exuded both authority and a deep sense of community pride.

The door to her office opened quietly, and Mr. Jenkins stepped in, his expression earnest and slightly nervous. Mayor Emma looked up, her face softening into a welcoming smile.

"Mr. Jenkins, please, have a seat," she invited, gesturing to the chair across from her desk.

Jenkins nodded, taking the seat with a respectful demeanor. "Thank you, Mayor Emma."

Before he could speak, Pastor Daniel Thompson entered the room, his presence calm and reassuring. He stood beside Jenkins, offering a supportive nod to Emma. "Good evening, Mayor. May I?" he asked, indicating a seat beside Jenkins.

"Of course, Dad," Emma replied warmly. "Please, make yourselves comfortable."

Once settled, Mr. Jenkins took a deep breath, gathering his thoughts. "Mayor Emma, Pastor Daniel, thank you both for meeting with me on such short notice."

Emma leaned forward, her eyes filled with genuine concern. "Of course, Mr. Jenkins. What's on your mind?"

Jenkins began, his voice steady and focused. "I wanted to update you on our recent activities at the Masonic Lodge. As you know, Gabe and his team have been uncovering significant historical items related to Captain Morgan. During our latest investigation, we discovered several artifacts that are crucial to preserving Carter's Creek's heritage."

Emma listened intently, her expression serious. "I'm glad to hear progress is being made. But is everything secure? Any signs of interference or threats?"

Jenkins shook his head. "No immediate threats, but the discovery underscores the importance of securing these items properly. We're aware that Mr. and Sadie's cousin, Ethan, are conducting their own searches. To mitigate any potential interference, we left a decoy artifact to divert their attention from the true locations we're investigating. With the increased interest, both legitimate and otherwise, we need to ensure that our historical treasures are protected for future generations."

Emma nodded thoughtfully. "I agree. Protecting our heritage is paramount. How can the town support this effort?"

Before Jenkins could respond, Pastor Daniel interjected, his tone measured and supportive. "Mr. Jenkins, your dedication to this cause reflects your commitment to the community. After last year's incident with Kevin's project, it's crucial that we reinforce our collaborative efforts."

Jenkins maintained eye contact, conveying his determination. "I understand, Pastor. My involvement in Kevin's project was a lapse in judgment. Turning in the evidence was necessary to protect our town, but I recognize the impact it had on trust. Since then, I've stepped back from the town council to focus on restoring that trust through direct action and supporting initiatives like this investigation."

Emma reached out, placing a reassuring hand on his shoulder. "Mr. Jenkins, we all make mistakes. What matters is how we move forward. Your actions last year were instrumental in safeguarding Carter's Creek, and your continued dedication is appreciated."

Pastor Daniel nodded in agreement. "Accountability is key, and I see that you're taking the necessary steps to make amends. Rejoining community service and supporting projects like this are excellent ways to rebuild trust."

Jenkins met Emma's gaze with determination. "Thank you, Mayor. Ensuring our town's safety and preserving its history are my top priorities. Collaborating on these projects is essential not just for safeguarding artifacts but also for restoring faith within our community."

Emma smiled, a sense of renewed purpose evident in her demeanor. "Absolutely. Let's collaborate closely to ensure that all historical items are documented, stored securely, and accessible for future research. We'll need to coordinate with the library, the town council, and other key stakeholders to make this happen."

Pastor Daniel added, "And I'll be here to support both of you, ensuring that our efforts remain transparent and uphold the values Carter's Creek stands for."

Jenkins felt a sense of relief and motivation. "Thank you both. Your support is invaluable. Together, we can honor Captain Morgan's legacy and ensure that Carter's Creek thrives for generations to come."

Emma stood, signaling the end of the meeting. "Let's get to work. We have a town to protect and a legacy to preserve."

As Jenkins and Pastor Daniel left the office, the atmosphere felt more focused and collaborative. The past was acknowledged, mistakes were addressed, and the path forward was clear. Together, they would ensure that Carter's Creek's rich history remained intact, safeguarded by the very community that cherished it.

***

Later that evening, Gabe sat in his office, the day's conversation with Ms. Jameson replaying in his mind. He placed the ornate key and map on his desk, the symbols catching the fading light and reminding him of both the mission and his growing feelings for Sadie.

The words from Captain Morgan's journal lingered in his thoughts, intertwining with his personal reflections:

"The true treasure lies not in gold or jewels, but in the heart of the one who seeks it. Follow the whispers of your soul, and let them guide you to the hidden truths of our heritage."

Gabe leaned back, closing his eyes as he tried to make sense of the emotions battling within him. The responsibilities of protecting the town's secrets were immense, but now there was another layer to his life—his connection with Sadie.

"Follow the whispers of your soul..." he mused. The journal seemed to suggest that his journey was about more than just uncovering historical relics; it was also about discovering what truly mattered to him on a personal level. He pulled out the journal to read that entire section again, perhaps it was time to go back to where this all began, the entry in the Captain's Journal that he received from his father when he turned 21:

April 18, 1865

"The war is lost. General Lee surrendered at Appomattox just days ago, and I fear our cause has all but crumbled into dust. I write these words with a heavy heart, knowing the country I fought for will never be. But duty, even in defeat, binds me still.

As the Union forces push deeper into the South, we are ordered to ensure that certain valuables – treasures that could fund a new Confederacy or protect our people from complete ruin – are not seized by the enemy. Today, I was commissioned with a grave responsibility: to secure a portion of the gold from the treasury, lest it fall into Northern Hands.

I cannot entrust this mission to anyone. Only through this journal do I leave the faintest trace of its location, and even this trace is hidden inverse, so that no common thief may steal it. This burden I carry alone, though it shall be my family who decides its fate.

> *If you are reading these words, then perhaps the time has come for the gold to see the light once more. Or perhaps I was wrong to ever hide it. Either way, the path to it lies within these lines:*
>
> *The Treasure's Rest*
> *Where the trees in twin formation stand,*
> *Their roots entwined in Southern land,*
> *Beyond the creek that winds and bends,*
> *Beneath the oak where daylight ends.*
> *To find the prize, in shadows deep,*
> *Dig where the weeping willows weep,*
> *But heed the stones, old moss and gray,*
> *The ones with words, now worn away.*
> *The sun at dusk will point your way,*
> *A single beam where gold does lay.*
> *But rush not forth with greed in hand,*
> *For patience guides the honest man.*
>
> *The gold awaits, buried where only those with clear hearts and sharp minds may find it. The Union may take our homes, our pride, and our future, but they will never take this.*
>
> *May God guide you in what you choose to do.*
> *Captain Gabriel Morgan*
> *4th Virginia Infantry, Army of Northern Virginia**

Gabe stared at the verses, his mind working to decode the cryptic clues. He began by breaking down each stanza, mapping the references to real locations in Carter's Creek in his journal.

> "Where the trees in twin formation stand,
> Their roots entwined in Southern land,
> Beyond the creek that winds and bends,
> Beneath the oak where daylight ends."

Gabe pondered "twin formation trees" and then recalled a pair of ancient sycamore trees located near the old mill, their branches almost touching. He marked it on the map, then noticed that mark was on the town's southern edge bordered the meandering creek, providing a natural landmark. Huh, could it be that easy.

The next phrase, "beneath the oak where daylight ends," could be one of many oak trees, but the most obvious one was the large oak tree still standing on the town square, often silhouetted against the setting sun. Perhaps they needed to do some more research about the Town Square and that old oak tree. They'd want to be sure before they starting digging around in the middle of town, where every eye was on them.

They'd skipped over the clues to the Weeping Willow Grove, when they went to the Old Mill, and Gabe remembered Sadie holding up a photo on their first visit to the Town Archives, saying, it was an old tree next to the grove.

Time to revisit that clue, perhaps plan a visit to the grove as they headed out on their first date, a date to go fishing. That thought made Gabe smile big, and he felt confident again about the next steps, especially since the last section of the riddle made no sense, not yet anyway.

> *"The sun at dusk will point your way,*
> *A single beam where gold does lay.*

> *But rush not forth with greed in hand,*
> *For patience guides the honest man."*

No worry, none of the others had made sense until they'd made progress on their journey. With these interpretations, Gabe began to plot the locations on his map. The clues pointed towards the old mill area, the weeping willows by the creek, and the prominent oak tree in the town square. Each spot held significance, possibly leading to different parts of the hidden treasure Captain Morgan had worked so diligently to protect.

As he connected the dots, Gabe felt a surge of anticipation mixed with determination. The path was becoming clearer, but he knew the journey would require meticulous planning and unwavering focus.

***

Feeling the weight of the day's discoveries and the emotional complexities of his relationship with Sadie, Gabe decided it was time to reach out. He picked up his phone and dialed her number, waiting for it to ring.

Click... Click... Click...

"Hey, Sadie," he greeted softly when she answered.

"Hi, Gabe. How was your day?" Sadie's voice was warm and inviting, instantly putting him at ease.

"It was productive," he replied, a smile evident in his tone. "Ms. Jameson shared more about Captain Morgan's past, including his relationship with Eleanor Whitaker. She was his fiancée back home when he left for the war. She died while he was away, and he never married after settling here. It's given me a lot to think about."

"That sounds intense. I just knew of him as part of Carter's Creek history, but I never knew about his life before Carter's Creek. That's so sad," Sadie responded, her empathy palpable.

Gabe paused for a moment, feeling the weight of the story resonate within him. "Yeah, it's made me reflect on what truly matters. Losing someone you love changes everything. It makes me realize how important it is to cherish the connections we have now. It feels like I've taken all the people in my life for granted up until now."

Sadie's voice softened. "You didn't think you'd go on this great adventure and not be changed, did you? Sounds like you're embracing what you've learned in a positive way. I'm so glad I'm along for the ride to see you working through this both to discover the treasure, but also applying it to your life personally. You're a good man, Gabe, I'm glad to be your partner."

He took a deep breath, his feelings bubbling to the surface. "That means so much coming from you, Sadie. You have a great mind and so much compassion. It hit me today that the tension I've often felt leaves when we're together. Another mystery, you calm my soul. I'm really looking forward to our date, and I bet I'll catch more fish than you."

There was a brief pause before Sadie replied, her tone filled with warmth. "I've been looking forward to it too, Gabe. Challenge accepted – and I seldom lose. In fact, my grandpa used to say, 'if you can't win fair, there's no reason to lose.' Unfortunately, I don't know how to cheat at fishing."

Gabe felt a surge of gratitude and hope. "I'll tell you a story about my dad and grandpa cheating at fishing as our first tall tale on our fishing date. ... Hey, do you remember that photo we found at the

Town Archives that you said showed an oak and the Weeping Willow Grove, we never followed up on that," Gabe reminded her, "Shall we drive past that as we go fishing for our first date? ... I just love saying that!"

Sadie laughed, "We did forget about that, that sounds like a good plan to me!"

"Now that we have a plan and a fishing challenge, I just want to say good night and let you know how much I appreciate you. I was just thinking how much I want to build something meaningful with you, so I just needed to hear your voice before going to sleep."

"Good night, Gabe. Sleep well," Sadie said softly. "Talk to you tomorrow."

"Good night, Sadie. Talk soon," he replied before ending the call.

Gabe set his phone down, feeling a sense of calm wash over him. Balancing the mission with his personal life was proving to be challenging, but the support from Sadie provided him with the strength he needed to continue.

He glanced back at the journal, the cryptic entry now making more sense as he pieced together the locations. Tomorrow would be crucial in their quest to uncover the hidden treasures of Carter's Creek, and Gabe felt ready to face whatever challenges lay ahead.

Chapter Ten

Shadows and Reflections

THE FIRST LIGHT OF dawn painted the sky in hues of pink and gold as Carter's Creek slowly awakened. Inside Sadie's Sweet Rolls, the aroma of freshly baked bread and pastries filled the air. Sadie moved gracefully through the morning routine, her hands deftly kneading dough and placing trays into the oven. Each movement was synchronized with the upbeat rhythm of "Happy" by Pharrell Williams, playing on the radio. She couldn't help but sway her hips to the melody, a genuine smile lighting up her face – she was going on a date with Gabe. She'd slept so well after his call last night.

Lost in her own world, Sadie didn't notice the small bell above the door jingling as Mayor Emma Hunter slipped inside. Emma's eyes were weary, the exhaustion from a restless night evident in her drooping eyelids. The baby had been unusually active, making sleep elusive. She glanced around the bakery, her gaze landing on Sadie's radiant smile.

Emma paused, taking in the sight of Sadie's carefree demeanor. "You look really happy today, Sadie."

Sadie turned, her eyes sparkling. "Good morning, Emma! Yes, I'm feeling great today, plus this batch of cinnamon rolls turned out perfectly."

Before Emma could respond, Hannah appeared behind her, tying her apron on, and leaning casually against the counter. "Emma, you're out and about early. Did you even sleep last night?"

Emma forced a small smile. "Not really. The baby was quite the little night owl."

Hannah chuckled, her presence bringing an extra layer of warmth to the room. "Well, at least the bakery opens early, a great place to hang for a while, until time to head to your office in the Town Hall. Clearly, Sadie's in a good mood."

Sadie laughed, wiping her hands on her apron. "I try to be a positive person, but today I have a reason why I'm in such a good mood. Glad you're both here, because I have some exciting news."

Emma raised an eyebrow, intrigued. "Oh? What's that?"

Hannah nudged Emma playfully. "I bet it's got something to do with Gabe, every time he leaves, she's dancing and smiling all over the kitchen!"

Sadie rolled her eyes, a playful grin spreading across her face. "It's nothing big. We're going fishing. I don't have to dress up, I'm just packing lunch! But, I'm so excited."

Emma walked over, her tiredness momentarily forgotten by Sadie's enthusiasm. "Fishing sounds wonderful. A perfect way to spend the day. Is this your first date with him?"

Hannah nodded across the counter, "I think the story has been 'we're just good friends working on this project together' up until now."

Sadie pulled out her phone, tapping on it thoughtfully. "He's picking me up shortly, and we're going to drive out to the Weeping Willow

Grove. It's one of the clues we haven't followed up on yet, then we're headed to the creek to fish – he thinks he's going to catch more fish than me."

"Clearly, he doesn't know our Sadie, who always catches the most fish even though she's talking and singing the whole time. We call her the 'Piped Piper of Fish'," Hannah said, while laughing.

Emma smiled, "Just have fun. You guys are already good friends, so no stress, just enjoy yourselves."

Sadie gasped, remembering, "I've got to get a lunch packed here real quick. Time for chatting is over if I'm to get done with all I have to do before taking the rest of the day off."

Hannah offered, "I'm here, I can finish the bakery stuff for the day. You focus on the picnic basket, and you'll be set to go."

Sadie's eyes shone with gratitude. "Thanks, Hannah. That would be great. And Emma, thank you for your support. It means a lot."

Emma squeezed her shoulder gently. "Anytime, Sadie. Enjoy your day. You deserve it."

Sadie waved goodbye, as Emma stepped out the door for the short walk to Town Hall. Today felt like the beginning of something new and hopeful, and she felt ready!

***

The early morning sun cast a soft glow over Dew Drop Inn, a beloved local spot where regulars gathered for hearty breakfasts and warm conversations. Inside, the clatter of cutlery and the hum of friendly chatter filled the air. Gabe, Luke, and Mr. Jenkins sat in a corner booth, plates piled high with eggs, bacon, and pancakes steaming before them.

Gabe stirred his coffee nervously, glancing between his friends. "I can't believe today's the day," he admitted, taking a tentative sip. "I'm really looking forward to my first date with Sadie, but I'm a bit nervous."

Luke grinned, flipping a pancake with practiced ease. "I didn't know you asked her out officially. Congrats, and don't worry, man. Sadie's awesome. What's your plan?"

"Well, I had so much fun fishing with you guys the other day, I thought that might be a fun first date," Gabe grinned, "She loved the idea, so since she isn't a novice, I bet her I could catch more fish than her."

Luke smirked, saying, "Well, that was your only mistake. Sadie is notorious in these parts for always catching the most fish. I hope you'll be a good sport, when you lose, because that's what's going to happen!"

Mr. Jenkins chuckled, leaning back in his seat. "Yeah, and if she starts talking and singing while fishing, you'll have nothing to do but enjoy the show."

Gabe laughed, the tension easing slightly. "True. I just hope I can keep up with her. She's got this incredible energy that's contagious."

Before Luke could respond, Mr. Jenkins leaned forward, his expression turning serious. "Speaking of energy, we've had some developments with the Masonic Lodge trap we set up."

Gabe's smile faded as he listened intently. "What happened?"

Jenkins sighed, running a hand through his hair. "It was tripped twice in the past 24 hours. The first time was Mr. Mattison. He didn't find the hidden compartment, but it confirmed he's following the same leads as us."

Luke raised an eyebrow. "And the second time?"

Mr. Jenkins nodded grimly. "Ethan. He found the hidden compartment and took the decoy artifact with him. Now, the Sheriff is looking for Mr. Mattison since he left his job at the Town Archives under suspicion. Ethan seems to have headed out of town on his own, and there's no sign of Lily and Maya with him."

Gabe leaned back, processing the information. "So, Mattison is a target now, and Ethan's left town. Were Lily and Maya with him?"

Jenkins shook his head. "No sign of anyone accompanying him on that search. We need to stay vigilant, because Ethan seems really determined."

Luke tapped his fork against his plate thoughtfully. "This just keeps getting more complicated. We need to ensure our next moves are calculated."

Gabe nodded, a sense of determination settling in. "Agreed. We can't let them undermine our efforts to protect Carter's Creek's heritage. But first, I need to focus on today. If things go well with Sadie, it might help clear my mind."

Mr. Jenkins gave him a reassuring pat on the back. "You've got this, Gabe. Just be yourself."

Gabe took a deep breath, the weight of his responsibilities momentarily balanced by the support of his friends. "Thanks, both of you. I appreciate it."

As they continued their breakfast, the conversation shifted between the looming challenges and lighter topics, offering Gabe a brief respite before the day ahead. The camaraderie at the diner provided a much-needed anchor, reminding him that he wasn't alone in this journey.

***

The morning sun cast a warm glow over Carter's Creek as Gabe and Sadie loaded her picnic basket, sliding it in next to the fishing gear in the back of Gabe's SUV. Nervous energy buzzed between them, a mix of excitement and anticipation for their first official date. The Weeping Willow Grove was not just a picturesque location but also a critical clue in their ongoing quest to uncover Captain Morgan's hidden treasures.

As they buckled their seatbelts and started the engine, Sadie reached over to Gabe, pulling out her phone. "Remember this?" she asked, displaying a photo they had taken at the Town Archives. The image showed a detailed sketch of the oak tree and the weeping willows, annotated with notes from the archivist.

Gabe leaned forward, studying the picture. "Yeah, this is exactly what we need to find. It's like a map within a map."

Sadie nodded, her eyes reflecting determination. "Aunt Clara's book had a couple more clues that we should keep in mind. She wrote, 'Within the Grove, a marker will point the way.' It sounds like we're getting close."

Gabe glanced at her, his nerves easing slightly with her confidence. "I had breakfast with Luke and Mr. Jenkins this morning. The trap at the Masonic Lodge was tripped by first Mr. Mattison – he found nothing, then by Ethan, he found the hidden compartment, and we think he left town with what he found. Lily and Maya were not there!"

Sadie shrugged, trying to mask her own worries. "Well, that's some good news, but we're still trying to stay ahead of everyone else. I can't believe we forgot to check this out previously."

They drove in comfortable silence for a while, the hum of the engine and the gentle sway of the SUV creating a rhythm that mirrored their synchronized steps. The radio played "Can't Stop the Feeling!" by Justin Timberlake, prompting them to sing along softly, their voices blending harmoniously with the upbeat melody. Gabe stole a glance at Sadie, marveling at how her positivity seemed to brighten his entire day.

As they approached the outskirts of town, the landscape began to change. The paved roads gave way to gravel paths, and the dense canopy of trees enveloped them in a serene, almost mystical atmosphere. The Weeping Willow Grove came into view, its iconic trees swaying gently in the breeze, their long branches cascading towards the ground.

Gabe slowed the car, pulling into a small clearing where they could park. "Here we are," he said, stepping out and stretching his legs. "Looks peaceful."

Sadie smiled, "It is. And according to the clues, the marker should be somewhere around here, probably hidden by overgrowth after all these years."

They began walking along a narrow trail that snaked through the grove, the ground soft under their feet. The air was thick with the scent of damp earth and blooming wildflowers. As they ventured deeper, Sadie paused, holding up the photo for Gabe to see again.

"This is the exact spot," she said, pointing to a specific area where the oak tree and the weeping willows intersected. "Man, this is almost like a jungle after all this time, it's hard to get through all these vines and stuff."

Gabe scanned the area, his eyes darting around for any signs of the hidden marker. "Do you see anything?"

Sadie crouched down, brushing aside some tangled vines. "Not yet. Maybe we need to look more closely."

Just as they were about to continue their search, Gabe noticed something unusual near the base of one of the weeping willows. Footprints and tire marks marred the otherwise pristine ground, indicating that others had been here recently.

"Hey, check this out," Gabe called, pointing to the disturbed soil and the faint impressions of large tires, like you'd see on an ATV. "Looks like someone else was here before us."

Sadie approached cautiously, her eyes narrowing as she examined the footprints. "Mr. Mattison and/or Ethan. They must have beaten us to whatever is here."

Gabe felt a chill run down his spine. "So they're one step ahead of us. We need to be careful."

Sadie nodded, her expression serious. "Let's keep looking, but keep what we've learned in mind. They may have overlooked something that we will see because of how we're searching."

They resumed their search, carefully navigating through the dense underbrush. Only minutes passed, but it felt like hours, as they methodically combed the area, their determination unwavering despite the lingering threat of their competitors. Finally, near the base of the oak tree, hidden beneath a thick blanket of moss and fallen leaves, they found a small, weathered marker partially obscured by overgrowth.

"This must be it," Sadie whispered, her heart pounding with excitement and relief. "We knew we'd find something here."

Gabe knelt beside the marker, tracing the faded engravings with his fingers. "We did it. Now, we just need to follow the next steps."

As he examined the marker, a hidden latch caught his attention. He pressed it gently, and with a soft click, the marker swung open, revealing a concealed compartment. Inside lay a rolled-up parchment, sealed with an old, tarnished wax stamp bearing Captain Morgan's initials.

Sadie carefully unrolled the parchment, her eyes scanning the delicate script. "Here's the next clue," she murmured, reading aloud:

> *To uncover the treasure you seek,*
> *Start when the sun shifts to shadows,*
> *Through windows to the world,*
> *Where light meets the hidden path.*

Gabe pondered the words, trying to decipher their meaning. "Let's tuck this away, because we need to review it with all the other clues we've received. There was a part I didn't understand last night, but they all become clearer when we see them together."

"Agreed," Sadie says, tucking the old scroll in Gabe's glove compartment. "Now what?"

Gabe smiled, reaching across for her hand, "Did you forget? We're going to the creek for our first date, and I was forewarned that you hustled me last night, accepting my challenge to see who could catch the most fish!"

Sadie laughed, saying, "I warned you I seldom lose. Let's head on down to the creek and get this challenge started. No matter what, you owe me some grilled fish to go with the picnic lunch I packed, plus ... pie for dessert!"

They arrived at the creek, where the breeze felt good even with the afternoon sun glaring down on them. The spot was tranquil, the gentle ripples creating a soothing backdrop to their conversation.

Sadie set aside the packed picnic basket, and reached for a fishing pole, baiting it with worm quickly, and casting it in the creek. "Alright, let's set up here. Once we settle in, we can discuss the next clue in more detail."

As they fished, the conversation naturally flowed from their personal lives to the mystery they were unraveling. Gabe found himself sharing more about his feelings, inspired by the supportive environment and Sadie's unwavering positivity.

"Thanks for doing this with me, Sadie. It means a lot," Gabe said, his voice tinged with gratitude.

Sadie smiled warmly. "Of course, Gabe. We're a team, both in this quest and now on our date."

Their fishing session was a blend of friendly competition and shared joy. Sadie's hands worked with practiced ease, effortlessly reeling in fish after fish—three for every one Gabe managed to catch. All the while, she sang and talked non-stop, her laughter ringing through the grove.

Gabe watched in amazement as she caught another fish, her energy infectious. "How do you do that? I've never seen anyone catch so many fish in one morning."

Sadie shrugged playfully, her eyes twinkling with mischief. "Guess I just have a knack for it. You'd be surprised what a little singing can do."

Gabe laughed, shaking his head in disbelief. "Well, I'm impressed. What else don't I know about you?"

As Sadie continued to chat animatedly, her line of fishing never faltered. Gabe couldn't help but marvel at her ability to accomplish whatever she set her mind to, all while maintaining such a vibrant spirit.

After a few more successful catches, Sadie finally called a halt. "Alright, I think that's enough for today. Time for you to clean these fish, build a fire, and grill those fish, while I set out the rest of our dinner!"

They spread out a blanket under the shade of a large willow tree, the fish perfectly grilled by Gabe were perfect with the sides Sadie had meticulously prepared. The peaceful ambiance of the creek provided the perfect setting for their meal, the sounds of nature complementing their lighthearted banter.

As they ate, Gabe couldn't shake the feeling that they were on the verge of another breakthrough. The new clue they had found seemed to point them toward the next location, but he wasn't quite sure how to interpret it yet.

Sadie, noticing his pensive expression, leaned closer. "What's on your mind?"

Gabe sighed, setting down his fork. "This new clue, it's tied to Captain Morgan's last entry. I think it's hinting at a time and a place, but I'm not exactly sure how to connect the dots."

Sadie nodded, thoughtful. "When we're done here, let's go back where we can look at this whole timeline and clues spread out together. We work best putting our two heads together."

Gabe smiled, the pieces beginning to fit together. "Agreed, and I want to thank you for a most memorable first date. You win the fishing challenge, so I'd like to offer you a prize of a second date. Does that work for you?"

"Sounds good to me, but I don't know how you're going to beat this one. This is my first ever fishing date, and I was excited when you asked, and this was so relaxing today, I'd forgotten how much I loved to fish." Sadie sighing, adding, "So, your challenge is planning another date that lives up to this one. Are you up for that challenge?"

Gabe smiled, and grabbed her hand to pull her up, "I accept your challenge! Let's head back to the bakery and eat our pie there as we study these clues again. Come on, let's load up the car!"

They packed up their belongings, ready to leave the creek behind for the day. As they walked back to the SUV, Gabe felt a renewed sense of purpose. Not only was he gaining valuable insights into the mystery of Captain Morgan's treasure, but he was also building something meaningful with Sadie.

As they drove back to town, the setting sun cast long shadows across the landscape, creating a beautiful interplay of light and dark. Gabe glanced over at Sadie, her content smile reflecting the warmth of the day. "Today was great. I'm really glad we did this."

Sadie smiled back, her eyes shining with happiness. "Me too, Gabe. It's nice to take a break from the mystery and just enjoy the moment."

They rode together in a companionable silence, with just the radio playing softly in the background. Something good was happening here, with the treasure and with the two of them.

***

Meanwhile, sunset in Carter's Creek carried a sense of urgency as the Sheriff and his deputies arrived at the secluded hunting cabin nestled deep within the woods near the creek. They'd received a call from a neighbor driving by that it looked like it was occupied, so they'd headed out to check it out. The cabin, once a popular spot for local hunters, now stood as a silent witness to the unfolding mystery surrounding Captain Morgan's hidden treasures.

Sheriff Daniels approached the cabin cautiously, his flashlight piercing through the dense foliage that obscured the entrance. Inside, Mr. Mattison sat uneasily at a rustic wooden table, his hands cuffed in front of him. The room was sparsely furnished, but among the usual hunting gear and worn furniture lay several items that immediately caught Thompson's attention: old maps, vintage tools, and artifacts unmistakably tied to Carter's Creek's heritage.

"Mr. Mattison," Sheriff Daniels began, his tone firm but not unkind, "you've been apprehended for attempted trespassing and interference with town heritage sites."

Mr. Mattison glanced up, a flicker of defiance in his eyes. "I was just curious, history is my life. There's nothing wrong with that."

Thompson shook his head. "Unfortunately, in this case, you've taken historical documents that were the property of the Town Archive, after you'd resigned and left without notice as the Town Archivist. These belong to Carter's Creek and are part of our protected heritage."

Mr. Mattison sighed, glancing at the artifacts with a mix of frustration and longing. "I didn't mean any harm. I just wanted to uncover the truth about Captain Morgan, to find the treasure if there's even one to be found."

Before Thompson could respond, the door to the cabin swung open, and Mayor Emma Hunter and Mr. Jenkins stepped inside. Their presence added a layer of gravity to the situation, signaling the importance of the interrogation.

Emma approached the table, her expression a blend of concern and authority. "Mr. Mattison, we need to understand your intentions. Why were you interfering with our preservation efforts?"

Mr. Jenkins stood beside her, his demeanor supportive yet stern. "Captain Morgan's legacy is invaluable to our town. Your actions could have jeopardized years of hard work and dedication."

Mattison met their gazes, his resolve wavering slightly. "I believed there was more to Captain Morgan's story. These artifacts could hold secrets that have been buried for too long."

Sheriff Daniels interjected, "Your intentions might be misguided, but possessing and tampering with these items is a serious offense. You're charged with attempted trespassing, interference with town heritage sites, and possession of protected historical artifacts."

Emma took a step closer, her voice softening. "We understand the desire to uncover the past, but there are proper channels and procedures to follow. Your actions have consequences not just for you, but for the entire community."

Mr. Jenkins added, "We need to ensure that our town's history is preserved accurately and respectfully. Tampering with artifacts can distort our understanding and appreciation of our heritage."

Mattison looked down, the weight of their words pressing upon him. "I just wanted to make a meaningful discovery, something that would honor Captain Morgan's legacy, while demonstrating to the world my knowledge."

Sheriff Daniels nodded in agreement. "For now, you'll remain in custody until further investigations are complete. We'll determine the full extent of your involvement and any additional charges if necessary."

As the interrogation concluded, Mattison was led out of the cabin, his demeanor subdued but still defiant. Emma and Mr. Jenkins exchanged a glance, both aware of the delicate balance between preserving the past and addressing the present threats to their town's legacy.

Back at the police station, Emma and Mr. Jenkins sat across from Sheriff Daniels, reviewing the evidence and discussing the implications of Mattison' actions.

"We need to ensure that Ethan doesn't find out about Mattison' capture," Emma said thoughtfully. "I don't know if they're connected at this point – it looks like they're not, but I want to be careful."

Mr. Jenkins nodded, tapping a finger against his chin. "Agreed. We should tighten security around the Masonic Lodge and any other key locations. And perhaps it's time to consider bringing Lily and Maya back into the fold. Their expertise could be invaluable right now."

Emma leaned forward, determination shining in her eyes. "I'll coordinate with the library and the town council to reinforce our preservation efforts. We can't afford any more interference."

As they strategized, the gravity of the situation settled over them. The capture of Mr. Mattison was a significant victory, but it also underscored the lengths to which others would go to claim Captain Morgan's treasure. The town of Carter's Creek stood at a crossroads, its history hanging in the balance between preservation and obsession.

Chapter Eleven
Tangled Legacies

THE EARLY MORNING SUN just rising over Carter's Creek, casting a golden hue across **Gabe's** modest home. Inside, he sat at his cluttered desk, surrounded by maps, journals, and photographs related to Captain Morgan's treasure hunt. His phone buzzed, pulling him from his focused research. Seeing the word "Mom" flash on the screen, he felt a surge of warmth. They lived miles away in the Outer Banks, but Gabe cherished their regular calls.

He swiped to answer, smiling as he saw their faces appear on the screen.

"Hey, Dad! Hey, Mom!" Gabe greeted, his voice filled with enthusiasm.

"Hi, Gabe! How's everything going?" Rachel, his mother, responded with her usual cheerful tone.

Gabe leaned back, taking a deep breath. "It's been a busy week, but good. Sadie and I made some progress on the treasure hunt. We found a marker in the Weeping Willow Grove that led us to a new clue. It's getting exciting!"

Lee, his father, nodded thoughtfully. "Captain Morgan's treasures, huh? That brings back memories. Your grandfather used to tell stories about that when I was a kid."

Gabe's eyes sparkled with curiosity. "Really? What did he say?"

Lee chuckled softly, a hint of nostalgia in his eyes. "He always said that the treasure was 'hidden in plain sight.' We never found anything concrete, but I always believed there was some truth to those tales."

Rachel chimed in, "Gabe, do you think there might still be something out there? Maybe something that's been overlooked all these years?"

Gabe nodded, feeling a deeper connection to his family's lore. "I believe so. Sadie and I have been piecing together clues, and it seems like we're getting closer. Plus ... yesterday we had our first date, we went fishing, she can really catch fish, and not quietly either, like you guys taught me."

Lee raised an eyebrow, a playful smile tugging at his lips. "Fishing, huh? Did I hear correctly—you're dating a Whitmore now? Now, that's something!"

Gabe laughed, a blush creeping up his cheeks. "Yeah, when I'm with her it's like coming home, my soul is content. Sadie is incredible—she's smart, determined, and she has this amazing ability to catch fish. I marvel at her ability to accomplish whatever she sets her mind to."

Rachel smiled warmly. "Sounds like you've found someone special, Gabe. I'm happy for you, and I can't wait to meet her. Lee, it may be time for us to plan a trip to Carter's Creek again."

Lee leaned closer, his expression turning serious. "There was something else my grandfather mentioned that might help you. Besides being 'hidden in plain sight,' he also talked about 'reflections and shadows' playing a role in finding the treasure. It's vague, but maybe the next clue involves how light interacts with the surroundings."

Gabe's mind raced as he connected the dots. "That makes a lot of sense. We've already found clues related to light and shadows, especially with the latest parchment we uncovered. It might be pointing us toward another significant location in Carter's Creek."

Rachel's eyes sparkled with pride. "Your grandfather would be proud to see you continuing the hunt. Just be careful, Gabe. There are always risks when you dig into history and treasure hunts."

Gabe nodded firmly. "We will. Sadie and I are more determined than ever. We're not just doing this for the treasure, but to preserve Carter's Creek's heritage and honor those who came before us."

Lee placed a reassuring hand on Gabe's shoulder. "That's the right mindset. Remember, treasure hunts can be unpredictable, so always prioritize your safety and the integrity of the artifacts you find."

Gabe felt a surge of gratitude for his parents' support. "Thanks, Dad, Mom. Your insights and encouragement mean a lot. We'll keep you updated on our progress."

Rachel's voice softened with love. "We're always here for you, Gabe. Take care and good luck. I'll call once Dad and I pick a date to visit, to make sure it works for you."

Gabe smiled, feeling a renewed sense of purpose. "Thanks, I will. Talk to you soon."

As the call ended, Gabe turned back to his notes, the conversation with his parents fueling his determination. With Sadie by his side and his family's legacy guiding him, he felt more prepared than ever to uncover the secrets hidden within Carter's Creek.

***

The cozy interior of Dew Drop Inn buzzed with the midday rush, the clatter of cutlery and murmur of conversations creating a lively backdrop. Emma, Linda, Sadie, and Hannah found a quiet corner near the window, their table already adorned with plates of sandwiches, salads, and steaming bowls of soup.

Sadie beamed as she set down her bag, a satisfied sigh escaping her lips. "I'm really glad you all could make it today. I closed the bakery for an hour so Hannah and I could both join you for lunch."

Emma, her baby bump gently highlighted by her loose-fitting blouse, reached out and squeezed Sadie's hand reassuringly. "Carter's Creek is small enough that they'll hang around town for an hour if they need something. Now, how was your first date with Gabe? We want details."

Sadie laughed, a playful glint in her eye. "Well, first, we stopped by the Weeping Willows Grove to check out a clue there. We could see where others had been there ahead of us, so we were concerned they had beaten us to whatever was there, but we kept looking, hoping. Finally, we found a marker, with another hidden latch, that opened a box beneath the marker, and ... another scroll with another clue. Everything leads to another clue ... exciting, but ... I'm ready to see the pot of gold at the end of the rainbow."

Linda, leaned forward with genuine interest. "Sounds like you're having fun, so enjoy the journey – this will be an adventure to tell your grandkids about. Speaking of grandkids, tell us about the date, or was that it?"

"Oh, we still went fishing, and, just as we already knew, I won the fishing competition. The picnic with the grilled fish was perfect. I couldn't have planned this date any better, and ... it brought back so many great memories I had fishing with my folks. I won the prize in the fishing competition, he's planning our second date – and trying to make it as great as our first date. I'm betting on him!"

Emma smiled, "Of course you are. Sounds perfect, and, Sadie, you do realize you're in love, don't you?"

"Love is a strong word," Sadie said, flinching slightly. "I really care for Gabe, and he's pretty amazing. I'm trying to take it slow, but ... we'll see. I have hopes anyway! Now, Emma, tell us what's happening with baby?!?"

Emma nodded, her expression softening. "Yes, we're really excited. It's been a busy time, balancing work and preparing for the baby. ... and, I almost forgot to tell you, next week is our ultrasound! We've decided to find out the gender, if they know."

Hannah, always the supportive friend, chimed in with a warm smile. "Ahhh, that's exciting. And, once you tell us, we'll help you decorate the nursery, and we'll plan a shower .... we want to shower you with our love and lots of cool baby gifts!"

Before the conversation could continue, Emma's phone buzzed on the table. She glanced at the screen, her expression shifting from warmth to concern as she read the incoming message. "Excuse me for a moment," she said, excusing herself to take the call.

Moments later, Emma returned to the table, her face etched with seriousness. "I'm sorry about that. It was Sheriff calling with some important news. I forgot to tell you, they arrested Mr. Mattison at an old hunting cabin just outside of town, and he had some historical documents that he'd stolen from the Town Archive as he quit."

Sadie frowned, the news adding another layer of complexity to their ongoing mystery. "That's a significant development. Why was the sheriff calling today then?"

"They had his first hearing today, and his bail was set at $500,000, based on the fact he stole priceless historical documents that he had pledged to protect in his role as Town Archivist. He's still being held at this point, but they expect he may make bail soon."

Linda's eyes widened in surprise. "Mr. Mattison? What exactly did he steal?"

Emma continued, her voice steady despite the tension. "He took several original manuscripts and artifacts from the Town Archive. These documents are irreplaceable and hold significant historical value for Carter's Creek. His actions not only violate his position but also threaten the integrity of our town's history."

Hannah leaned back, her expression thoughtful. "This complicates things even more. If Mattison was involved in stealing these artifacts, it might mean he was looking for specific items related to Captain Morgan's treasure. Do we know if any of the stolen documents were linked to our clues?"

Emma nodded, "The Sheriff called me yesterday when they found him, so Mr. Jenkins and I headed there. Mr. Mattison was searching for the treasure, but also for the history hidden with it. He basically said he was trying to be recognized for the great historian he is. Apparently, being town archivist wasn't enough for him! The items he took have been placed in evidence for now."

"Do you think Gabe and I could have a look at what they're holding in evidence," Sadie asked.

"I suspect I could arrange it. You can't take it, but definitely have a look, let me speak to the Sheriff, and I'll let you know," Emma agreed.

Linda added, smiling at Hannah, "We're going to start planning the shower ... you know that's what I do now, right, Emma? And, let's have a night out for all of us once you know the gender, we'll want to celebrate. Sadie, let us know how we can help or support you, it's one for all, and one for all in Carter's Creek!"

And, with that, the girls headed out for their day, all feeling loved and loved on, and that was enough.

***

Gabe loved working at Southern Roots, Carter's Creek's cherished tavern, because he felt connected to the entire town as he served and interacted with everyone who walked through its doors. The soft hum of conversations and the clinking of glasses spilled out into the street, creating a welcoming atmosphere. Inside, the dim lighting and wooden décor provided a cozy setting for heartfelt discussions and strategic planning.

Gabe was restocking glasses, a necessary duty after happy hour, taking a moment to steady his thoughts before Sadie walked through the door. She spotted him behind the bar, his expression a mix of determination and concern. As she approached, he gestured for her to sit down.

"Hey," Gabe greeted softly, his voice tinged with urgency. "Thanks for meeting me here so late. It's the only time we could get together today, between your bakery and my shift here. Were you able to reach Lily and Maya?"

Sadie smiled warmly. "Of course, Gabe. I'm always happy to fit you into my day. Lily and Maya were glad I called and are eager to help, but they're driving from the city, so it may be a few more minutes before they get here."

Gabe took a deep breath, leaning forward. "My parents called this morning, and we talked about our search, but... I told them about our date. I'm sorry if it was too soon, but I'm so happy... it just spilled out.

Now, my mom is planning to visit; she wants to meet you, and my dad was surprised I'm dating a Whitmore."

Sadie's smile faltered slightly, a shadow crossing her features. She glanced away for a moment, her eyes filling with unbidden tears. "Don't get me wrong... I'd love to meet them, Gabe. It's just a reminder that my parents are gone and will never meet you, and they would have loved you."

Gabe reached out, gently taking her hand in his. "I know, Sadie, and I understand how that makes you sad. Don't cry, because I'm going to promise you something. My parents love everyone they meet. They welcomed every friend I brought home from school, especially those who didn't have good support at home. You had fabulous parents, I can tell because of who you are now, so they're really going to love you."

Sadie squeezed his hand back, drawing strength from his words. "Thank you, Gabe. It means a lot to hear that. Let's lay out our clues so we're ready when Lily and Maya get here. We're going to have to catch them up."

Just then, the door to Southern Roots swung open, and Lily and Maya walked in. Lily, an archaeologist and the oldest of the three cousins, exuded confidence with her keen eye for detail, while Maya, Lily's younger sister with a background in cryptography, carried an air of quiet intelligence. They spotted Gabe and Sadie and made their way over to the table.

"Hey, you two," Lily greeted, pulling up a chair. "Thanks for inviting us this evening. I know you have no reason to trust us, but I'm glad you did. We really want to help."

Maya nodded politely, placing her own set of notes on the table. "But, before we dig into clues, I suspect you need an update about what Ethan's up to, right?"

Gabe gestured for them to join. "Glad you could make it tonight. We would love any update you can provide us about your brother, Ethan."

Lily began, "We haven't seen him, but we've heard from other family members that after leaving here, he immediately headed to the Outer Banks. For some reason, he's searching there."

"He's told family there that he believes the Whitmore treasure, as he calls it, is hidden in plain sight there. I'm not sure how he got that in his head, but he's searching day and night," finished Maya.

Gabe and Sadie looked at one another in shock, then burst out laughing before Sadie explained, "When we made our find in the Masonic Lodge, we left behind a decoy, hoping it would steer anyone else searching away from the truth. And, apparently, Ethan took the bait, which is good for all of us. You're not upset with us, are you?"

Maya and Lily started laughing with them, and Maya reached out for Sadie's hand. "You guys worked him perfectly. We would have never thought to do that, so you guys are truly protectors of the truth!"

Gabe sighed, saying, "But... my parents just mentioned that clue to me, something that's been passed down through our family. Captain Morgan's treasure is 'hidden in plain sight,' and that's one of the things we'd planned to discuss tonight. I wonder how Ethan got that information?"

Lily leaned back, her expression thoughtful. "It's possible that Ethan has been digging into old family records or archives that we haven't accessed yet. He might have found something that ties directly to our clues."

Maya nodded in agreement. "Or perhaps he's been leveraging connections in the Outer Banks to get insider information. People with knowledge of local histories or hidden spots could have inadvertently or intentionally shared details that aligned with our clues."

Sadie interjected, "No worries, our clues are definitely centered around Carter's Creek. And we've uncovered enough that it's clear this is a joint effort between Henry Whitmore, our uncle from way back when who lived here his whole life, and Gabe's namesake, Captain Gabriel Morgan, who moved here after the Civil War was ending."

Gabe frowned, his mind racing. "I need to warn my parents about Ethan's search in the Outer Banks and send him a picture of him. Since he's searching in their neck of the woods, I definitely want them to know and be safe. Can one of you text me a picture of him so I can send it to my folks?"

Lily quickly texted Gabe a picture of Ethan, and Gabe stepped away to send the text and picture to his parents, considering it pretty urgent since Ethan was already there.

Sadie continued the conversation in Gabe's brief absence, "We just want to show you what we've found, give you an opportunity to do the same, then we all need some time to let that settle in our minds to see if something becomes more obvious. The clues aren't as obvious as an 'X' on a map. I'm sure we're meant to have to figure it out, so it's not easily found."

Maya nodded, agreeing, "That's right, and I'm excited... I studied cryptology because I love solving puzzles!"

Gabe rejoined the group, sharing, "My parents probably won't see that text until the morning, with the time difference and their early bedtimes, so now let's see if we can solve this puzzle. One of Captain Morgan's journals has been passed down through my family over the years, always to the eldest son on his 21st birthday. It passed to me several years ago now, and it's the reason I moved here last year. I felt drawn here to find whatever Captain Morgan had hidden. Here's his last entry that we've been following:

> *The Treasure's Rest*
> *Where the trees in twin formation stand,*
> *Their roots entwined in Southern land,*
> *Beyond the creek that winds and bends,*
> *Beneath the oak where daylight ends.*
> *To find the prize, in shadows deep,*
> *Dig where the weeping willows weep,*
> *But heed the stones, old moss and gray,*
> *The ones with words, now worn away.*
> *The sun at dusk will point your way,*
> *A single beam where gold does lay.*
> *But rush not forth with greed in hand,*
> *For patience guides the honest man.*

Lily handled the journal as the treasure it was, while Maya focused on the words and solving the puzzle. Finally, she smiled, saying, "So, tell us where this has led you so far. I know we all ran into one another the first time at the Old Mill when we were still working alongside our brother, Ethan. What did you find in the Old Mill?"

Gabe and Sadie smiled at one another, knowing they had trusted the right people and that Lily and Maya were perfect additions to their team. Now they'd be unstoppable.

"We saw a picture—you guys probably saw it, too—of Uncle Henry and Captain Morgan posing in front of the Old Mill. That's what drew us there. Inside one room, we found a hidden button in some trim that made a wall swing open, revealing a whole room with another hidden compartment containing another journal and another riddle. This is the pattern of everything we've found: symbols reveal a hidden latch, which reveals a hidden compartment with a journal or scroll containing another riddle. Here's the riddle we found at the Old Mill:"

> *Beneath the watchful gaze of the ancient tree,*
> *Where light meets shadow, the path shall be.*
> *Seek the place where brothers convene,*
> *There lies the legacy unseen.*

"Ahhh, so that's what led you to the Masonic Lodge... 'seek the place where brothers convene,'" Maya realized.

Gabe laughed, "Well, that was super easy for you to figure out after the fact, but we pondered that for days with lots of other ideas before we even learned of the existence of the Masonic Lodge, especially since it's long since been abandoned. But it was indeed another location with hidden secrets."

"Mr. Mattison put us onto the Masonic Lodge. He knew about it and was sure the next clue would be there. He had promised to work with us, and we were pretty sure he was double-crossing us. It was during that meeting that Maya and I began to realize we were on the wrong side of this search—that both Mattison and Ethan had their own agendas that had nothing to do with securing history for future generations," Lily shared, sadness clouding her eyes.

"Lily, we're so glad you and Maya are working with us now, not against us. In case you haven't heard, Mr. Mattison was arrested yesterday, and he's sitting in jail. Ethan is off on a wild goose chase in the Outer Banks. And we found another hidden compartment at the Masonic Lodge, holding a chest filled with some cool old stuff.

Captain Morgan would have been a writer in our generation," Sadie smiled, encouraging them that all was forgiven.

Gabe reached into a box, sitting beside him on the table, and pulled out a stone that had a map carved on it and an ornate key. "These are the most significant items we found at the Masonic Lodge," he said, laying them on the table in front of them.

Lily was mesmerized. "Can I touch it?" Gabe nodded with a big smile, feeling the same excitement.

As Lily thoroughly examined the key, Maya delicately spread out the map to study it carefully.

Lily spoke first, "This key has some of the same symbols we've been following all along. Were there any clues about what it unlocks?"

"Interesting way to create a map," Maya finished. "Clearly, these were meant to be found together, so perhaps that's part of the puzzle. Have you figured out where this leads you yet?"

"We have other clues that seem to lead to the Town Hall, but we haven't really focused our search there yet because wouldn't it have been found already if the treasure was there?" Sadie answered, thinking hard to piece the puzzle together in her mind. "But we've seen the same symbols as are on this key inside the Town Hall, and this map seems to highlight the Masonic Lodge and the Town Hall, perhaps indicating the path between the two. So, perhaps we are being guided in that direction."

"And one last thing you may not have connected to this search yet: Aunt Clara's book, *The Willow's Secret*, seems to be providing confirming guidance every step of the way. If we are unsure, her book confirms it," Gabe added.

Lily and Maya looked at one another before glancing over toward Sadie. Then Lily spoke softly, "When your parents died, we were just starting our careers and were so interested in history. Aunt Clara invited us back to her house and told us so many fabulous stories that ignited our young minds. We felt like she was inviting us to a treasure hunt, and that's how the three of us ended up on this search in the first place—she gave us her book as a parting gift."

"That sounds just like her," Sadie said, her eyes clouded with tears. "I miss her so much! I understand how you felt, young and idealistic, ready to make your mark in the world. I was so used to her stories—they felt like fairy tales to me—until Gabe started telling me about the Captain's Journal he had."

"So, I feel that puts us all on the same page for now," Gabe said, standing. "It's late, Sadie has to open the bakery early tomorrow, so let's head our separate ways and roll this around in our brains tonight to see what thoughts it sparks. I need to warn you, I often dream of Captain Morgan after sessions like this. I know it's just my subconscious working on the puzzle, but it seems really real to me."

Sadie stood, turning to her cousins. "Will you drive home tonight? When can we connect again? I suddenly feel like I have family again when I've felt so alone recently."

"I had a feeling we'd need to stay close. I found an Airbnb near here, so we'll set up there indefinitely. This is the most fun we've had in a long time," Maya said with a big smile.

Gabe gathered up what he'd laid out, walking the ladies to the door and locking up the tavern behind him. Sadie grabbed her cousins in a big hug, and they all held on, laughing. Lily and Maya jumped into their cars to head to their new lodgings, while Gabe insisted on driving Sadie home. Life felt good in Carter's Creek right now, and they all looked forward to seeing what was around the next bend.

Chapter Twelve
Family Ties and Friendships

THE MORNING SUN STREAMED through the large windows of Sadie's Sweet Rolls, casting a warm glow over the bustling shop. The aroma of freshly baked bread and sweet pastries filled the air, creating an inviting atmosphere for the early risers. Sadie stood behind the counter, expertly arranging a display of cinnamon rolls, her mind already racing with the day's plans. Hannah stood by her side, diligently filling the cookie tray.

Just as Sadie turned to check the oven, the door swung open, and Lily and Maya walked in. They spotted Sadie behind the counter and made their way over to the table at the center of the bakery.

"Good morning, you two," Sadie greeted with a welcoming smile. "Thanks for coming so early. We have a lot to discuss."

Lily smiled warmly. "Good morning, Sadie. We're glad to be here and ready to help with anything you need."

Before Sadie could respond, the door opened again, and **Linda** and Mary walked in, carrying bags.

Linda greeted everyone with a warm smile. "Hey, everyone. We're just popping in before the Ladies Bible Study at church, hoping to get a box of donuts, but it looks like the ladies are already gathering here!"

Sadie stood to greet them. "Good morning, Linda, Mary. I'll get that ready for you, but please, sit and visit with my cousins, Lily and Maya, who are visiting from the city."

As everyone settled around the table, Ms. Beatrice and Mabel walked in. With a quick glance, they made themselves at home at the large table with the other ladies. "Good morning, and who are these two lovely young ladies?" Ms. Beatrice asked.

Sadie laughed. "Hannah, can you get Ms. Beatrice and Mabel their teas? And Linda, would you be the official hostess and make the introductions?"

Linda nodded, starting to introduce everyone around the table just as Ms. Jameson, the librarian, stepped through the door. She looked a little startled by the crowd in the bakery—unusual for Carter's Creek—but Linda invited her to join, and she sat down as introductions began again.

Hannah popped back behind the counter after dropping off the teas. "Okay, just making sure we're both keeping up. Linda and Mary want a dozen donuts boxed up for the Ladies Bible Study, Ms. Jameson wants two dozen mixed assortment cookies for the Library Book Club this afternoon, and Ms. Beatrice said she's bringing pastries for the table."

"Great, Hannah," Sadie replied with a smile. "You plate the pastries and take them to the table so everyone can enjoy them before they scatter again. And see if anyone else needs a drink? I'm going to box the donuts and cookies. This is kind of exciting, isn't it?"

The bell above the door rang again as Mayor Emma walked in, and everyone shouted, "Emma's here, join us at the table!"

Her presence brought a fresh spark of excitement to the gathering, and the women began talking all at once, eager to hear any news about the baby.

"Morning, everyone!" Mayor Emma greeted, her eyes twinkling with enthusiasm. "The baby is fine. I stopped in today, and it looks like everyone else did too, eager to hear any exciting news about the treasure hunt. Care to share?"

"Everyone, this is Lily and Maya, my cousins," Sadie began, gesturing towards the cousins. "Lily is an archaeologist with a sharp eye for detail, and Maya specializes in cryptography. They're working with us to move this adventure forward more quickly. I'm sure you've all heard through the grapevine that Mr. Mattison has been arrested and my other cousin, Lily and Maya's brother, Ethan, is off on a wild goose chase that we sent him on."

Linda chimed in, adding, "We're all here to support each other and ensure you stay ahead of Ethan in your quest to uncover Captain Morgan's treasure."

The table buzzed with conversation as everyone discussed what they had heard. Mayor Emma, always keen to stay involved, couldn't help but bring up her own excitement. "Speaking of progress, my ultrasound is coming up next week. I'm feeling a mix of excitement and nerves, but everything is going well so far."

Hannah, who worked alongside Sadie at the bakery, joined in the conversation. "That's wonderful, Emma! We're all so happy for you. Linda and I have started making preliminary plans for the baby shower."

Linda added, "Of course, we're holding off on invitations until after the ultrasound. You're all invited—we can't wait to celebrate Emma and Luke and this little one arriving one day soon."

As the women chatted about Emma's upcoming ultrasound and how she was feeling, the atmosphere remained light and supportive, blending personal joys with the intensity of their treasure hunt.

The camaraderie among the women was strong, each bringing their unique strengths to the table. The blend of personal support and collective determination set the stage for the challenges ahead.

As the plate filled with pastries emptied, the women paid Hannah for their purchases and started scattering to their various events and responsibilities across Carter's Creek, leaving just Emma, Lily, and Maya seated at the table, and Hannah and Sadie behind the counter.

Sadie had never experienced that many people in her bakery at one time, but she was tickled pink by their support and the friendships new and old.

***

The bakery was just settling back into normal mode, as Gabe and Luke arrived, their presence adding to the feminine energy still circling the room. Gabe, holding a stack of maps and notes, took a seat beside Lily and Maya, while Luke glanced around, slipping a quick kiss with Emma, before joining the conversation.

"Morning, everyone," Gabe greeted, laying out the maps on the table, as Sadie came to sit beside him. "We need to discuss the Town Hall as a possible location for the treasure hunt."

Sadie leaned forward, her curiosity piqued. "Does anyone have the architectural plans for the Town Hall? We really haven't searched about the Town Hall yet, because we thought ... if anything were there, everyone would know. Emma, do you have access to something like that."

Emma shook her head. "I don't have them on hand, but I believe Mr. Jenkins can locate them. I'll get on that first thing when I return to the Town Hall."

Luke, always the pragmatic one, insisted, "Let me drive you there, Emma. Even though it's just a short walk, it's better if we stick together, especially with everything that's going on."

Emma smiled gratefully. "Thank you, Luke. I appreciate it."

As Emma and Luke prepared to leave, Hannah remained at the counter, keeping the bakery running smoothly. Sadie, Gabe, Lily, and Maya leaned closer to the table, diving back into their discussion.

"We need to map out the Town Hall layout based on the architectural plans once we have them," Lily said, pointing to specific areas on the map. "Based on what you've already found, there may be hidden rooms or secret passages that align with Captain Morgan's clues."

Maya nodded, her mind racing with possibilities. "I've been analyzing the journal entries, and there are mentions of specific architectural features that could be present in the Town Hall. If we can match those descriptions with the actual layout, we might pinpoint the exact location of the next clue."

Gabe tapped a note on the map. "And with Ethan searching the Outer Banks, it's crucial that we stay organized and keep track of all potential sites. The Town Hall could be a central hub that connects other key locations in Carter's Creek."

Sadie added, "Once Emma gets the plans from Mr. Jenkins, we can cross-reference them with our clues and see where they intersect. It might reveal something we've missed."

Lily looked up from her notes. "We should also consider any historical events or gatherings that took place at the Town Hall. Captain Morgan might have chosen a location with significant historical value to hide his treasure."

Maya agreed, "That's a great point. We can research any major events that happened there and see if they coincide with the timeline of Captain Morgan's activities."

As the discussion continued, the group meticulously pieced together the puzzle, their combined expertise creating a comprehensive strategy to tackle the treasure hunt. The synergy between Sadie, Gabe, Lily, and Maya was palpable, each contributing their unique skills to advance their quest.

With Emma and Luke en route to secure the architectural plans, the team felt a renewed sense of purpose. They knew that every piece of information brought them closer to uncovering the secrets of Captain Morgan's treasure and protecting Carter's Creek's heritage.

As Emma and Luke left the bakery, Lily and Maya headed back to their place to work on this some more together, and Sadie and Hannah had more work to restock the bakery after the morning's sales, so Gabe headed out on his own. The path ahead was challenging, but with their collective effort and unwavering support for one another, they were ready to face whatever obstacles lay in their way.

***

As Gabe headed to his SUV, he felt his phone buzzing in his pocket. Glancing at the screen, he saw it was his parents calling. He was expecting this call, since he'd texted them so late last night about Ethan.

He answered the call, smiling as he saw his parents' faces on the screen. "Hey, Mom, Dad."

Lee, his father, greeted him warmly. "Hi, Gabe! We saw the picture you sent. Looks like you and Sadie are really making progress."

Rachel, his mother, chimed in, "We had heard some rumors about a young man searching the Outer Banks for some treasure, I assume it must be Ethan, based on your text."

Gabe nodded, leaning against the SUV. "Yes, Ethan's supposedly in the Outer Banks now, your part of the world. We set a decoy that sent him on a wild goose chase, but I never expected he'd end up there with you guys. Apparently Sadie's cousins had already researched that area, since it's where Captain Morgan was before the war."

Lee reassured him, "We promise to keep an ear out and let you know if we hear anything more. And please, stay safe out there, just as we'll do here."

"Hey, Gabe, Dad and I were wondering if we could visit you in a couple weeks. We miss you so much, and we really want to meet Sadie, and … we really just want to visit. Not too soon, is it, " his Mom asked, hesitatingly.

Gabe smiled, grateful for his parents' support. "Thanks, Dad. I appreciate it. That's perfect, Mom, schools will be back in session after the summer break, and the weather is starting to cool off. Sadie is excited to meet both of you as well. I need to warn you though, the idea of you visiting made her a little misty, because she is an only child and her parents both passed several year after a car accident. She may need a minute to warm to my own family."

Rachel nodded, answering softly, "That sounds great. We know exactly how to love on her, no worries. Can you arrange some lodging for us? I know you don't have room to put us up."

"Thank you, Mom and Dad," Gabe said sincerely. "I'll get you something for a week if you have that much time. I've missed you, too, and I'd love some quality time with both of you. We'll keep you updated on our progress. Stay safe, too."

They exchanged goodbyes, and Gabe felt a renewed sense of support from his family. He jumped in his car for the drive home.

***

Later that afternoon, the sun began its descent, casting long shadows across Carter's Creek. Sadie stepped out of Sadie's Sweet Rolls, the bell above the door jingling softly behind her. As she glanced around, she spotted Gabe heading towards his shift at the tavern, a little earlier than usual.

She matched his pace, a playful smile tugging at her lips. "Hey, Gabe," Sadie called out, catching up to him just outside the bakery.

"Hey, Sadie," Gabe replied, his face lighting up. "Wrapping up our day at the bakery already?"

"It was quite the morning," Sadie began, her tone a mix of amusement and exhaustion. "The bakery was packed. All those ladies stopping by for their treats and updates. It's good to see everyone so engaged, but it definitely kept us on our toes. And everyone wanted to know the latest about our treasure hunt and Emma's baby news. They're getting their ultrasound next week! Have you heard from your parents, since you texted them last night."

Gabe sighed, glancing down the street. "They're supportive as always, Mom and Dad are eager to help out however they can, but I'm hoping they stay safe in the process. I don't really trust Ethan not to use them to get to us. I need to tell you though – they're planning to visit us in just a couple of weeks. It'll be nice to have them here, I've really missed them."

Sadie smiled softly, appreciating the support. "I'm glad your parents are so understanding. It means a lot to have that kind of backing."

Their conversation naturally flowed into updates about their ongoing search. "So, how are things progressing with the clues?" Sadie asked, her curiosity piqued.

Gabe glanced at her, determination evident in his eyes. "We're making steady progress. With Lily and Maya's help, we've been able to piece together more of Captain Morgan's riddles. The Town Hall is our next big target once Emma gets those architectural plans from Mr. Jenkins."

"Sounds promising," Sadie replied. "And how are things going with the Outer Banks search? Any new leads on Ethan?"

Gabe shook his head slightly. "Not yet. Ethan's relentless, but so are we. We're staying one step ahead, hoping to intercept his findings before he gets too far."

Sadie chuckled, shaking her head. "Well, we have been busy, haven't we! But enough about the treasure hunt. I seem to remember winning the fish competition on our first date, and you promised me my reward would be a second special date you are planning. ."

Gabe's face broke into a triumphant grin. "Sadie, I haven't forgotten that at all. You didn't think I would forget, did you?."

Sadie raised an eyebrow, teasingly, as he reached for her hand. "I just wanted to make sure you weren't reneging on our second date. A deals a deal!."

Gabe laughed, scratching the back of his neck. "It takes time to plan something special. Anyone can pick up a girl and take her out to eat and to a movie. Not everyone takes their girlfriend fishing on their first date."

Sadie smiled, feeling a warmth in her chest. "So, I'm your girlfriend now, am I?"

"My parents will tell you, I've never brought a girlfriend to meet them before. Will you be my girlfriend, pretty girl," he asked shyly, still holding her hand.

"Gabe, until further notice, I am your girl," Sadie answered confidently, then added, with a wink, "Of course, that could change if you're not forthcoming with a second date. A girl can't wait for her Prince Charming forever, can she?"

He pecked her on forehead, hugging her quickly as they arrived to the tavern doors for his shift, "Stay tuned, pretty lady, I'll be calling soon with the details!"

As Sadie walked on, she smiled, pleased with their conversation, so she did a little jig as she headed down the street alone. She was unaware that he was still watching, and he smiled to himself. She was a catch, and he needed to do everything in his power to make sure she didn't get away from him!

Chapter Thirteen
Mapping the Unknown

THE LATE MORNING SUN filtered through the tall windows of Carter's Creek Town Hall, casting long shadows across the historic building's meeting room. Mayor Emma Hunter had called an impromptu gathering, pulling together key people who had been involved in the treasure hunt. Around the large wooden table sat Gabe, Sadie, Luke, and the Whitmore cousins, Lily and Maya. Mr. Jenkins, with a thick roll of blueprints under his arm, entered last and took a seat across from Emma.

"Thank you all for coming on such short notice," Emma began, her tone steady and focused. "Mr. Jenkins has found something significant in the old architectural plans of this building, and I thought it was best if we went over everything together."

Mr. Jenkins unrolled the blueprints with care, smoothing them flat across the table as everyone leaned in. The crisp lines and careful details illustrated the town hall's original structure, complete with notations in faded ink. He pointed to a section labeled "Sub-Basement Storage."

"This," he said, tapping his finger on the blueprint, "is where it gets interesting. As you all know, this building has been updated and renovated over the years, but certain areas have remained untouched.

The sub-basement, according to these plans, was meant to serve as a secure vault for town records and artifacts during the town's founding years."

Gabe exchanged a glance with Sadie, feeling the thrill of discovery brewing as they took in the details of the hidden level.

Mr. Jenkins continued, "What's particularly unusual is this small room marked off here, adjoining the main basement storage. I don't believe it's ever been accessed—at least not officially. There are no documented entries or exits recorded after the building's renovations in the 1920s. And, I really don't know how to access it, given the walls in place now."

Maya's eyes lit up. "Do you think it could have been intentionally hidden during the renovations? Maybe as a way to protect certain items?"

"Could be," Jenkins agreed. "It wouldn't be unusual for people at that time to take extra steps to safeguard important possessions. And if Captain Morgan and Henry Whitmore were working together, they might have been clever enough to make this room seem invisible on purpose."

Emma leaned forward, her gaze intent. "So, what do you all think? Is this the lead we need?"

Sadie nodded, the excitement evident in her voice. "It has to be. Everything we've found so far suggests they would have chosen somewhere meaningful, right under our noses."

Luke spoke up, "If we're going to check it out, we'll need to see where it is in relation to the other rooms that are accessible now. Jenkins, do you have any idea how we might get in there?"

Mr. Jenkins tapped on the blueprint. "I'd suggest just walking the basement, with the plans in hand, to see what jumps out at you. I haven't been spent any time in the basement over the years, until just recently, while I'm currently filling in at the Town Archives in the basement. Even that, I've just been coming and going from there directly to the stairs. There's so much stored down there in dusty forgotten rooms."

As the group absorbed this, Mr. Jenkins glanced at his watch, then looked to Emma apologetically. "I'll have to leave you all to continue without me. I have an appointment with Linda I can't miss. I've set up the conference room down the hall for you all to spread out these plans and review anything you need."

Emma smiled, nodding her thanks. "Of course, Mr. Jenkins. Thank you for everything."

He stood, gathering his things and nodding to the others. "Good luck—and be careful down there."

With Mr. Jenkins gone, the group moved to the conference room, each feeling the weight of the discovery ahead. As they set up around the table, the excitement in the air was palpable. The clues were coming together, and the heart of Carter's Creek was about to reveal one of its deepest secrets.

***

The group filed into the conference room, a modest space with a large rectangular table surrounded by mismatched chairs. The architectural plans Mr. Jenkins had left were spread out on the table, and Luke immediately took his place at the head, ready to guide everyone through the blueprints.

"Alright, let's get a closer look," Luke said, scanning the detailed plans. "I can help point out any areas that might have been updated over the years. And since I'm used to reading these layouts, hopefully, I'll spot anything that seems out of place."

Emma took a seat beside him, her eyes sharp as she studied the blueprints. "Thank you, Luke. Anything you can identify will be a huge help."

Gabe leaned in from across the table, his eyes trained on the notations marking each section. "Do you think any of these spaces could still be hidden?"

"Maybe," Luke replied thoughtfully. "But the trick with these old buildings is that renovations sometimes miss hidden rooms or passageways, either by accident or because they were intended to stay concealed."

Maya tapped the area marked as the original basement entry. "So if we're looking for clues, we should start with places that wouldn't have been completely renovated. Here," she pointed, "this wing and these adjoining corridors might still hold traces of the original structure."

Sadie looked to Luke, her curiosity piqued. "Are there specific signs we can look for? Maybe more of those symbols we've been finding?"

"Exactly," Luke replied. "Those symbols could be key. If they used certain markings back then to signify hidden passages or rooms, we might find them in places that haven't been completely redone."

Emma glanced at the plans, then back at Luke. "So, you think it's worth walking through the halls and seeing if any of these areas line up with what we're seeing here on the plans?"

Luke nodded, his expression serious. "Definitely. It's the only way to see if the space we're after even exists in its original form. If there are any inconsistencies—walls that don't quite match or symbols hidden in plain sight—they might lead us in the right direction."

Emma closed the blueprint folder and stood. "Alright, let's walk the corridors and see what we find. We'll stick to these areas and check for any markers. And, based on what Mr. Jenkins said, we should definitely spend some time in the basement."

With a collective feeling of anticipation, the group gathered their things and prepared to walk through the heart of Carter's Creek's Town Hall, eyes peeled for symbols, codes, or any clues that could bring them one step closer to uncovering the town's hidden secrets.

***

At the cozy parsonage living room, Linda, Hannah, and Mary gathered with notebooks and swatches of pastel-colored fabrics spread across the coffee table. Mary poured tea for everyone, her smile warm and motherly.

Hannah flipped open her notebook, her eyes sparkling with excitement. "I can't believe we're finally planning Emma's baby shower! And finding out if it's a boy or girl? That's going to make it even more fun!"

Linda nodded, glancing through some of the decoration ideas they'd brainstormed. "It feels like we've all been waiting forever. And, Emma mentioned she has no color preferences, so I thought we'd do a soft mix of greens and yellows. Keep it cozy and neutral but still festive."

Mary clasped her hands, beaming. "That sounds perfect, Linda. The whole town's buzzing with excitement over this baby, and, you know, this will be my first grandchild... I'm so excited to be a grandma. Emma and Luke are really looking forward to the ultrasound, but Daniel and I are really excited as well."

"Oh, Mary, I know this is a big deal for the whole family. I'm so glad you're helping us with the shower, since you know Emma so well,"

Hannah chimed in. "We could even have a little reveal moment at the shower. Even though everyone will already know the gender by then, it would be nice to have a little surprise for the gender at the shower. Imagine a cake, cupcakes or a bunch of balloons—something simple but meaningful."

Linda looked up, a hint of excitement in her expression. "And speaking of plans, I have some news that I've been saving just for you two." She paused, glancing at their curious faces. "I met with Mr. Jenkins this morning, and he's accepted me into the business incubator program. I'll be opening my own event planning business—Southern Charm Events—right here in Carter's Creek."

Hannah and Mary gasped, exchanging thrilled looks. Mary leaned over and squeezed Linda's hand. "Linda, that's wonderful! You'll be amazing. Southern Charm Events—just the name sounds perfect for you."

"Thank you, Mary. I appreciate you and Daniel helping me find a new path for my life last year, so I didn't want you to think I'm abandoning you. I'm still available for whatever you need. I just wanted a fresh start with something of my own, and this feels right," Linda said, her voice filled with gratitude. "Plus, I think Carter's Creek could use some extra 'charm' for all the weddings, birthdays, and, of course, baby showers we'll be celebrating."

Hannah laughed, a look of pride in her eyes. "You're going to bring so much joy to this town, Linda. And we get to be your first big project with Emma's shower!"

Linda grinned, already envisioning the touches she'd add. "Exactly! I want it to be special, memorable—and full of Carter's Creek charm. This baby is bringing so many new beginnings."

The three women continued discussing shower details with a renewed energy, knowing that they were all supporting each other in more ways than one. With friends like these, every celebration felt like a new chapter for them all.

***

The group moved quietly through the corridors of the Town Hall, their footsteps echoing faintly against the old wooden floors. Emma returned to duties in her office, while Gabe, Sadie, Luke, Maya, and Lily headed downstairs to tour the basement. The basement was vast, filled with numerous rooms connected by narrow, shadowy corridors. Dust particles floated lazily in the beams of light that managed to pierce through the small, grimy windows, giving the entire area an eerie, forgotten atmosphere.

Gabe held a flashlight steady, its beam sweeping across the room. "Wow, this place is massive," he said, his voice echoing slightly in the expansive space. "Look at all these rooms—storage, old furniture, boxes of forgotten stuff."

Sadie stepped cautiously forward, her eyes immediately drawn to a stack of antique trunks in the corner. "It's like a labyrinth down here," she observed, a hint of concern in her voice. "We need to keep track of everything we find."

Maya, ever the organizer, pulled out her phone and began taking pictures of the various items scattered around. "I agree," she said. "This could take a while if we don't stay organized."

As they ventured deeper into the basement, each room revealed a new array of eclectic items: vintage clothing hung neatly in one area, old books were stacked in another, rusty tools lay scattered on workbenches, and peculiar artifacts were displayed on dusty shelves.

The air was thick with the scent of aged wood and musty paper, adding to the sense of mystery that enveloped them.

Luke, always the thinker of the group, studied the layout thoughtfully. He pulled out a notebook from his backpack and began to sketch. "Guys, I have an idea," he said, his eyes lighting up with excitement. "I think I can draw a floorplan of the current basement, based on what we're seeing. I can produce it with the same dimensions as these plans. We can then overlay the two, and anything we haven't found will immediately be visible, and we can search that area more thoroughly. Sound like a good plan to ya'll?"

Lily smiled, nodding, "That's perfect. How long will that take you to finish?"

"Hmm, probably a couple days, because I have to create it then reproduce it in the right dimensions," Luke answered. "Why don't you guys leave me here with the flashlight to get this etched out in my notebook, while you go search the rest of the building. A better use of all our time."

Everyone agreed, so everyone but Luke hiked back up the stairs, as he began the arduous task of sketching out the basement outline based on rooms they could access.

The group examined every corner, wall, and crevice as they went along, searching for any of the hidden compartments or latches that had become so familiar in their treasure hunt. Several times, they spotted the unique codes and symbols they'd uncovered in previous locations—etched subtly on baseboards, carved into a beam, or tucked within a decorative trim.

Lily traced her finger along a faintly carved symbol near a window ledge. "These symbols are definitely part of the trail, but whoever put these here didn't want them found easily. No obvious latches this time."

Sadie leaned in, studying the symbol alongside him. "They're teasing us, I swear," she joked with a smile. "Leaving just enough for us to keep looking but no easy answers."

After another sweep of the corridor without any luck, they regrouped in the conference room. Gabe glanced at his watch, sighing reluctantly. "Well, it's time for me to head to work. Southern Roots needs their bartender."

Maya smiled, a hint of amusement in her eyes. "Go on, Gabe, we'll continue this puzzle later. We've made progress, even if it doesn't feel like it yet."

Sadie shot him a mischievous grin. "Actually, I think Maya, Lily, and I might follow you over to Southern Roots. After all, dinner sounds good, and we could use some fun."

Gabe laughed, feeling a warmth spread through him at her words. "Well, then I guess I'll see you all in a few minutes," he said, grabbing his bag. With a wave to the group, he headed out, his steps light with anticipation.

The rest of them gathered their things, the excitement still buzzing in the air from their discoveries, even if no hidden compartments had revealed themselves yet. There was a sense of camaraderie and optimism that made it easy for them to keep going, trusting that they were on the right path. And for tonight, a little dinner and laughter sounded like just the right way to end the day.

Chapter Fourteen

Matters of the Heart

That afternoon, Gabe stepped behind the bar at Southern Roots, mentally mapping out the perfect second date with Sadie. He'd been turning the idea over in his mind all day, refining the details to make it just right. With the plan fully taking shape, he pulled out his phone and quickly shot a text to Luke and Tommy:

Hey, I've got a plan for Monday night, need your help to make it happen. Think you guys are up for it?

Within seconds, both friends replied with enthusiastic thumbs-up emojis. He knew he could count on them to help bring this idea to life, and his excitement grew as he pictured the look on Sadie's face when she saw what he had planned.

Just then, the bell above the tavern door chimed, and in walked Sadie, Lily, and Maya, laughter spilling over as they found a table near the bar. Sadie caught Gabe's eye, flashing him a bright smile before heading his way to grab drinks for the table.

"Hey, Sadie," he greeted, his voice softening as he leaned forward over the counter. "Glad you're here."

"Hey, Gabe," Sadie replied, her smile widening. "Could I get three lemonades?"

As he filled the glasses, Gabe took a breath, feeling his pulse quicken slightly. "So... Sadie, would you like to go out with me on our second date Monday night? It's my regular night off."

Sadie's eyes sparkled as she answered. "Sure! Where are we going?"

Gabe chuckled, sliding the lemonades toward her. "That's a surprise. Just dress comfortably—nothing fancy."

She nodded, biting back a grin as she took the glasses back to the table. Gabe watched her go, the warmth in his chest growing as she shared the news with Lily and Maya. The three of them exchanged glances and broke into giggles, the kind of girl talk he could only imagine but knew was all about him.

Just then, the upbeat tune of *"Boot Scootin' Boogie"* started playing on the jukebox, and before anyone could blink, Sadie, Lily, and Maya were up on their feet, starting a line dance as the music filled the room. Gabe's heart skipped a beat as he watched Sadie sway with the music, her laughter carrying across the room.

Other regulars joined in, creating a lively scene that brought Southern Roots to life. Gabe leaned against the counter, unable to take his eyes off Sadie. In that moment, it was clear as day—he was sunk.

***

That same afternoon, Luke was seated in his home office, focused on the current basement floor plan he was sketching out. He adjusted his pencil, glancing over his shoulder to where Emma stood, leaning close as she studied his work.

"So many storage rooms in that basement, that's why I tried to sketch it out there before heading back here, but it's so hard to remember one over another sitting here trying to finish this," he said, sighing, looking up at her for a moment, appreciating the soft glow in her eyes.

Emma tilted her head thoughtfully. "Hmm ... I was just thinking what a brilliant mind you have, pulling this all together so quickly."

Luke smiled, setting down his pencil and tugging her gently onto his lap. She laughed, settling in comfortably as he wrapped his arms around her. Just as he pressed a kiss to her forehead, they both felt a sudden, strong kick.

Emma gasped, her eyes lighting up. "Oh, I think someone wanted to say hello."

Luke grinned, placing a hand over her growing belly. "Hey, Daddy's here. Talk to me, little one," he murmured softly, his voice warm with affection.

Emma smiled, resting her hand over his. "Your daddy loves your momma so much, sweet baby, and he loves you, too."

He leaned down, close to Emma's belly. "You're already part of the team, little one, and we'll know if you're a boy or a girl tomorrow. Have you thought about any baby names, Emma?"

Emma's eyes softened. "I have a few in mind, but I'm excited to decide together, once we know a little more about our tiny kicker here."

Luke chuckled, feeling another tiny tap against his hand. "Good, because I can't wait to start calling you by name, baby. You're already loved so much."

They sat in contented silence, savoring the moment as a family, the anticipation of tomorrow making everything feel all the more real.

***

The tavern was buzzing that evening, packed with townsfolk who seemed ready to dance all night long. The girls had been leading the crowd onto the floor, stirring up the energy and keeping everyone on their feet. Gabe worked the bar with his usual skill, stealing glances at Sadie every chance he got, his heart swelling as he watched her laughing and dancing with her friends.

Hannah and Linda had both arrived earlier in the evening, quickly joining the group. Tommy came in not long after, sliding into an empty seat next to Gabe for a quick hello before heading over to the others. Between dances, the group gathered around the table, diving into a plate of cheese fries and sharing stories over the music.

Linda, her cheeks flushed with excitement, leaned in with a grin. "Ladies and gentlemen, I have news. Big news." She paused for dramatic effect, then said, "Southern Charm Events is official. Mr. Jenkins accepted me into the business incubator, and I'm finally launching my own event planning business!"

The group erupted in cheers, and Tommy, with a big smile, stood up just as "Better Together" by Luke Combs began to play. He held out a hand to Linda, bowing slightly. "Well then, Miss Business Owner, I'd love to have the first dance with the newest entrepreneur in Carter's Creek. May I?"

Linda's smile turned even brighter as she took his hand, letting him lead her to the dance floor. Gabe, inspired by the moment, motioned for a server to cover the bar, then walked over to Sadie with a soft grin.

"May I have this dance, too?" he asked, holding out his hand.

Sadie beamed, sliding her hand into his. "I'd love nothing more."

As they danced, Gabe and Tommy exchanged a nod of camaraderie, both of them clearly comfortable on the floor. Gabe twirled Sadie expertly, her laughter blending with the warm, soulful melody. Tommy, meanwhile, had Linda laughing with his enthusiastic moves, leading her in a lively two-step. When the song ended, Tommy made a point of dancing with each of the other ladies, bringing laughter to Hannah, Lily and Maya, while the ladies continued dancing together in between.

After his last dance, Tommy clapped Gabe on the back, grinning. "Gotta keep the charm going, you know? Don't want any of these ladies getting ideas—I'm not looking to get hitched!" he teased, winking at the girls who all laughed in response.

The night wound down on a high note, the warmth of friendship and laughter lingering long after the last song had played.

***

As the night wrapped up, Tommy rounded up Hannah, Lily, and Maya, ushering them out to his truck. "No worries, ladies," he said with a grin. "I'll be by in the morning to get you back to your cars." With a wink and a wave, he promised them a safe ride home, leaving Gabe and Sadie to walk together in the quiet, moonlit streets of Carter's Creek.

The town felt peaceful, bathed in the soft glow of streetlights, and the air was pleasantly cool after the lively evening at Southern Roots. Gabe held out his arm, and Sadie took it with a smile, her laughter still lingering from the fun they'd had all evening. She leaned into him slightly, her voice soft as they walked side by side.

"You know, I feel like we're on the edge of something amazing, Gabe. Like ... I know we'll find the treasure. I really believe it." She gazed up at the night sky, her voice filled with a dreamy excitement. "And I wonder what else might change when we do. Because things always change, don't they?"

Gabe chuckled softly, glancing over at her. "Yeah, they do. Sometimes in ways we'd never expect. But you know, some changes can be pretty wonderful too."

She looked up at him, her expression thoughtful. "You're right, but it makes me a little nervous too. We've worked so hard on this search—it's taken on a life of its own. And then there's everything else that's changed for me since you came along. But ... it all feels good. Like a shift I've been waiting for."

Gabe paused, guiding her to a stop beneath one of the old oak trees that lined the street. He turned to face her, his gaze warm and steady. "Sadie, whether we find treasure or just a dusty old relic, I want you to know ... I'm here for all of it. This whole journey with you, it's been the best thing to happen to me. And it feels like just the beginning."

Sadie blushed, a soft smile spreading across her face. "I like the sound of that," she said, her voice barely above a whisper. "Maybe ... maybe the best treasure I could find is right here."

Gabe's eyes softened, his hand reaching up to brush a stray strand of hair from her face. "Well, I think you're already a treasure," he murmured, a smile tugging at the corners of his mouth. "Just one I was lucky enough to stumble upon."

They shared a moment in comfortable silence, then began walking again, the comfortable quiet between them filled with a deeper sense of understanding.

As they reached her front door, Sadie turned to face him, her eyes shining. "Thanks for walking me home, Gabe. And for tonight—it was perfect."

"Anytime, Sadie. Get some rest. Monday night is going to be a night to remember," he promised, the hint of a playful smile lighting up his face.

She laughed softly, her gaze lingering on him before finally slipping inside. Gabe stood there for a moment, feeling as though something significant had shifted. This was more than just a search for treasure now—it was a journey that had brought him to her doorstep, and he knew he was exactly where he was meant to be.

***

Gabe drifted into a deep sleep, the day's events playing softly at the edges of his mind. Slowly, his dreams took shape, transporting him to a grand ballroom he had never seen, yet somehow felt familiar. Music filled the air, a gentle waltz that seemed to come from nowhere and everywhere at once, surrounding him with warmth. People dressed in elegant attire moved about, but Gabe's focus was drawn to a particular couple at the center of the room.

Captain Gabriel Morgan, tall and handsome in his military uniform, held a beautiful woman in his arms. She wore a flowing blue gown, her dark curls pinned elegantly back as she gazed up at him with unmistakable love in her eyes. They swayed together, their steps light and graceful, each movement filled with a quiet intimacy that needed no words. Gabe watched them, mesmerized, recognizing the profound connection they shared.

As the music softened, the Captain gently kissed Eleanor's hand before stepping away, his gaze now fixed on Gabe. Walking slowly across the room, the Captain approached, his face warm with an understanding that seemed to bridge centuries.

"Gabriel Hunter," he said, his voice steady and filled with something like amusement. "You're walking a similar path to mine—entangled in a treasure hunt, yes, but more so, bound by love." His eyes grew serious as he placed a hand on Gabe's shoulder. "Don't waste time, son. I let the world pull me away, and when I came back, it was too late. Love—real love—only comes around once in a lifetime if a man is lucky."

The words resonated deeply, filling Gabe with a strange urgency that tugged at his heart. As the Captain gave him a final, encouraging nod, the ballroom began to dissolve, the scene blurring until only the memory of it remained.

Gabe stirred awake, the remnants of the dream lingering in his mind. He lay there in the quiet of his room, his heart pounding with clarity. He knew now, with absolute certainty, that he wasn't going to let anything come between him and Sadie—not time, not hesitation, not fear.

He sat up, filled with a renewed sense of purpose. This treasure hunt was important, but there was something even more valuable in his life now. He was determined not to wait too long to win the love he had found, not to let history repeat itself.

Chapter Fifteen

Looking to the Future

THE MORNING SUN FILTERED softly through the blinds of the Sheriff's office as Sheriff Daniels and Mayor Emma Hunter sat across from each other, reviewing the findings from the investigation into Mr. Mattison. A stack of reports and evidence sat between them on the desk, each piece connecting Mr. Mattison to the stolen historical relics he'd secretly stashed in his home.

"Mayor, it's looking like this case is a lock. The FBI's will be taking the lead of this investigation going forward, and with the evidence we've gathered, there's little doubt he'll be behind bars for quite a while," Sheriff Daniels said, tapping a report. "He was holding onto those relics to build himself up in the historical community, hoping to make his mark."

Emma nodded thoughtfully, her mind already churning with questions. "Good riddance, then. But before they cart him off too far, I'd like to speak to him. He's been tied up in this town's secrets for so long; maybe he knows something valuable about the treasure we've been piecing together—or even about Ethan."

Sheriff Daniels considered her request, then nodded. "I think I can arrange that. But I'd be cautious, Emma. Mattison isn't exactly known for being straightforward."

Minutes later, Emma found herself in the dimly lit holding room where Mr. Mattison, looking weary but still defiant, sat across the table from her. He gave her a curt nod as she settled into her seat, but his gaze held a resigned acceptance.

"Mayor," he greeted, his voice even. "To what do I owe this visit?"

Emma leaned forward, meeting his gaze firmly. "Mr. Mattison, I'm here for answers. You've tampered with history, twisted our town's legacy for personal gain. You could save yourself a bit of dignity by sharing what you know—about the treasure hunt, Ethan's involvement, and anything else you think we should be aware of."

Mattison chuckled softly, a glimmer of amusement in his eyes. "Ah, the treasure hunt. Quite the local legend, isn't it? You all think it's some grand tale. Well, there's truth to it. Carter's Creek does hold secrets—layers of history hidden from the public eye. But it's more complicated than a simple buried treasure chest."

Emma raised an eyebrow, waiting for him to continue.

Mattison sighed, finally leaning back. "I'll tell you this: I believe Gabe stands a chance. He's looking for the right reasons—preservation, honor, understanding. He's the type who just might stumble upon things that others have missed for centuries. And yes, some of it may not be so pretty."

Emma's gaze intensified. "And Ethan? What's his role in all this?"

Mattison rolled his eyes. "Ethan's a different story. Greedy, impatient, reckless. He's as lost in this search as I am in here. He'll never find anything of real value, not with that mindset. The treasure you all seek doesn't reveal itself to those with greed in their hearts."

Emma considered his words carefully. "So you're saying there are hidden parts of our town's history, things even Gabe might not be expecting."

"Exactly," Mattison said, nodding. "Some things were meant to be kept in the past, and others ... well, others just need the right eyes to see them. I suspect young Gabe might be the one to bring both light and shadows to Carter's Creek's story."

Emma studied his face, searching for any sign of deceit, but there was only a weary honesty in his expression.

"Thank you for sharing this, Mr. Mattison. I believe you, in part." She stood, glancing back at him with a slight nod. "Perhaps there's still a chance for some redemption in your story."

Mattison gave her a small, somber smile. "Redemption isn't in the cards for me, Mayor. But perhaps it's not too late for Carter's Creek."

***

Emma and Luke's cozy living room buzzed with the voices of friends and family who had gathered for the evening. The group, including Hannah, Tommy, Gabe, Sadie, Linda, Lily, and Maya, settled in as Emma set a tray of snacks on the coffee table, the room warm with the glow of conversation and shared purpose.

Luke took a seat next to Emma, glancing around with a serious expression. "Thanks for coming, everyone. We've got some important updates after Emma's meeting with Mr. Mattison earlier today. Turns out, he had quite a bit to say."

Emma leaned forward, her gaze moving around the circle. "Mr. Mattison admitted that there are secrets about Carter's Creek's history that have been hidden intentionally—some might be things we didn't expect. According to him, Gabe might be the only one to find the real treasure because he's searching for the right reasons. As for Ethan... well, Mr. Mattison had a pretty dim view of him."

Lily exchanged a glance with Maya, then spoke up. "That sounds about right. Ethan's always been competitive to a fault, even with us. I hate to say it, but his impulsive side often gets the better of him."

Maya nodded, her tone thoughtful. "I never wanted to believe he'd take it this far, but if he's chasing something purely for himself, I can see him going down the wrong path entirely. The thing is, it's almost like he's lost his way in this, more focused on winning than on understanding the legacy we're trying to preserve."

Gabe frowned, a mix of sympathy and resolve in his eyes. "I just hope Ethan finds his way without causing any more damage. But I have to admit, Mr. Mattison' hints about secrets in Carter's Creek have me wondering... what's still left to uncover?"

Emma looked at Luke, who gave a small nod. "We think the next step is talking to some of the older members of the community," he said. "Mr. Jenkins, our parents, anyone who's got that long-standing knowledge of the town's history. They might know something about the legacy Captain Morgan left behind, and even if it's just a small piece, it could help us."

"Definitely," Sadie chimed in. "This whole search has revealed pieces of the past that none of us expected, and talking to people who've been here longer could be the key."

Luke nodded and then reached for the rolled-up plans he'd brought to the meeting. Unfurling them on the coffee table, he layered the modern floor plan of the Town Hall over the original blueprint. "Take a look. I've been working on this layout, marking the locations where we've seen the symbols and clues. This here—" he pointed to an area outlined in red, "—appears to be the location of a hidden room. It's hidden between some of the newer walls and the original foundation, but I haven't found any signs of an entrance."

Hannah leaned over the plans, her brow furrowing. "The symbols... they're all around this area, almost as if they're creating a border."

Linda peered closer, her eyes lighting up. "Maybe those symbols are markers for something below. It's almost like they're pointing down to whatever's underneath them."

Emma nodded thoughtfully. "That's exactly what it looks like. And the room is well-hidden, probably deliberately so. But it's clear that we need to investigate this spot thoroughly. Just not tonight." She glanced at Luke with a smile. "Tomorrow morning is our ultrasound appointment, and I don't think I'll get much sleep if we try digging into this tonight."

The group chuckled, and Tommy clapped Luke on the shoulder. "Smart thinking, buddy. Besides, if there's a secret room tucked away somewhere, it's not going anywhere before Tuesday."

Sadie looked over at Emma, her expression warm. "We can wait a day or two—especially if it means getting to hear about the ultrasound. I think we're all excited for you two."

Emma beamed, her hand resting on her stomach. "Thank you, everyone. Tuesday, we'll get back to treasure hunting. But for now, it's time to get ready to meet our little one. And, you're all invited to our house Tuesday evening to hear more about baby – our parents are going with us to the appointment."

***

The morning was filled with eager anticipation as Emma, Luke, and their parents gathered in the doctor's waiting room for her ultrasound. The hum of soft music played overhead, but their attention was fixed solely on each other and the milestone they were about to share. Emma squeezed Luke's hand, a warm smile on her face as she took in the presence of their family around them. Tom Hunter, Luke's father, and Pastor Daniel and Mary Thompson, Emma's parents, exchanged excited glances as they waited, equally thrilled to be part of the moment.

As they settled in, Luke leaned forward, and asked the parents. "Hey, have any of you ever heard any old stories about hidden history here in Carter's Creek? You know, things people didn't want to be revealed?"

Tom and Daniel shared a knowing look, an expression that was easy to miss but hinted at a shared memory. Daniel cleared his throat, glancing back at Luke. "Well, son, that's an interesting question. Let us put our heads together and think on that."

Before Luke could press further, the technician appeared in the doorway, clipboard in hand, and called them back. Luke and Emma waved to their parents who were staying behind, following the technician with eager steps, and Emma's heart raced as they entered the dimly lit room where the ultrasound machine awaited. She lay back, Luke's hand firmly in hers, while the technician prepped the equipment.

"Alright, let's take a look at your little one," the technician said warmly as she spread the cool gel on Emma's belly and began moving the wand over her abdomen. Moments later, a small, flickering image appeared on the screen.

"There's the baby," the technician announced, pointing at the tiny form. "You can see the arms and legs here, and this is the baby's heart." She turned on the audio, filling the room with the steady, rhythmic heartbeat of their child. Emma's eyes misted, and Luke's hand tightened around hers as they shared a glance full of awe and love.

"The heartbeat sounds perfect," the technician said, smiling. "Everything looks healthy and right on track."

Emma and Luke breathed a sigh of relief, their joy growing by the second. The technician paused, looking at them with a grin. "Now, I have to ask—do you want to know your baby's gender?"

Emma and Luke exchanged a look, and with matching smiles, they responded in unison, "Yes."

The technician focused on the screen, moving the wand gently. "Alright, now remember, it's not always 100% accurate, but I believe you're having a beautiful, healthy baby girl!"

Emma's heart swelled as she looked at Luke, his eyes shining with pride and excitement. They shared a quiet moment of joy, then made their way back to the waiting room to announce the news.

As they entered, all eyes turned to them, eager and hopeful. Luke grinned and, holding Emma close, he said, "We're having a baby girl!"

Cheers and hugs filled the room, but Luke's expression grew soft as he turned to his father, pulling him into a heartfelt embrace. "I just wish Mom could be here to meet her."

Tom's eyes glistened, and he patted Luke's back, his voice thick with emotion. "She'd be so proud, son."

Luke took a deep breath, still holding his father's arm as he looked around at the beaming faces surrounding them. "Last night, Emma and I decided... if we were having a girl, we'd name her Sarah, after my mother."

Mary reached out, her hand gently resting on Emma's belly. "Sarah. It's a beautiful name for a beautiful baby." Tears shone in her eyes as she spoke, and the room grew quiet with the depth of love shared.

Emma glanced down at her belly, feeling a fresh wave of emotion as they welcomed baby Sarah into their lives, surrounded by the family who would love and cherish her from the very beginning.

***

As the sun began to sink below the horizon, casting long shadows over Carter's Creek, Gabe met Luke and Tommy behind the town's gazebo. The trio had been huddling in secret over the past hour, discussing Gabe's grand plan for a special evening with Sadie. The air buzzed with a blend of anticipation and amusement as they began unloading boxes and bags, working swiftly to get everything set up before dusk fully claimed the town.

Luke chuckled, glancing at Gabe as he hung a string of twinkling lights along the railing of the gazebo. "Gabe, I've never seen you this worked up over a date. You sure you're not setting the bar a bit high?"

Gabe grinned, unfazed by his friend's teasing. "What can I say? She deserves the best, and I want tonight to be memorable."

Tommy finished arranging a cluster of wildflowers he'd brought from his shop, adding pops of color along the gazebo steps. "I don't think I've ever seen you like this, man," he said with a smirk. "Running around, planning a surprise date like this—it's almost like you're...well, in love."

Luke laughed, slapping Gabe on the back. "Almost? Pretty sure he's already gone, Tommy. No one else would go to these lengths."

Gabe rolled his eyes, but a faint blush crept up his neck. "You two can say whatever you want. Just help me set this up before Sadie catches wind of it. I need every detail to be perfect."

Tommy stepped back, admiring their work. The gazebo, bathed in soft light from the string of bulbs and surrounded by fresh flowers, looked like something straight out of a storybook. "Well, she's bound to be impressed. And, if this doesn't win her over completely, nothing will."

Luke handed Gabe a small box with a satin ribbon tied around it. "Just remember to thank us in your wedding speech one day," he joked. "Now, what's the plan for when she arrives?"

Gabe shook his head, laughing. "I owe you both. When she gets here, I'll have the candles lit, the music ready, and—"

"Music? What kind of music are we talking about here?" Tommy asked, his eyebrow raised.

Gabe shrugged. "I thought I'd play something she loves—something nostalgic, maybe. The kind of song that makes you feel like you're the only two people in the world."

Luke gave a mock sigh, clutching his heart. "That's it. You're officially a goner."

"Alright, alright," Gabe said, grabbing the last bag from his truck. "Laugh all you want. Just help me finish this up before she gets here."

Luke laughed, nudging Tommy as they headed back to the truck for some extra supplies. "Come on, Tommy, let's do this right. We can rig up a sound system that'll do a lot better than some old boom box. Never say we didn't pull out all the stops for a friend."

Tommy grinned, nodding. "Alright, now you're talking. If we're doing this, we're doing it all the way."

Before long, the two had set up a small, hidden sound system around the gazebo, placing speakers just out of sight and running the cords back to a portable setup they'd stashed under the steps. Luke plugged in Gabe's playlist and ran a quick test, filling the air with a rich, warm melody that seemed to make the lights glow even brighter.

"There we go," Luke said, satisfied. "Now, this is a proper setup. She won't forget this night anytime soon, that's for sure."

Gabe grinned, shaking his head in gratitude. "I owe you both, big time. This is perfect."

Tommy chuckled, giving him a thumbs up. "Just don't forget to invite us to the wedding."

As they placed the final touches, they couldn't hide their pride in how it all looked. The setting sun cast a warm glow over the scene, adding to the cozy, intimate atmosphere they'd created. Luke and Tommy stood back, arms crossed, satisfied with their work.

Tommy gave Gabe one last pat on the back. "Good luck, man. You're setting a new standard here in Carter's Creek. Just don't mess it up."

Gabe laughed, feeling his nerves and excitement swell. "Thanks, guys. I think I'm ready."

As his friends left, Gabe took a deep breath, glancing around to make sure everything was in place. The evening was set, and now all that was left was for Sadie to arrive.

Chapter Sixteen
A Town's Embrace

Gabe parked his truck at the edge of Town Square, catching the hint of surprise on Sadie's face as she looked around at the quiet, familiar space. A small smile played on her lips. "A date in Town Square?" she teased, arching an eyebrow.

"Have a little faith," he replied, smiling as he slipped out of the truck and into the shadows, leaving her waiting in curious silence.

Moments later, lights began to flicker on in the trees, casting a soft, warm glow throughout the square. A few seconds later, Michael Bublé's voice drifted through the square, filling the air with his rendition of "Fly Me to the Moon." The song's smooth notes mingled with the glow of the lights, transforming the square into something magical. Gabe reappeared, holding out a hand to her, his expression both proud and tender.

"May I escort you to your table, Miss?"

Sadie laughed, her smile bright as she took his hand. He led her to a small, beautifully set table in the center of the square, where candles flickered gently between them. The music played on softly in the background as they began to eat, and Gabe could sense her eyes studying him, curious and thoughtful.

"So, tell me, Gabe," she began, a gentle smile on her face, "what's one thing you're absolutely set on achieving in your life?"

Gabe paused, surprised by the depth of the question. He glanced down, taking a moment before looking back up at her, his expression thoughtful. "Honestly? I've always wanted to build something real for myself... to feel like I made a difference, even in a small way. To leave something behind, maybe. That's why I love working in this town, helping with the tavern, and even all those little renovations I do for friends." He hesitated, then smiled softly. "But lately, that vision has started to feel less complete without someone to share it with."

Sadie's eyes softened. She nodded, clearly understanding more than she was saying. "I get that," she murmured. "I think it's easy to get caught up in going after things we think we want, only to find out that what matters most is simpler than we realized."

"What about you?" he asked. "What's something you'd never want to give up?"

Sadie's eyes drifted to the candlelight for a moment. "The ability to laugh. To find joy, even in the mess. I know it might sound silly, but I think laughter's my way of keeping the world light, no matter what it throws at me."

They shared a smile, each recognizing something kindred in the other's words. They talked about dreams and disappointments, their childhood memories, and small moments that shaped them. There were stories of Sadie's bakery mishaps and Gabe's awkward attempts at learning guitar in high school, each story bringing them closer, one laugh at a time.

When they'd finished eating, Gabe stood, extending his hand once again with a smile. "Care to dance?"

As they moved beneath the lights, Michael Bublé's soft melody surrounded them, the world fading to just the two of them in the heart of their town. The rhythm of their steps matched perfectly, an easy flow of movement and laughter.

Later, as the evening began to wind down, Gabe switched off the lights and the music, and they started back toward his truck. But the night wasn't done surprising them just yet. As they paused to take in the starlit sky, a full moon emerged from behind a cloud, casting a bright silver glow across the square.

They both stopped, noticing the Oak tree's shadow stretching across Town Hall. There, against the pale stone, the shadow formed a strange shape—a faint, etched pattern they hadn't noticed before, revealed only in the moonlight.

Sadie's breath caught as she stared, her eyes wide with excitement. "Do you see that?"

Gabe's gaze remained fixed on the shadow. He nodded, his voice barely a whisper. "The Oak tree and Town Hall... I think we're onto something."

They stood in silence, letting the moment settle. A quiet thrill filled the air between them, the night deepening their bond. Finally, Gabe glanced at Sadie, his eyes still bright with wonder. "Too late to solve this tonight," he said with a grin. "Let's get some sleep and come back tomorrow."

Sadie nodded, her eyes sparkling with anticipation. They walked back to the truck, hand in hand, their steps echoing in the moonlit square. For tonight, the mystery would wait, but both knew this was just the beginning—of their search and, perhaps, of something even more lasting between them.

***

As Sadie settled into bed, her mind lingered on the evening she'd shared with Gabe. The glow of the town square lights, their laughter, and the easy, meaningful conversation had left her feeling warm and content. But it was the discovery under the moonlight—the Oak tree's shadow, hinting at a secret long hidden—that filled her thoughts. Nature itself seemed to be revealing the town's secrets to them, as if pulling back a veil just for them.

As her eyes grew heavy, she drifted into a dream where she was once again a child, curled up beside her Aunt Clara. They were sitting on the front porch of her aunt's house, where countless stories had been shared over the years. Aunt Clara's voice was warm and steady, her words weaving pictures as vivid as they were comforting.

"Sadie, my dear," Aunt Clara said, her eyes twinkling. "You know this town holds secrets, don't you? They're like treasures hidden in plain sight, waiting for the right heart to come along and understand them."

Young Sadie, in the dream, nodded, feeling the familiar magic in her aunt's words. She'd heard these stories countless times, but tonight, Aunt Clara's voice held a new kind of clarity, as if she were revealing truths she'd only hinted at before.

"Life's more than mysteries, though," Aunt Clara continued, her voice softening. "You've got to live it fully, Sadie—take risks, love deeply, laugh even in the hard times. That's the only way to truly find your place in this world."

Aunt Clara's words filled Sadie's heart, wrapping her in a warmth that felt both timeless and deeply personal. She hadn't realized how much she'd longed to hear those words, words of encouragement to live boldly, to trust in herself, and to embrace whatever came next.

As morning light began to seep through the window, Sadie awoke with Aunt Clara's words echoing in her mind. She lay still for a moment, feeling the lingering comfort of her aunt's love, the confidence it inspired within her. Whatever lay ahead—whether in her budding relationship with Gabe or the mysteries that lay in Town Square—she knew she was ready. She felt loved, confident, and inspired, ready to embrace the next chapter.

***

The morning sun filtered through the windows of the Dew Drop Inn as Luke, Gabe, Tom, Tommy, and Daniel settled into their regular booth. The cozy hum of breakfast chatter surrounded them, and the smell of coffee and warm biscuits filled the air. Luke, Tom, and Daniel were practically glowing, still caught up in the joy and excitement of the ultrasound news, a fact that hadn't escaped Gabe or Tommy's notice.

But Luke's curiosity was stirring, his mind drifting back to the look on Daniel's and Tom's faces the day before when he'd brought up the idea of town secrets. He hadn't missed the way they'd exchanged a quick glance, something unspoken passing between them.

Setting down his coffee mug, Luke leaned forward, lowering his voice slightly. "So, about yesterday... I saw the way you both reacted when I mentioned town secrets. What do you know? Gabe and I need to understand what we're dealing with, in case it's something that's better left undiscovered."

Daniel exchanged a glance with Tom, who gave a slight nod, as if giving him permission. Daniel took a deep breath, his face settling into a look of quiet resolve.

"It's not in any history book," Daniel began, choosing his words carefully, "and it's not something folks have discussed openly. But it's a part of who we are—a story handed down. Back during the Civil War, this town was filled with impartial people, compassionate ones who believed in freedom. They didn't want the horrors of slavery touching their town, so they did something about it. They became part of the Underground Railroad, helping move those seeking freedom through secret routes."

Gabe and Luke exchanged glances, their curiosity growing as Daniel continued.

"By the time the war ended, it wasn't as necessary," Daniel went on, "but that's when Captain Gabriel Morgan moved to town. He was a man from the Confederacy, and folks here kept that part of our history hidden. They weren't sure about his values or whether he'd respect the choices they'd made to protect freedom."

"But something changed over time," Tom added, his voice thoughtful. "Captain Morgan wasn't just any Confederate officer; he was someone who'd been deeply in love with a woman named Eleanor Whitaker. They'd known each other for years, and when he left for the war, she became involved in women's groups supporting the war effort. Eleanor was educated, sharp as a tack, and she had a mind of her own."

Daniel nodded. "As the years passed and Eleanor began to understand the real issues behind the war—slavery, secession—her beliefs started to shift. She wrote to him about it, shared her doubts, and he held onto those letters like they were lifelines. You see, he loved her fiercely, and her words got under his skin."

Tom's gaze softened. "By the time he learned she'd passed, those letters had stirred something deep inside him. It changed him. He realized he couldn't live by old beliefs and decided to create something worthwhile, something she would have been proud of."

The table fell silent as the men took in the weight of the story, the legacy left by a man whose life had been transformed by love and loss. It was a story of redemption, of honoring one's beliefs and the people who shaped them.

Luke and Gabe sat back, a quiet understanding settling over them. This history—the secret that had shaped their town and bound its people together—wasn't just a tale of old. It was part of their present, something that connected them to the very heart of their community.

After a moment, Luke broke the silence, his voice barely a whisper. "It's more than just a secret. It's... a legacy."

Daniel nodded, a knowing look in his eyes. "Exactly. And if you're going to uncover anything about that legacy, you're not just uncovering the past. You're carrying it forward."

The men sat in silence, each one feeling the weight of the morning in a new way. Whatever lay ahead, it wasn't just their search anymore. It was a mission—to honor the past and to ensure that the values of compassion, courage, and love continued to shape their town's future.

***

The morning light poured in through Town Hall's high windows, casting an almost magical glow on the group gathered inside. Emma, Luke, Sadie, Gabe, Tommy, Hannah, Linda, Mr. Jenkins, Daniel, Mary, Tom, and now Lily and Maya, too, huddled together, each caught up in the thrill of what they might uncover. Luke had just finished recounting the story of the town's history, and his words hung in the air like an unbroken spell.

Sadie's eyes widened, her voice soft. "I never would have guessed... our town, part of the Underground Railroad?"

"Neither would most folks," Daniel replied, his voice thick with pride. "But that's the kind of people this town was built by—folks who couldn't stand by and watch others suffer."

Tommy shook his head, impressed. "Makes you feel proud to be part of a place with a history like that."

Lily, with a thoughtful expression, spoke up. "And Captain Morgan... he could have stayed the same, but he didn't. He chose to grow because of love. There's something powerful in that."

Mr. Jenkins, looking at her, nodded in agreement. "Exactly. That's why we need to keep this history alive, but also why it's been hidden for so long. Not everyone would see it as something to be proud of."

Emma stepped forward, setting her hands on the old plans they'd spread out across the table. "All right, everyone. Let's see what we're up against in that basement."

They made their way down, their footsteps echoing off the stone walls. Gabe and Tommy took the lead, overlaying the new building plans with the old. Gabe pointed to a spot near the back wall. "There it is. But, uh... I think we've got a little more work than expected."

They stared at the room ahead, stacked floor to ceiling with dusty files, boxes, and old furniture. It was the remnants of decades of town history—everything from forgotten chairs to file cabinets practically bursting with papers.

Hannah let out a low whistle. "You weren't kidding about spring cleaning, Tom."

Tom grinned, rolling up his sleeves. "I say we get to it. No time like the present."

Emma, already brainstorming, looked over at Mr. Jenkins. "We'll need a spot to store all this until we can go through it. And I'll definitely want to loop in the town council. I don't think we can keep a project like this completely under wraps."

Linda nodded thoughtfully. "Especially with Ethan lurking around, looking for this, too."

Luke, noticing Lily and Maya's excitement, chuckled. "Didn't expect to get your hands dusty on a day like this, did you?"

Maya laughed. "Are you kidding? This is the most exciting thing I've been part of since moving here!"

Lily added, grinning, "Same! I feel like we're in one of those adventure movies."

Emma turned to everyone, her gaze warm and grateful. "We'll need all the help we can get. But this is a job for the Town Hall, not all of you. Mr. Jenkins and I will come up with a game plan after the council meeting. I'll let you know if we need your help."

Everyone nodded, sharing determined glances as they took in the mountain of history they had to move before reaching their goal. The task felt both daunting and thrilling, a treasure waiting just beneath the surface.

As the group began to file out, Emma clapped her hands together. "Oh! One more thing before everyone goes." She looked around, her smile bright. "Luke and I are hosting a cookout tonight at our place. We're finally sharing our baby news with the whole town—and yes, that means you two are invited, Lily and Maya. You're family now, too."

The women beamed, touched by Emma's words, and the entire group buzzed with excitement for the night ahead. They left Town Hall with a renewed sense of purpose, knowing that tonight, they'd be gathering not just as friends but as family, celebrating the legacy of their town—and the new beginnings it promised.

***

The evening sun cast a golden glow over Emma and Luke's backyard as the entire town gathered for the cookout. Pink and white decorations adorned the space, from delicate streamers to balloons tied along the fence, each one bearing messages of love for the new arrival. Linda had gone all out with the decorations, her eye for detail transforming the yard into a warm, inviting celebration for Baby Sarah. Sadie's cake sat at the center of it all, beautifully decorated with the words, "Baby Sarah is coming!" in elegant pink script.

As Emma and Luke moved through the crowd, they were met with congratulations and warm smiles from every direction. Ms. Beatrice and Mabel shuffled up to Emma, looking uncharacteristically bashful before each took her hands.

"Congratulations, dear," Ms. Beatrice said, her smile broad.

"Couldn't be happier for you both," added Mabel, a mischievous glint in her eye. She shot a glance at Sadie, then whispered, "Mum's the word on the 'ownta allha!"

The words were met with laughter from all sides as people caught on—the town gossips were managing to keep the secret. Emma couldn't resist a laugh herself, squeezing their hands in gratitude.

As the celebration continued, Emma noticed Linda gathering the ladies together, gesturing toward the center of the yard. With a wink at Emma, Linda spoke just loud enough for everyone to hear, "As a new life has formed and will soon arrive to Carter's Creek, the ladies of our town offer a bud and a wish for this blossoming life, Luke and Emma's Baby Sarah!"

Emma and Luke sat surrounded by family, with her parents, Mary and Daniel, beside her and Luke's father beside him. The women of the town formed a line, and one by one, each woman stepped forward, offering Emma a pink rosebud and a note card with a single word written on it. The words were simple yet profound, each one chosen with love: *Joy, Love, Bounty, Strength, Kindness, Wonder.*

Emma's eyes filled with tears as the line continued, each woman placing her rosebud into a delicate bundle in her lap and handing her a note card with another word of blessing. It was a silent promise, an offering of the community's heart for her daughter's future. As she looked at the growing pile of rosebuds and read each word, Emma felt overwhelmed by the love and support of the people around her, her tribe, her home.

Luke reached over, squeezing her hand, and she looked at him, her heart swelling with gratitude. This was more than a celebration of new life—it was a testament to the strength and love of their community, and a reminder that Baby Sarah would grow up surrounded by people who cared deeply for her.

The women stepped back, the pile of roses now resting softly in Emma's lap. With a voice full of emotion, she managed, "Thank you, all of you, for surrounding our family with so much love. Sarah is blessed to be part of Carter's Creek."

Applause and cheers rang out as the sun dipped below the horizon, casting a soft glow over the town's celebration. Linda beamed, nodding to the group, and they all raised their glasses in a toast to Emma, Luke, and the little one on the way.

And as the evening continued, filled with laughter, good food, and heartfelt conversations, Emma knew this memory would be one they cherished forever—a moment when family, friends, and neighbors came together to welcome a new life, bound together by the love they shared.

Chapter Seventeen
Echoes of Unity

Morning sunlight streamed through the bakery windows as Sadie and Hannah arrived together, slipping into their familiar rhythm. The scent of flour and sugar filled the air as they mixed dough, kneaded, and prepped trays for the oven, each motion as natural as breathing.

Emma arrived a little earlier than expected, looking fresh and ready despite the busy day ahead. Hannah's face brightened as she saw her friend. "Good morning, Emma! Take a seat, let me bring you your favorite tea, and you can visit with us while we get things started here."

Emma smiled, taking a seat at a cozy table near the counter as Hannah brought over a steaming cup of tea. "Thank you, Hannah. Starting the day here feels perfect before diving into council meetings."

Sadie grinned as she folded a batch of dough. "And we're glad to have you! Yesterday was such a whirlwind—history, treasure hunts, baby celebrations. Almost feels like we're in the middle of a storybook."

Hannah chuckled, dusting her hands off before moving to check on a tray of cinnamon rolls in the oven. "And I think you just nailed our bakery's secret ingredient—comfort."

Emma wrapped her hands around the warm tea mug, relaxing into the bakery's welcoming atmosphere. As Sadie kneaded dough, her gaze shifted to Hannah, excitement in her eyes.

"Girls, we haven't had a chance to catch up," she began, looking both shy and thrilled. "I need to tell you about my second date with Gabe."

"Oh, I've been waiting to hear!" Hannah said, leaning in with interest. "What happened?"

Sadie's cheeks flushed as she continued kneading. "It was perfect. He took me to Town Square, he and the guys put up lights, a sound system played Michael Bublé... We ate, we danced, the whole thing. It just felt right." She paused, a soft smile on her face. "I think I love him."

Hannah gasped, clapping her hands together in delight. "Sadie! That's amazing! Does he know?"

Sadie glanced at Emma, who was watching with a warm smile. "I think he feels the same way. But there's so much going on right now with the treasure hunt, and I want to solve this mystery before I can fully focus on us. And, geez, this was just our second date, it's too soon to say 'I love you,' isn't it"

Emma placed a comforting hand on Sadie's shoulder. "Real love will wait for the right moment, Sadie. You're following your heart and doing what matters most to you, and that's what counts."

Hannah nodded as she arranged a fresh batch of muffins in the front display. "Exactly! And I've seen how Gabe looks at you ... when we were line dancing the other night, he only had eyes for you."

Sadie's face softened, feeling the encouragement from her friends as she placed finishing touches on the pastries. She returned to kneading, adding thoughtfully, "I think you're both right. I just hope Gabe knows how much he means to me, even if my focus is on this hunt for now. Oh, and in other news, his parents are coming for a visit next. I'm so nervous, they want to meet me."

"How exciting! I can't wait to meet his parents. As great a guy as he is, they have to be really special. Don't be nervous, they're gonna love you," Emma responded, sipping her tea.

As she kneaded, Sadie's excitement grew, and she turned to Hannah, a spark in her eye. "Oh! And there's something else I have to tell you—Gabe and I found a new clue last night at the end of our date."

Emma, intrigued, leaned forward, her tea forgotten for the moment. "A clue? What did you find?"

Sadie glanced at them both, her cheeks flushed with excitement. "So, after our dinner in Town Square, we looked up, and the full moon was casting this huge shadow of the Oak tree right across Town Hall. And in the shadow, there was... a shape, like something hidden on the building itself. It felt like a sign that the hunt might end right here in Town Square, with that oak tree and Town Hall."

Hannah gasped, her eyes widening. "Are you serious? That's incredible! I can't believe the moon would reveal a clue like that!"

Emma shook her head in amazement, her voice soft. "It's as if the town itself wants you to find this treasure, Sadie. What are the odds Captain Morgan and Henry saw a full moon as the town was being built and set it all up for us to find now?"

Sadie laughed, the thrill of the discovery lighting her up. "It sure felt like that. Gabe and I are getting close, I can feel it. But now, of course, we're both focused on this until we get to the bottom of it."

Hannah nodded, placing a fresh tray of cinnamon rolls in the front display. "You have to see this through. And Gabe seems just as excited as you are—if anyone can solve this, it's you two."

As Sadie worked on arranging muffins and pastries, she added quietly, "Honestly, I think I'm falling in love with him. But I need to focus on solving this mystery first so I can really give this new relationship my full attention."

Emma reached out, giving Sadie's arm a reassuring squeeze. "True love will wait, Sadie. And what you're building with Gabe will only grow deeper through this shared adventure."

Hannah gave Sadie an encouraging nod. "Exactly! And Gabe knows how much this hunt means to you, so he'll be right there by your side, no matter what."

The conversation shifted back to the cozy, comforting rhythm of the bakery as Sadie and Hannah moved through their morning tasks. Emma took a deep breath, savoring the aroma of the cinnamon rolls Hannah had just brought to the front.

"I shouldn't, but..." Emma's eyes sparkled, taking a deep breath, catching the warm scent of the cinnamon rolls. "Give me one of those fresh cinnamon rolls. It smells way too good to pass up."

Sadie chuckled, plating a roll for her friend. "For you, anything. You can't run council meetings on an empty stomach, anyway."

Emma took a blissful bite. "I'm convinced this is exactly what I need to make better town decisions. Who knows—maybe the council will agree with everything I say if I show up smelling like cinnamon."

As the three friends shared a laugh, the morning unfolded around them, filled with warm pastries, quiet conversation, and the comfortable flow of friendship. In that cozy bakery, surrounded by scents of cinnamon and sugar, they each felt ready for the day ahead.

***

Emma leaned back in her office chair, exhaling with satisfaction. The council meeting had gone better than she'd hoped. Most council members, having spent their entire lives in Carter's Creek, had grown up with the same rumors and stories about the town's founding. To her relief, they shared her view: this was a part of their history to be proud of—no shame, no regrets. The town's hidden legacy was something to honor and preserve.

Across from her, Mr. Jenkins sat, nodding in agreement as they recounted the council's response.

"I have to say, Emma," he began with a warm smile, "it's a blessing to see everyone so unified. They're ready to protect this piece of history, as they should."

Emma nodded. "Absolutely. And now, we've got some work to do in that basement if we're going to uncover whatever's been hidden down there. I took the liberty of arranging a dumpster and a mobile shredding service." She glanced out the window, where the two trucks had just pulled up outside Town Hall. "They've just arrived, right on time."

Emma glanced at the hallway, where several workers from the town maintenance department stood by, ready to get started. She turned back to Mr. Jenkins, handing him a clipboard with the outline of their plan.

"I'll leave you in charge of the project, Mr. Jenkins. Anything of no value can go straight to the dumpster. Old records that don't need to be kept should be shredded, and anything worth preserving can be lined up along the hallway for now."

Mr. Jenkins took the clipboard with a determined nod. "Sounds like a solid plan, Emma. With all the help we have, I think we can clear out the room by the end of the day. It's high time we uncover what's been sitting behind those piles for so long."

Emma smiled, feeling a renewed sense of purpose. "Agreed. I'll be down later to check in, but I trust you'll have everything under control."

Mr. Jenkins gave a salute, his eyes gleaming with the same excitement she felt. "Time to get to work, then."

With that, he headed down the hall, clipboard in hand, and called the maintenance workers to attention. In no time, the team had started their work, the sounds of boxes shifting, paper rustling, and old furniture being hauled out filling the air. Each step brought them closer to the hidden room, the secrets it held, and the history it would soon reveal.

Emma stood at her office window, watching the process begin. There was an energy in the air—a sense of unity and shared purpose—as the town came together to rediscover its past.

***

Sadie, Gabe, Lily, and Maya sat around the table at the back of the bakery, their notes and clues spread out like pieces of a puzzle, each with its own story and mystery. They began sorting through everything, organizing the clues in the order they'd found them, hoping that the sequence would offer some insight.

"Before we begin, there's a good update from the Town Hall," Gabe began. "The Town Council are all in and authorized moving forward with the search. Emma and Mr. Jenkins believes the room will be emptied by close of business today. Unfortunately, that's when my shift at Southern Roots begins, so if you're all good with it, let's plan to meet up there tomorrow morning, and hopefully we'll find something more!"

ECHOES OF UNITY

The ladies all nodded in agreement, and Sadie immediately texted Hannah to ask her to cover Sadie's Sweet Rolls tomorrow. She was really going to owe Hannah some time off after this was all over. And, as an afterthought, she texted Luke and Emma to let them know about their plans to begin the search in the Town Hall the next morning.

"All right," Sadie said, flipping to the beginning of her notebook. "Let's go over everything, one clue at a time."

Gabe started, "First, there was Captain Morgan's last journal entry about *The Treasure's Rest*. At the time, we didn't know what it meant, but it guided us in the beginning, but not all of it made sense at the time – I'm still trying to figure out the last part – 'the sun at dusk will point your way, a single beam where gold does lay' – huh, Sadie, do you reckon what we saw from the full moon light the other night might be this exactly?"

Sadie's eyes widened, her mind racing as she considered Gabe's question. "The single beam... maybe the moon's light was showing us where we need to be, just like the journal hinted the sun does. I don't think we would have seen that, if we hadn't just turned off all those twinkling lights, it was like a spotlight from the tree to the Town Hall."

Maya starts placing markers, attaching the clues that led to that destination, on the map. "This should help us see where we've been and where we are going clearly."

"Ah, with that in mind, we saw a picture in the Town Archives, of Captain Morgan and Henry Whitmore, standing near where the Old Mill is, and we saw 'where the trees in twin formation stand,' so that's how we decided to search, the Old Mill, Sadie reminded, and Maya added those words to the Old Mill on the map.

"Right," Gabe said, leaning forward. "Then, in the Old Mill, we found the next journal with that riddle: 'Beneath the watchful gaze of the ancient tree, where light meets shadow, the path shall be. Seek the place where brothers convene; there lies the legacy unseen.' That's what led us to the Masonic Lodge."

Sadie nodded. "And at the Lodge, we found the key and the map etched on the stone. The map led from the Masonic Lodge to the Town Hall, that's significant. Still don't know what the key unlocks, but it feels like we're getting close."

"Then we reached the marker near the weeping willows," Maya added, reading from her notes. "'To uncover the treasure you seek, start when the sun shifts to shadows, through windows to the world, where light meets the hidden path.' Wow, guys, that sounds like what you saw in the Town Square at the end of your date."

Lily chimed in. "I concur, Maya, it feel like all these clues led to what you saw in the moonlight—the Oak tree's shadow cast by the full moon on Town Hall. I hope that means it's right there in the center of town. I've been on these hunts so many time in the past few years, and so often, when we think we're almost done – we just find one more clue that leads us on. I'm hopeful this time, though, because all signs are leading there!"

Gabe nodded, a grin forming as he thought it over. "So, we're close to the end of this. The Oak tree, Town Hall, and the shadows—maybe all of these are signals that we're exactly where we need to be."

Lily leaned forward, her voice dropping slightly. "And I have news about Ethan. He called last night, asking for Maya and I to join him in the Outer Banks. He's convinced he's about to find the treasure out there."

Gabe burst out laughing. "Oh, that's perfect. I heard my parents and their friends have been planting fake clues and evidence to keep him tied up there. Looks like it's working."

Sadie chuckled, shaking her head. "I don't think he'll be back anytime soon, then. But with him out of the way, we have a clear path to see this through."

"So here's the plan," Gabe said, outlining their next steps. "Tomorrow morning, then. We'll meet at Town Hall, dressed for demolition. We have to break through that wall to find what's behind it. Let's hope this finally leads us to Captain Morgan's legacy. Sadie, bring the key, hopefully it will be useful tomorrow."

With the plan set, they gathered their papers and notes, each of them feeling the weight of history and the thrill of discovery.

***

As dusk settled over Carter's Creek, a soft golden light filtered through the basement windows of Town Hall, casting warm shadows across the bustling scene. Emma, Luke, Daniel, Tom, and Mr. Jenkins stood shoulder to shoulder, overseeing the last few steps of clearing out the storage room. The hallway outside was lined with boxes, stacked high with old furniture and stacks of records awaiting further review.

Inside, the room that had once been a chaotic jumble of forgotten town history now stood empty, its walls and floors cleared and open. There was a quiet energy in the space, as though it held its breath, ready to reveal whatever secrets it had kept hidden for so long.

Mr. Jenkins wiped a dusty hand across his forehead, his gaze scanning the empty room with a look of satisfaction. "Well, we did it. All that's left is to see what the morning brings."

Daniel gave a nod, his voice soft with pride. "Tomorrow's the day. After all these years of hearing whispers and rumors, we'll finally see if there's any truth to them."

Luke clapped a hand on his father's shoulder, grinning. "Invited or not, I think we'll all be here bright and early, work gloves ready."

Emma laughed, glancing around at the group. "I wouldn't have it any other way. This is part of our town's story, and I can't think of better people to uncover it with."

Tom chuckled, adjusting his hat. "Seems fitting that we're all here for this. And I have a feeling it's going to be something we'll remember for a long time."

Mr. Jenkins nodded, a hint of excitement in his eyes. "Well then, it's settled. Tomorrow, we'll come back, prepared to do whatever it takes to unlock the secrets of this room."

The group shared a silent look of understanding, each of them filled with a sense of promise and purpose. They knew that whatever they uncovered would be a part of Carter's Creek's legacy, a piece of history that would bind them together. As they left the basement, the empty room remained behind, ready to reveal its mysteries to those determined enough to find them.

Chapter Eighteen
Breaking Barriers

A NEW MORNING DAWNED over Carter's Creek, bathing the historic Town Hall in warm, golden light. The early hour had not deterred the dedicated group that gathered outside, each carrying a mixture of tools, coffee mugs, and expressions of excitement. Emma, Luke, Gabe, Sadie, Hannah, Linda, Tommy, Lily, Maya, and Mr. Jenkins exchanged glances and grins, feeling the energy of the moment as they prepared for what lay ahead.

Emma unlocked the Town Hall's front doors, and they made their way to the basement with a collective sense of purpose. The basement was dimly lit, its walls lined with old wooden shelves and forgotten relics of Carter's Creek's past. Dust hung in the air, stirred by the movement of so many people, and each step echoed with an almost reverent anticipation. Today, they hoped, they would uncover the next chapter of the town's history.

"Well, here we are," Luke said, rolling up his sleeves and setting his tools down. "Let's get to work."

The group began to organize themselves, with Gabe, Tommy, and Luke taking the lead on the demolition, while the others cleared space and set aside anything that might be important. Each hammer strike and chisel blow rang out with purpose, filling the basement with the sounds of eager effort. Bits of old plaster and brick fell away, revealing layers beneath the surface as they worked, their determination unshaken.

After nearly an hour of effort, Tommy wiped his brow, exchanging a look with Gabe. "Feels like we're making progress, doesn't it?"

"Definitely," Gabe replied, his voice carrying a hint of excitement. "We're getting close."

Finally, as the last pieces of the outer wall crumbled away, they stepped back, expecting to see an open space. Instead, they were met with a much more formidable sight: another wall, this one reinforced with thick stone and plaster, and at its center, an ornate door unlike anything they'd seen in the building.

The door was set deep into the wall, its frame carved with intricate designs that looked almost as if they were etched in centuries past. Its surface was weathered yet beautiful, with curling vines and symbolic patterns running along the edges, like a portal meant to keep secrets safe. An iron lock, heavy and adorned with a finely crafted emblem, held the door firmly shut.

Sadie's eyes widened as she reached out to run her fingers along the carvings. "This...this is incredible. It's like a piece of history standing right in front of us."

Emma moved closer, her expression a mixture of awe and frustration. "It's so secure. We can't just break it down, not without risking damage to the door or whatever's behind it."

Mr. Jenkins, who had been studying the door in silent contemplation, nodded. "This isn't just any wall. Whoever built this was protecting something important. We're going to have to rethink our approach."

Luke knelt beside the door, examining the lock closely. "I've never seen one quite like this. It's not just old; it's intricate. This lock was designed to keep people out."

Hannah leaned in, tilting her head as she studied the carvings along the frame. "There's definitely more to this door than meets the eye. These patterns look like they might be telling a story... or hiding another clue."

Frustration settled over the group as they took a step back to assess their options. They had come so close, only to be met with another barrier, one that required more than brute force to overcome. The tools they had brought were suddenly inadequate, and the sense of urgency they had felt now mingled with an unspoken sense of respect for the task at hand.

"We've got to be careful," Luke said finally, rising to his feet. "This door might be the only way in, and we could end up ruining something important if we try to break it."

Gabe nodded, his expression thoughtful. "Agreed. Let's regroup, figure out how to approach this without damaging anything."

Emma took a deep breath, trying to steady the surge of disappointment. "We'll find a way. If Captain Morgan went to these lengths, there has to be a key or a method to unlock it without breaking it down."

As the group stood in the quiet basement, facing the unexpected obstacle, their frustration was tempered by a renewed sense of purpose. The door, with its ancient carvings and steadfast lock, seemed to challenge them to dig deeper, to respect the mystery that lay beyond. This wasn't just a treasure hunt anymore—it was a journey through history, one that demanded patience, cleverness, and, perhaps, a little luck.

***

The group stood in silent awe before the door, each detail drawing them in: intricate carvings covered the wood, vines and symbols interwoven with the faded elegance of a forgotten era. The iron lock gleamed dully in the dim basement light, a steadfast guardian hinting at the historical importance of what lay beyond. As they stepped closer, their faces were a blend of fascination and frustration.

Emma ran her fingers along the edge of the door. "This is no ordinary door. Look at the craftsmanship. It's like something you'd see in a historic manor. Mr. Jenkins, could this be older than the Town Hall itself?"

Mr. Jenkins squinted at the carvings, nodding. "It's possible. This could predate the building. Whoever constructed this intended it to be hidden and protected. We have to be careful."

Sadie, eyes locked on the carvings, shook her head thoughtfully. "There's something here... I can feel it. I think we're missing something right in front of us."

Luke stepped back, studying the framework around the door. "Let's check for keyholes or compartments—anything that could give us a way in without risking damage."

As they searched the door's surface, Sadie traced a familiar symbol carved into the wood. "This symbol... It's the same one we've seen in Captain Morgan's journals. He used it to mark significance, like a treasure map."

Gabe, sensing the rising frustration, attempted to lighten the mood. "Alright, folks, maybe we need to say the magic word—'please.' Or perhaps the door's waiting for a compliment. You're looking great for your age, Mr. Door."

The group chuckled, but the lightheartedness quickly faded as the search continued fruitlessly. After a few more tense minutes, Hannah noticed a small recess near the bottom left of the door.

"Look here!" she called out, crouching down. "There's something—it might be a keyhole."

Gabe, heart racing with renewed excitement, pulled out the ornate key they had discovered in the hidden compartment at the Masonic Lodge. He took a deep breath and slid it into the keyhole. For a moment, they all held their breath, watching as he tried to turn it.

Nothing.

He jiggled it, pulled it out, and tried again, but the key stubbornly refused to budge.

Sadie crossed her arms, her frustration barely contained. "It's got to be the right key, Gabe. Why isn't it working?"

Gabe sighed, slipping the key back into his pocket. "Looks like this door has other plans. We're so close... but something's still off."

Emma exchanged a tense glance with Mr. Jenkins. "If this key doesn't fit, there's either another key, or... maybe something we haven't figured out yet in the carvings."

The room fell into silence as the weight of their challenge set in, their excitement dampened by the realization that this was going to be much more complicated than anticipated.

***

The group stood around the ornate door, their energy waning as the reality of their situation settled in. An hour of searching had yielded no new insights. Each carving and crevice had been examined, but no mechanism, no hidden compartment, and no key seemed to fit.

Gabe sighed, checking his watch with a frown. "I hate to do this, but I'm officially late for my shift. If I don't get over to Southern Roots soon, Tom will have to cover for me, and that won't make him happy with me."

Sadie reached out to squeeze his arm. "It's alright, Gabe. We'll take a breather too, and then maybe circle back with some fresh ideas."

Mr. Jenkins nodded, removing his glasses to clean them as he gave Emma a resigned look. "Sometimes, stepping back is the best way to gain clarity. Perhaps after we rest a bit, we'll have a new idea to follow."

Emma agreed reluctantly, "Maybe Gabe's shift could work in our favor—taking a break together might help us brainstorm better than staring at this door. But I'll admit, I'm not ready to split up just yet. How about we all head over to Southern Roots and keep Gabe company while he's working?"

Luke perked up, nodding in agreement. "That's the best idea I've heard all day. And knowing Gabe, he could use some familiar faces around while he stews over this."

The group chuckled, the atmosphere lightening just a little as they turned to leave the basement. They filed out of Town Hall together, the afternoon sun casting long shadows over the steps as they lingered, each of them feeling the weight of the unsolved puzzle.

Emma gave a quick nod. "Alright, let's head over and give Gabe some much-needed support. Maybe a round of cheese fries and a bit of laughter is exactly what we all need right now."

With that, they set off down the street together, hopeful that a little camaraderie would spark the breakthrough they needed.

***

At Southern Roots, Gabe was already behind the bar, polishing glasses with a focused, somewhat frustrated energy. The familiar hum of the tavern usually felt comforting, but tonight, he couldn't shake the nagging feeling that the group had been so close, only to hit yet another wall.

As he lined up the last few glasses, he noticed a familiar group filling up the tavern's entrance. Sadie, Emma, Luke, Tommy, Mr. Jenkins, Linda, Lily, Maya, and Hannah were filing in, grins on their faces as they made their way to his bar.

"Look who decided to join me," Gabe chuckled, surprised and grateful. "Couldn't get enough of the door-watching business, or what?"

Sadie leaned over the bar, eyes twinkling. "What can we say? No one wanted to sit home stewing about it. We'd rather be here, bothering you."

Tommy nudged Gabe playfully. "I don't know about you all, but I say we turn this whole frustration fest around. Why not dance it out, loosen up a little?"

Linda's eyes sparkled with mischief as she caught the eye of the tavern's server, motioning for her to queue up something lively on the jukebox. Moments later, "Fishin' in the Dark" began to play, the twangy, upbeat tune pulling the whole group into the tavern's small dance floor.

Gabe laughed, setting his bar towel down and nodding to one of his coworkers to cover him. He held out his hand to Sadie, giving her a wink. "Care to dance, Miss Whitmore?"

She accepted, laughing as he spun her out onto the floor. "I thought you'd never ask, Mr. Hunter."

Emma, Luke, Linda, and the rest soon joined in, the group losing themselves to the rhythm, the tension easing with every step and laugh.

Gabe found himself in sync with Sadie, grinning as he watched Tommy trying to keep up with Linda's energetic moves, and Luke holding Emma close, laughing as she spun him unexpectedly.

When "Fishin' in the Dark" ended, Tommy threw an arm around Gabe's shoulder, grinning. "Not a bad way to end a frustrating day, right? And don't worry, friend—we'll crack that mystery soon enough."

Gabe nodded, catching Sadie's gaze. "Yeah, we will. Just gotta take it one step at a time."

As another upbeat tune started, the group dove back into dancing and laughing, leaving the frustrations of the day behind them, at least for the night. For now, they had each other, and that was enough.

Chapter Nineteen
A Town United

Gabe's heart lifted as he spotted his parents, Lee and Rachel, waving enthusiastically from the edge of Carter's Creek's bustling main street. Their faces lit up with joy, and he couldn't help but smile back, momentarily forgetting the treasure hunt and the wall of mystery he'd left unsolved at Town Hall.

"Gabe!" Rachel enveloped him in a warm hug, her eyes filled with pride. "It's so good to be here. And look at you—our own adventurer, all settled in Carter's Creek!"

"Hey, Mom, Dad." Gabe's tone was relaxed, but his mind was already jumping to his friends. Sadie and the others were probably gathering to plan their next steps, but it felt wrong to rush this moment. "I can't wait to show you both around."

Lee clapped him on the shoulder. "We're here to see it all. Show us your world—and that includes meeting this famous Sadie we've been hearing about."

Gabe chuckled, scratching the back of his neck. "She'll meet us later. For now, let's get some coffee at Dew Drop Inn, and I'll catch you up on everything."

They spent the morning wandering through Carter's Creek, stopping by landmarks, shops, and his favorite local spots. Every time his phone buzzed with an update from Sadie, he felt that tug back toward the hunt but tried to stay focused on the time with his family. His parents' excitement about the town's charm, paired with their endless questions about the treasure, kept him grounded in the moment.

By lunchtime, they'd walked nearly every street in town, and Gabe's phone vibrated with a new message from Sadie: *No new updates here, so enjoy your parents. We're all just taking it easy today, keeping the energy up for when you're ready to jump back in.*

Gabe relaxed, pocketing his phone with a grateful smile. "Mom, Dad, you've got a lot of Carter's Creek to see. And if you're up for it, there's a great tavern here I think you'll love."

The treasure hunt could wait another day.

***

Linda, with her notebook open and pen poised, took a deep breath, glancing around the table. "Alright, ladies," she began, with a sparkle of excitement in her eyes. "Let's get down to business. This baby shower is going to be our first official Southern Charm event—and we're going to make it absolutely perfect for Emma."

Sadie leaned back with a grin, clearly happy to see Linda in her element. "Lead the way, Linda. You know Emma better than anyone when it comes to style."

Linda smiled, jotting notes as she spoke. "So, we'll start with the basics. I'm thinking a color scheme of soft pinks and greens, with just a touch of gold for that classic feel. Light and airy but still elegant—just what Emma loves."

Mary clapped her hands in agreement. "That sounds beautiful, Linda! And for flowers, I know the florist can do peonies, roses, and a touch of eucalyptus for that fresh, green look."

Linda nodded, her pen moving swiftly. "Perfect! We'll arrange those in small, mixed vases across the tables. And speaking of tables, I'm thinking white linens with pink runners and a few gold accents."

Hannah jumped in, her enthusiasm contagious. "And for games! What do we think? I thought a 'Guess the Baby Traits' game could be fun, like guessing if the baby will have Luke's eyes or Emma's smile."

"Oh, that's a fantastic idea, Hannah!" Linda agreed, jotting it down. "And I thought we could have a message board where everyone leaves notes or advice for the new parents. That way, they have something to look back on later, kind of like a little time capsule of love."

Sadie smiled as she listened, feeling the warmth of friendship and excitement in the room. "What about food, Linda? I was planning a mix of sweet and savory bites. Mini quiches, finger sandwiches, cupcakes, and a beautiful cake as a centerpiece."

Linda beamed. "Perfect, Sadie. Your baking is already legendary around here! For drinks, I was thinking a signature mocktail station and maybe some infused waters. Emma's favorite lemonade, too, of course."

They all exchanged glances, picturing the layout of the baby shower, and Linda's vision began to take shape with every detail.

"And what about favors?" Mary asked, clearly delighted by how the plan was unfolding.

Linda thought for a moment, then nodded decisively. "How about little potted succulents or herbs? Something that grows, symbolizing new life—Emma's going to love that!"

The women murmured their agreement, and Linda looked around the table, her voice softening. "This is a special moment for Emma and

Luke, but it's also special for us. We're her village, her support, and we're going to make this a celebration she'll never forget."

Sadie reached over, giving Linda's hand a squeeze. "You're going to make Southern Charm the best event planning business in Carter's Creek. And, honestly, I don't think anyone else could pull off an event quite like you."

Linda, touched, smiled back. "Thank you, Sadie. Now, let's make this baby shower one for the books."

As they wrapped up the shower planning, Hannah leaned forward with a playful smirk. "Alright, so... Sadie, what can you tell us about Gabe and you! "

Sadie blushed, laughing as she glanced around the table, realizing she wasn't getting out of this. "When we started this search, we were only friends, and we are still friends. But, two dates later, I'm hoping we're becoming something more."

Linda raised an eyebrow, a teasing smile on her face. "Well, his parents are here to visit ... and I'm sure you are one of the reasons for their visit!"

Sadie laughed. "Well, no pressure, right?!?s I'm meeting them tonight at the church potluck, and I'm feeling ... nervous. The treasure hunt is the most important thing happening with us right now, I think all of this ... may be premature."

The table erupted in laughter, and Mary shook her head with a smile. "Sadie, no worries, relax and enjoy them. Knowing Gabe, we know they're good people."

Hannah grinned, winking at Sadie. "It's a lot harder the deeper you are in the relationship when meeting the parents. Right now, they're just nice people you'll hang with for a week."

Sadie's blush deepened, but she couldn't hide her grin. "This is the first time I've ever felt like this, I hope I don't embarrass Gabe."

Linda chuckled, sharing a knowing look with the others. "Girl, they are gonna love you! No worries."

Mary patted Sadie's hand, her voice warm. "You're a part of our family too, Sadie. And I think Gabe's parents can see just how special you are to him."

Sadie smiled, her heart full as the women continued to chat, each of them sharing in her happiness as eagerly as they planned for Emma's. The friendship, support, and light-hearted teasing filled the bakery, leaving Sadie feeling grateful—and maybe just a little more ready for whatever her future with Gabe might hold.

***

In the cozy warmth of the church's fellowship hall, the Carter's Creek community bustled with excitement. The smell of homemade casseroles, fresh bread, and sweet desserts filled the air as families gathered around tables, chatting and sharing stories. Lee and Rachel, Gabe's parents, were the guests of honor, and the evening quickly became a blend of laughter, reunion, and good-hearted gossip.

Pastor Daniel and Mary moved through the crowd, warmly introducing Lee and Rachel to everyone. Linda, Mary, and Hannah made their way to a table where several neighbors had already gathered, each holding plates piled with food and grins that hinted at more than just potluck cheer.

Linda, eager to share her progress, couldn't contain her excitement. "Emma's baby shower is coming together beautifully!" she announced, earning an enthusiastic cheer from the group. "We're going classic, elegant, with some fun, modern touches. Mary's homemade cupcakes will be there, and Hannah's going to make sure everyone has a great time with the games."

As they chatted, someone from the next table leaned over, chuckling. "So, is this baby shower going to be bigger than the treasure hunt, or what?"

"Oh, don't worry," Sadie laughed, "we're not giving up on the treasure. It's just...on hold for a bit. Gabe's got his hands full with his parents in town, and we can't let him miss out."

A neighbor nodded, nudging Linda. "Well, with Gabe's parents here, things must be getting serious between him and Sadie, don't you think?"

Linda, ever the organizer and supporter, couldn't resist a playful grin. "I'd say so. Sadie's practically part of their family now, and it's only been a couple of days!"

Sadie laughed, trying to deflect some of the attention, though she was clearly touched. "Well, I'm just happy they like Carter's Creek. Lee and Rachel are wonderful people, and...yes, it's been special to get to know them."

Meanwhile, the conversation turned to Ethan's latest escapade. "I heard he's still down in the Outer Banks, chasing down ghost clues," someone said with a smirk. "Guess the treasure's not coming home with him anytime soon."

"Knowing Ethan, he'll keep at it until he's dug up every beach dune from here to Cape Hatteras," another neighbor added with a chuckle.

The whole room erupted in laughter, and even Rachel and Lee, who had overheard the chatter, shared amused glances. Lee spoke up, "Well, if Gabe's got the town's support, I think he's on the right path."

Pastor Daniel, overhearing the conversation, joined in with a smile. "We'll let Ethan keep digging in the sand while the real treasure hunters are right here in Carter's Creek."

The room buzzed with anticipation and speculation about the baby, the treasure, and the enduring community ties that bound everyone together. As the evening carried on, the joy of being together felt like a treasure in its own right, one only a small, close-knit town like Carter's Creek could truly understand.

***

As the evening settled in, Gabe sat with his parents in the cozy living room of his house, a small fire crackling in the fireplace. The night air was cool, a gentle reminder of autumn creeping into Carter's Creek. Lee and Rachel had taken their seats across from Gabe, visibly relaxed after the lively potluck but clearly curious.

"So," Rachel began, leaning forward with an eager smile, "I've been hearing bits and pieces about this treasure hunt around town. Why don't you fill us in a little more? Sounds like there's quite a story there."

Gabe hesitated, choosing his words carefully. "Well, there's definitely a story," he said with a smile. "This treasure hunt is all about Captain Gabriel Morgan's lost riches. He was a Confederate officer who supposedly buried gold and other artifacts to keep them safe during the war. The clues he left behind have been hidden around town, and they're... not exactly straightforward."

Lee chuckled, looking impressed. "You've been running all over town, huh? Sounds like a scavenger hunt for adults. How close do you think you are to finding anything real?"

Gabe shrugged, keeping his tone casual. "Hard to say. We've found some clues that seem promising, but it's complicated. Each time we think we're close, something new pops up. And, you know, a lot of the clues seem to hint at things that might be more symbolic than actual treasure. Like it's as much about discovering history as it is about finding gold."

Rachel raised an eyebrow. "That sounds like a lot of work, Gabe. But it also sounds like something you'd love."

He nodded, a small smile playing on his lips. "Yeah, it is. I mean, it's been great—especially with Sadie and everyone else involved. It feels like we're uncovering something important together, something that's part of the town's soul. But," he paused, the conflict evident in his eyes, "I'll admit, it's been tough balancing it all. Especially now that you two are here."

Rachel reached over and patted his hand. "We don't want to interfere, sweetheart. We'll be around for a few days, but if you need to spend time with your friends on this, we understand."

Lee chimed in with a grin. "Besides, we're not leaving until after that baby shower you've been telling us about. And I'm sure the tavern still needs its best bartender."

Gabe laughed. "Alright, you've got me there. I'm scheduled for some shifts, and I'll have a few hours each day set aside for the search. I just don't want you to feel like I'm rushing off all the time."

Rachel smiled warmly. "Gabe, we're here to spend time with you, no matter how that time looks. And besides, this town has its own charm. We're already talking about coming back soon."

Gabe's expression softened, his heart torn between his sense of duty to his family and his eagerness to see the treasure hunt through with his friends. "Thanks, Mom, Dad. That means a lot."

As they sat back, enjoying the peaceful evening together, Gabe felt a renewed determination. He'd find a way to honor both commitments—to his family and to the mystery that had brought him and his friends closer than ever. And with his parents here, he felt more supported than ever to do just that.

Chapter Twenty

At the Heart of It All

THE MORNING SUN CAST a golden hue over Carter's Creek, its rays filtering through the tall oak trees that bordered Daniel and Mary's quaint home. The air was crisp, carrying the faint scent of blooming jasmine from Mary's meticulously tended garden. Inside, the house was a haven of warmth and hospitality, the rustic wooden furniture complemented by soft, inviting cushions and delicate lace curtains that danced gently with the breeze.

Daniel stood in the kitchen, deftly arranging a platter of assorted sandwiches and freshly baked pastries on the dining table. His movements were fluid, a testament to years spent perfecting the art of hosting. Mary, her auburn hair tied back in a loose bun, was in the adjacent room, meticulously setting out bowls of fruit and pitchers of homemade lemonade. The kitchen was alive with the sounds of clinking glassware and the low hum of cheerful conversation from the living room.

The doorbell rang, and Daniel made his way to the entrance, greeting each guest with a warm smile and a firm handshake. Lee and Rachel arrived together, their youthful energy a stark contrast to the more seasoned townsfolk who followed. Tom Hunter, a tall man with a broad smile and a penchant for storytelling, was the first to enter after them. Next came Ms. Beatrice, a retired schoolteacher whose sharp wit was as renowned as her delectable pies. Mabel, the town's beloved librarian, followed, her glasses perched precariously on the bridge of her nose, and finally, Mr. Jenkins, a jovial fisherman whose tales of the creek were legendary.

Gabe's parents, Mr. and Mrs. Morgan, were among the early arrivals. They were welcomed with open arms, their eyes lighting up at the sight of familiar faces and the comforting ambiance of Daniel and Mary's home. Mr. Morgan, a portly man with a hearty laugh, immediately gravitated toward Tom Hunter, eager to hear his latest anecdote about a peculiar fish spotted in the creek. Mrs. Morgan found herself in deep conversation with Ms. Beatrice, the two women exchanging recipes and reminiscing about old town gatherings.

As the guests settled into the living room, the atmosphere was one of relaxed camaraderie. Laughter bubbled from every corner, punctuated by the occasional clink of a glass or the soft murmur of shared stories. Daniel moved gracefully among the groups, engaging each guest with genuine interest, while Mary floated from one conversation to the next, ensuring everyone felt attended to.

Unbeknownst to the adults, the younger members of the group—Lee, Rachel, and their friends—had discreetly stepped out earlier that morning to prepare for the treasure hunt. They had taken care of essential tasks: securing supplies, mapping out routes, and ensuring everyone was ready for the adventure ahead. Their absence was subtle, masked by the natural flow of guests arriving and the bustling activity of the gathering.

Lee and Rachel found themselves drawn to a corner where Daniel and Mary were reminiscing about Carter's Creek's rich history. The

AT THE HEART OF IT ALL   231

couple spoke animatedly about the town's early days, their voices tinged with nostalgia.

"You know," Daniel began, his eyes twinkling, "Carter's Creek wasn't always this peaceful. Back in the early 1900s, we had a bustling market right here where the house stands. Farmers from miles around would come to trade their goods."

Mary nodded, adding, "And the old mill by the river—remember that? They say there's still a hidden room beneath it, filled with secrets from those times."

Lee leaned in, his curiosity piqued. "A hidden room? That sounds like something out of a storybook."

Rachel exchanged a glance with Lee, both recognizing the significance of the information. "Do you think there are still undiscovered places in town?" Rachel mused.

Daniel smiled knowingly. "Every town has its secrets. It's the history that keeps it alive, don't you think?"

Meanwhile, Gabe's parents were thoroughly entertained, their conversations with other guests flowing effortlessly. Mrs. Morgan laughed heartily at Mr. Jenkins' exaggerated tales of river adventures, while Mr. Morgan was captivated by Ms. Beatrice's detailed recounting of the town's first schoolhouse.

Tom Hunter, ever the raconteur, gathered a small group around him, animatedly describing his latest fishing expedition. His gestures were grand, his stories embellished just enough to keep his audience enthralled. Mabel, always eager to share her love for books, contributed tidbits about old manuscripts and forgotten legends that seemed to align eerily with Daniel and Mary's stories.

As the afternoon sun began to wane, the conversations naturally began to ebb, allowing for quieter moments of reflection. Lee and

Rachel found themselves alone with Daniel and Mary, the earlier hints about the town's history resonating deeply with their own plans.

"Thank you for hosting today," Lee said sincerely. "It's been wonderful getting to know everyone."

Mary smiled warmly. "We're glad you could all make it. Carter's Creek is special, and it's always a pleasure to share its stories."

Rachel nodded, her mind already racing with possibilities. "There's so much more to discover here. I feel like we're just scratching the surface."

Daniel placed a reassuring hand on Rachel's shoulder. "That's the beauty of it. There are always new adventures waiting just around the corner."

Throughout the gathering, the adults remained blissfully unaware of the young adults' absence. Their attention was fully engaged with the guests before them—discussing old memories, sharing laughs, and enjoying the delectable spread prepared by Daniel and Mary. The subtle orchestration by the hosts ensured that any hint of the younger group's whereabouts was seamlessly hidden, allowing the treasure hunt to proceed without interference.

As the guests began to depart, the house gradually quieted, the last of the laughter fading into the gentle evening sounds of the town. Daniel and Mary exchanged a satisfied glance, knowing their subtle guidance had planted the seeds of curiosity in Lee and Rachel's minds.

Outside, the young group of friends, unaware of the orchestrated gathering inside, prepared for their own adventure. The space created by Daniel and Mary had achieved its purpose, allowing the younger generation to embark on their treasure hunt with renewed enthusiasm and a deeper connection to the heart of Carter's Creek.

The sun dipped below the horizon, casting a serene twilight over the town, as the promise of discovery lingered in the air. At Daniel and

Mary's home, the night settled in with a sense of accomplishment and anticipation, the threads of community and mystery weaving together to form the tapestry of the town's ongoing story.

***

The soft afternoon light filtered through the tall, narrow windows of Carter's Creek Town Hall, casting a warm glow over the group gathered around a large oak table. Sadie, Gabe, Emma, Luke, and Mr. Jenkins sat quietly, focused on the collection of papers, photos, and maps spread out before them. The room was almost silent, save for the occasional murmur as they sifted through the clues once more, trying to find connections that may have slipped by them before.

Mr. Jenkins leaned forward, squinting at one of the documents. "Let's start by putting everything in the order we discovered it. Sometimes patterns emerge when you look at things with fresh eyes."

Gabe nodded, organizing the papers by memory. "Alright, so first we found Captain Morgan's journal, right? That mentioned 'The Treasure's Rest' and talked about dusk and shadows—our first clue that timing was important."

Emma picked up the journal, flipping through its worn pages. "And remember this line? 'Where shadows stretch long, and light fades low, look where brothers' paths did once flow.' It was right after that we found the map."

Sadie traced her finger over the map they'd uncovered at the Masonic Lodge. "This map led us to the old oak tree in the town square and the Masonic Lodge, both places where we've seen shadows cast in a specific way—like a guide."

Luke studied the map, his brow furrowed. "Every place we've been to has symbols and markers that only show up at a certain time of day. And most of those times are at dusk, right?"

Sadie nodded thoughtfully. "Exactly. Every reference to light and shadows has pointed us to dusk. But we never thought to look at the timing more carefully. Maybe this treasure can only be uncovered in a specific way, and at a specific time."

Gabe's face lit up with realization. "That's true—and remember what happened after our second date, Sadie?" He looked at her, a spark of excitement in his eyes.

Sadie's face brightened as she recalled the moment. "Yes! When we turned off the lights, we looked up, and the full moon was casting a huge shadow of the oak tree across Town Hall. Right there, on the building itself, was a shape we hadn't seen before—a shadow that seemed to line up with the designs on this map."

Luke's eyes widened, leaning forward with newfound intensity. "Wait, you're saying the moonlight created a shadow that pointed directly to the Town Hall?"

Sadie nodded, her voice full of conviction. "It was like the tree and the Town Hall were working together to show us something. Gabe and I thought it was a sign we needed to be there at a specific time—but we didn't know what."

Mr. Jenkins rubbed his chin, nodding slowly. "If that's true, we need to time this precisely. It's not just about the place; it's about being there when the light hits just right. It has to be at dusk."

Emma picked up a piece of paper with the Captain's writing, her voice thoughtful. "It keeps coming back to that line we found in the journal: *'The sun at dusk will point your way, a single beam where gold does lay.'* Maybe the sun sets at just the right angle to reveal something in the town square."

Sadie leaned back, crossing her arms as she looked at the table filled with clues. "You know, this whole search has felt like a wild goose chase at times, but now it's all starting to make sense. The Captain didn't want just anyone finding this. Whoever found it had to understand timing, patience... and maybe a bit of intuition."

Gabe grinned, glancing over at her. "Lucky for us, we have all three of those covered."

Luke pointed to a line in one of the old letters they'd found at the Old Mill. "Look at this—'The heart of the town is where legacies remain, yet only in shadow's embrace will you find what is hidden.' It's right here, too. It's always been in the town square, hidden in plain sight."

Mr. Jenkins nodded, a hint of pride in his eyes. "You've all done well, following this as far as you have. But now we know: it's about timing. If we're going to find this treasure, we'll need to be there just as the sun sets. That's when everything will align."

Emma picked up the journal again, as if seeing it in a new light. "This was more than a treasure map. It was the Captain's way of making sure that the only people who would find it would be those who valued what he did."

Sadie's face lit up with excitement. "Alright, so tonight at dusk, we'll be in the town square. We've already seen how the shadow of the oak tree lines up with Town Hall, but maybe it'll show us more if we're paying close attention. This is it, isn't it? This is our final chance."

Emma nodded, a determined glint in her eye. "Tonight, we'll be there. We've got one shot to get this right, and I say we're ready for it."

Gabe looked around at the group, his voice steady. "This is what we've been waiting for, what we've worked toward together. Tonight, we're not just chasing a legend; we're seeing it through."

With a shared look of resolve, the group silently agreed: tonight, as the sun set over Carter's Creek, they'd be there, ready to uncover the truth hidden for generations.

***

The group settled around the table in Town Hall, the weight of anticipation growing heavier with each conversation. They had poured over clues, prepared for dusk in the town square, and now, with a quiet moment to breathe, their minds wandered to what might truly be waiting for them.

Mr. Jenkins leaned back, folding his hands behind his head as he gazed thoughtfully at the ceiling. "You know," he began, his voice carrying the wisdom of someone who'd lived long enough to know a good mystery from an average one, "I keep coming back to Carter's Creek's role in the Underground Railroad. Captain Morgan might have started out on one side of things, but those letters from Eleanor—we know they had an effect on him. Maybe he ended up using his resources to help others."

Sadie leaned forward, nodding thoughtfully. "That makes sense, Mr. Jenkins. If his mind really did change because of Eleanor, he might've wanted to leave a record of the lives he helped or even a diary showing his transformation. Maybe that's his legacy to us: a record of change, of doing what's right."

Gabe tilted his head, his expression contemplative. "I wonder... what if the treasure is more than personal records? Like, what if he left artifacts—pieces of the town's history that we don't even know about? Tools, maps, even letters from other people involved in the Underground Railroad. If he wanted to show us who the town really was, it could be something that honors Carter's Creek and everyone who came through here seeking freedom."

Emma leaned her chin on her hands, her eyes bright with curiosity. "If that's what's waiting for us, we'd be discovering pieces of people's lives, right here in the heart of town. Imagine finding letters from those who passed through, their hopes and dreams preserved. It would make this town more than just a place we live in—it would be a place we're all connected to."

Luke, ever the realist but with a hopeful gleam, chimed in. "Or, it could be something even simpler. Like a time capsule that only shows up in the right light. Captain Morgan and Henry Whitmore might have left something that symbolizes their commitment to change—something small but meaningful."

Sadie smiled softly, looking around at her friends, feeling the warmth of their shared journey. "Or maybe," she said quietly, "it's a tribute to Eleanor herself. Think about it: everything Captain Morgan did, he did because of her influence. What if the treasure honors her—a marker of her life and legacy in this town, showing how love and understanding changed everything?"

Mr. Jenkins nodded slowly, his gaze drifting to the window as if he could see all the history they'd been talking about play out right there in the town square. "And you know, if it does connect to the Underground Railroad, we'd be holding something that reminds us of those who risked everything. That's not just treasure—that's an honor."

Gabe met Sadie's eyes, his smile thoughtful. "No matter what it is, we're uncovering something that matters. Not just to us, but to everyone who calls this town home. Captain Morgan, Eleanor, the people who came through this place—they're all part of Carter's Creek. And finding this, whatever it is, means carrying on that legacy."

They sat in silence for a moment, each one caught up in their thoughts, their hopes weaving together as they contemplated the legacy of Captain Morgan and what he might have left for them to find.

Emma finally broke the silence, her voice soft but filled with resolve. "We're not just looking for treasure. We're looking for understanding, for the truth about Carter's Creek. And tonight, we'll honor that legacy—together."

***

In the quiet conference room of Town Hall, the group gathered around a large wooden table, the map of the town square spread across its surface. Various tools and notes were scattered nearby, evidence of their preparations. Gabe leaned over the map, his finger tracing out the key spots for the following day, as everyone took their seats, the room buzzing with anticipation.

"Alright," Gabe began, looking around the table, "so tomorrow's the day. We'll need to have lanterns ready at these points—by the Oak tree, the steps of Town Hall, and just behind the gazebo." He tapped each location. "If we're right, shadows should fall somewhere along this line, especially as dusk approaches."

Emma nodded, leaning forward. "And if the light shifts like last time, we'll need backup flashlights. I'll bring extras for everyone. Just in case we end up searching past sunset."

Mr. Jenkins, his hands resting on his cane, added with a thoughtful smile, "Don't forget the journal and the key from the Masonic Lodge. It could be nothing, but if Captain Morgan went to the trouble of hiding it, we might as well keep it close."

Sadie nodded, her face alight with anticipation. "I'll have the journal ready, opened to the riddle: 'The sun at dusk will point your way, a single beam where gold does lay.' Every clue so far points to that line being critical. If we dim all the lights like last time, we might see something we'd otherwise miss."

Luke tapped the edge of the table thoughtfully. "Timing's going to be everything. We should meet at least half an hour before dusk. Let's set up quietly, get everything in place, and be ready to watch for any shifts in the light."

Sadie smiled, her voice soft but eager. "It feels like we're finally at the end of the path, doesn't it? All the clues—shadows, trees, the strange markings—they all lead to the town square."

Gabe nodded, but his tone was practical. "Let's make sure we're prepared for anything. I'll bring a rope and some basic tools. If there's something heavy to move or a space to reach, we'll have what we need."

Mr. Jenkins chuckled, giving Gabe an approving nod. "Good thinking. And remember, it might not be what we expect. Whether we find gold, records, or just a legacy left behind, we treat it with respect."

Emma added, "And if we do find something significant, I've been thinking it might be time we establish a small historical center in Carter's Creek. If this legacy has value, it deserves to be preserved and shared with the community."

Sadie's eyes lit up. "That's perfect, Emma. A place to share the real history of the town. We could even have a tribute to Captain Morgan's legacy and the town's role in the Underground Railroad."

Luke grinned, clapping his hands together. "Alright, then. We've got the plan, the gear, and the vision. Let's just make sure we're all here on time tomorrow. This feels like our one chance to do it right."

The group exchanged determined looks, each of them feeling the weight of the search but also the shared purpose of bringing the mystery to light. Whatever awaited them in the square, they knew that tomorrow would mark an unforgettable day for each of them and for the heart of Carter's Creek.

Chapter Twenty-One
A Shadowed Path

As the afternoon sun dipped lower in the sky, casting a warm glow over the town square, Sadie, Gabe, Emma, Luke, Mr. Jenkins, and the others arrived one by one, each carrying a sense of anticipation. They gathered in a loose circle near the Oak Tree, whose thick branches stretched out like arms over the square, casting long, sprawling shadows across the cobblestone ground. The air was thick with the quiet murmurs of the group as they settled into their roles for what promised to be a night steeped in discovery.

Emma opened the journal they'd been following, flipping to the page with the critical passage. "I still can't believe it all points to this square, here and now. Captain Morgan's words... 'The sun at dusk will point your way, a single beam where gold does lay.' Every clue, every symbol we've followed—it all leads us here."

Sadie nodded, a hand resting gently on the Oak Tree's bark as she looked around the square. "The tree, the Town Hall, even the gazebo... it's like this square was designed to keep something hidden, preserved in plain sight."

Mr. Jenkins chuckled, his eyes bright with curiosity. "Makes sense, don't you think? If you were hiding something valuable, why not put it where people pass by every day? They'd never suspect it's right underfoot."

Luke pulled out the map they'd reconstructed from the clues, laying it down on a stone bench beside him. He gestured toward a rough sketch of the square, marked with symbols they'd seen along their journey. "Look at this: every major clue—Captain Morgan's journal, the carvings on the Masonic Lodge, the key we found—they all have markings that line up right here. It's all connected to the center of town."

Gabe squinted at the Oak Tree, as if expecting it to speak. "This tree has stood here for what, centuries? It's witnessed everything—every change, every secret. It feels like it's been holding onto something all this time."

Emma, her eyes drifting to the lengthening shadows, spoke softly, "There's something sacred about this, isn't there? Like we're not just treasure hunting. We're discovering a piece of Carter's Creek that was meant to stay hidden until now."

As the light began to fade, Mr. Jenkins took out a flashlight, clicking it on briefly before turning it off. "We'll need these soon enough. Let's wait for dusk, just like the journal says, and see what the shadows show us."

Sadie glanced at Gabe, a flicker of excitement in her eyes. "Do you remember the shadow from the Oak Tree the night of our second date? How it fell against Town Hall? Maybe the timing needs to be just right for us to see the clue again."

Gabe nodded, his voice barely a whisper. "If the clues are right, then whatever we're looking for is only visible for a short time—dusk seems to be key."

Luke gathered everyone closer to review their plan. "Alright, here's the idea. We split up around the square to cover different angles. As the light fades, we'll look for anything that aligns, any shadow that falls differently or lights up. We don't move too far from the Oak Tree, and we'll check around the Town Hall and gazebo as well."

Mr. Jenkins raised his lantern, casting a warm glow on the group. "It's an honor to be a part of this with each of you. Whatever we find tonight, it's history in the making."

They all nodded, feeling the weight of his words and the legacy they were about to uncover. The last golden light faded from the sky, and a hushed quiet fell over the square as they took their positions, their eyes trained on the ancient Oak Tree and the shadows gathering around it.

***

The group fanned out across the square, each person moving slowly, their eyes trained on every nook, cranny, and crevice around the Town Hall and the Oak Tree. Gabe, his flashlight in hand, inspected the stone base of the gazebo, running his fingers along its edges, hoping for any kind of engraved symbol or hidden panel.

Sadie crouched near the roots of the Oak Tree, tracing her fingers along the bark. She squinted, catching a faint outline of a carved marking worn down by time. She leaned closer, trying to make it out. "Gabe! Emma! Come over here. I think there's something."

They hurried over, and as Gabe shone his flashlight over the tree's gnarled bark, they could make out faint symbols, half-faded, like a long-lost language that time had nearly erased.

"This looks like a mark we've seen before," Emma whispered, tracing the carvings. "Could this be another message left by Captain Morgan? It's almost like a wayfinder, something meant to guide us back here."

As they searched, Mr. Jenkins wandered around the base of the tree, spotting a small, circular indentation in the earth, barely visible among the fallen leaves. Kneeling, he brushed the soil aside and found the outline of what looked like an old stone. "Now, what have we here?" he murmured, calling over Luke.

Luke joined him, crouching down to inspect the spot. "It's almost like a stepping stone... but it's far too small for that. Maybe it marked something once?"

Mr. Jenkins chuckled. "Or maybe it's another part of the message—the Oak Tree marking the beginning and end of our search. All of these pieces, coming together right here."

Emma called out from a few feet away, "This tree must have seen so many gatherings. Look, there are even remnants of candle wax on some of the roots, as if people gathered here for something significant in the past."

Sadie nodded, standing up and brushing off her knees. "I can feel it, too. It's like the whole town has always known there was something special about this place, even if they couldn't put it into words."

The more they searched the square, the more they felt a magnetic pull drawing them back to the Oak Tree. It loomed tall, its branches stretching protectively above, each branch seemingly cradling the secrets it had guarded for generations. As they made their way back to the tree one by one, the sense of convergence became undeniable.

Gabe, glancing around at everyone, took a deep breath. "I think we all feel it. This tree is where the clues point, where everything leads."

Emma nodded, her eyes gleaming with excitement. "Captain Morgan was careful. He wanted this to be more than just a search for gold; he wanted us to understand its significance. And it all comes back to this tree, like it's been part of the town's soul from the beginning."

***

As the sun began to dip lower in the sky, the light softened, casting long shadows across the square. They watched in silence as the shadow of the Oak Tree grew, stretching across the square toward Town Hall in a striking, deliberate line. The air grew still, as if the town itself were holding its breath for this moment.

Suddenly, the shadow aligned with a specific point at the base of the Town Hall's stone wall, directly below a small, weathered plaque commemorating the town's founding. The line was sharp, clear, cutting across the ground as if someone had carefully drawn it there.

Sadie, eyes wide, whispered, "It's like Captain Morgan planned this exact moment—the sunset, the alignment. He must have known the tree would cast its shadow here."

Gabe's voice was low, filled with awe. "This can't be a coincidence. He left this for us to find, to uncover at exactly this time of day, so many years later."

Mr. Jenkins, reverent, stepped closer to the line where shadow met stone. "It's not just a marker; it's a passage of time, a story waiting to be told. We're not just here to find treasure, but to connect with the heart of Carter's Creek."

The group stood in silence, the significance of the shadow settling over them like a veil. They were on the edge of discovery, a culmination of their journey and Captain Morgan's legacy. But they also understood the importance of handling this with care.

Emma broke the silence, her voice steady. "If the treasure lies beneath the Oak Tree, we'll need to be cautious. This tree is part of our history. We can't risk its roots or its place in our town's legacy."

Luke nodded, placing a gentle hand on the trunk. "We're not just uncovering a mystery; we're protecting it. Whatever Captain Morgan left here, it's not just for us—it's for everyone in Carter's Creek, past and future."

With a shared look of determination and respect, they agreed: tomorrow, they'd carefully begin their search under the guidance of the Oak Tree's shadow, their hearts aligned with the very spirit of Carter's Creek.

***

As the shadow receded with the setting sun, the group huddled close, each member aware of the weight of what lay before them. Their discovery under the Oak Tree felt monumental, but none wanted to risk harming the town's ancient guardian in their pursuit of the past.

Emma was the first to speak, her voice steady but charged with excitement. "I think it's clear—this tree is as much a part of the treasure as whatever Captain Morgan left behind. We need to take every possible precaution before we dig."

Sadie nodded in agreement. "The Oak has stood here longer than any of us. If we're going to find anything, it has to be done with respect for the tree and its roots."

Mr. Jenkins, his gaze lingering thoughtfully on the Oak, nodded. "We'll need an arborist—someone who understands trees and can tell us exactly how to go about this without risking damage."

Emma reached for her phone, her expression resolute. "I'll make the call first thing tomorrow. I know a reputable arborist who has worked with the town on conservation projects before. I'll explain the situation and see if they can come out this week."

"Great idea," Gabe said, relief evident in his voice. "We've come this far together. Taking the time to do this right is the least we can do."

Luke turned to Mr. Jenkins, who was deep in thought. "Mr. Jenkins, are there any town approvals or permits we'll need to get started?"

Mr. Jenkins scratched his chin, considering. "We'll need clearance from the town council for any digging on public grounds, especially so close to a historical marker like this tree. I'll handle the paperwork and fast-track the approvals. Given what we've uncovered so far, I doubt anyone on the council will object."

The group shared a look of collective understanding—this was more than just a treasure hunt. They were stewards of the town's history, charged with the care of its legacy.

Emma slid her phone back into her pocket, addressing the group with a smile. "So, we'll take this one step at a time. First, we'll get the arborist's advice and approval, then we'll make a plan for the dig with minimal disruption."

Sadie beamed at her friends, pride and determination clear in her eyes. "We're going to do this right, for Carter's Creek. And whatever we find—if we find anything—it'll mean even more knowing we respected the town's roots, literally and figuratively."

Mr. Jenkins nodded approvingly. "Agreed. This treasure, whatever it may be, belongs to Carter's Creek and its future. We're just its caretakers, uncovering its story."

With their plan in place, the group felt a renewed sense of unity and purpose. They exchanged handshakes, hugs, and shared grins, each carrying the weight and pride of their task. And as they dispersed into the evening, the Oak Tree stood silent and resolute, watching over them as it always had, holding its secrets for just a little longer.

Chapter Twenty-Two
Unlocking Secrets

The morning sunlight cast a warm glow over the town square as Maggie Calloway, a tall, sturdy woman in her early fifties with sun-kissed skin and a calm, confident demeanor, approached the Oak Tree. She carried a few compact tools, a bag slung over her shoulder, and a keen, professional gaze that swept over the group waiting for her. Sadie, Gabe, Emma, Luke, and Mr. Jenkins stood in a semicircle near the tree, their faces a mix of anticipation and respect.

Maggie extended her hand to Emma, introducing herself with a friendly smile. "Good morning, everyone. I'm Maggie Calloway, certified arborist and—" she winked—"tree whisperer. I hear you've got a bit of a mystery under this beautiful oak?"

Emma shook her hand warmly. "We sure do, Maggie. This tree is significant, both to our town's history and, we hope, to what we're about to discover. We're so glad you could help us approach this in the best way possible."

Maggie nodded thoughtfully, glancing up at the towering branches. "This Oak Tree has been standing here for what looks like a few hundred years, and from what I've heard, it's pretty central to Carter's Creek's story. So, let's make sure we protect it as we work. I'll give you a clear plan to follow, step-by-step, to ensure the roots stay healthy while you dig."

Sadie stepped forward, her expression earnest. "What's the best way to get started without risking harm to the tree?"

Maggie crouched down, laying out a piece of chalk and starting to mark a line in a broad circle around the trunk. "First things first, we're setting a perimeter. This line here—" she pointed to the circle as she continued drawing it, "is where we'll start digging, just outside of it. You want to stay at least six inches away to avoid damaging any sensitive roots close to the surface."

The group nodded, watching intently as Maggie made her way around the base of the tree, completing the circle.

"Now," Maggie continued, standing up and dusting off her hands, "you're going to use small hand tools only. No shovels, no big garden forks—just little trowels and hands if necessary. Keep it slow, and dig down in shallow sections. I'd say no more than three inches at a time."

Luke glanced at his trowel with a grin. "So we're in for a long morning, then?"

Maggie chuckled. "Afraid so, but patience here will make all the difference. As you dig, keep an eye on any roots. If you encounter one, stop and don't try to move it. Just adjust your path slightly to work around it."

Gabe, leaning in with interest, raised his hand like a student with a burning question. "What if we find something that isn't a root? Like, say…a metallic object or something that doesn't feel like soil?"

Maggie smiled knowingly. "Then you call me over. But go slowly and carefully around it. Sometimes, in old sites like this, you'll encounter things from previous decades—bits of old pipes, brick fragments, sometimes even glass. Anything that feels different, just take your time and examine it closely."

Sadie nodded, taking mental notes. "Got it. And when we're done, do we fill in everything immediately?"

"Yes," Maggie replied. "Once you're sure there's nothing more in a given area, gently backfill the soil, keeping it loose around the roots. Don't pack it in too tight, and give the roots room to breathe."

Emma stepped forward, a sense of relief in her voice. "Thank you, Maggie. We really want to do this right, to honor both the tree and the history we might uncover."

Maggie gave the group an approving look. "You're on the right track. I'll be nearby, over by the benches if you need anything, but I'll leave you all to it now. This tree's been watching over Carter's Creek for centuries—whatever secrets it's holding, I'd say they're in good hands with you."

She stepped back with a wave, and after a quick nod of encouragement, she left them to the task at hand.

The group exchanged glances, each taking a deep breath as they held their trowels at the ready. With a final nod to each other, they took their places around the perimeter of the tree, prepared to start their careful, methodical dig to uncover Carter's Creek's long-buried secrets.

***

The group settled into a steady rhythm, carefully following Maggie's guidelines as they worked around the base of the Oak Tree. The atmosphere was tense but charged with anticipation; each scoop of soil removed felt like peeling back a layer of the past. They worked in near silence, occasionally sharing a glance or a nod to keep each other motivated.

Gabe wiped his brow, glancing at Sadie. "Feels like we're so close. Every bit of dirt moved feels like we're one inch closer to history."

Sadie nodded, her voice barely above a whisper. "I can feel it too. This has to be it—after all the clues, the nights spent combing through the journals. This feels...right."

Luke, a few feet away, let out a quiet laugh, though his hands trembled with the anticipation. "I never thought I'd be so invested in digging. But here we are—sweat, dirt, and mystery."

Mr. Jenkins, who had been quiet for most of the dig, suddenly stopped, his shovel poised mid-air. "Hold on," he murmured, leaning down. "I think...I think we've hit something."

Everyone froze, holding their breath. Gabe quickly moved over, kneeling beside Mr. Jenkins as he brushed away a thin layer of dirt with his hands. Beneath it, something solid and rectangular emerged from the soil, the unmistakable surface of aged wood reinforced with corroded metal bands.

As they brushed away the last bit of dirt, the full chest came into view—a weathered wooden box, banded with tarnished metal and deeply embedded in the soil. The group paused, each of them staring down at the chest as if afraid to believe what they were seeing.

As the last bits of dirt fell away, they revealed the edges of an old, wooden chest bound with tarnished metal bands. The group paused, staring down at the treasure chest as if it might vanish if they looked away.

Sadie let out a hushed, "We actually found it. Captain Morgan's treasure."

Gabe ran a hand along the rough wood, his expression filled with disbelief. "After everything, all those clues... it was right here under the Oak Tree."

Luke knelt beside Sadie, assessing the size and weight of the chest. "We need to get this somewhere safe—preferably without half the town noticing us lugging it across the square."

Emma nodded, glancing around the square. "Luke, run to Town Hall and grab a cart. We need to get this secured as soon as possible."

Without hesitation, Luke stood, brushing dirt from his knees. "I'll be right back."

As Luke jogged off, Mr. Jenkins kept an eye out while the others gently brushed dirt from the chest. Sadie whispered, a hint of awe in her voice, "This feels bigger than us. Like we're handling something sacred."

Gabe smiled, his hand still resting on the wood. "Feels like the town itself wanted us to find it."

Within minutes, Luke returned, wheeling a sturdy cart from Town Hall. Gabe and Mr. Jenkins positioned themselves at either side of the chest, lifting it slowly and setting it carefully onto the cart.

Sadie, noticing all the hole and all the dirt scattered around, speaks up, "Hey, we need to fill in these holes – no need to feed the gossip mill, plus we don't want anyone to get hurt stumbling in this hole!"

Luke secured the chest on the cart, as the others filled the hole with the freshly dug soil, tamping it down to avoid any visible sign of disturbance around the roots.

Emma gave one final look around, satisfied. "Let's get moving before we draw any attention."

The group exchanged silent nods, feeling the weight of the moment and the urgency to get the chest safely across the square and into Town Hall.

***

As they wheeled the chest through the town square, excitement buzzed through the group like electricity. The thrill of discovery was alive in each step, and every person in their little procession seemed to have a knowing grin or sparkling eyes.

Gabe nudged Sadie. "Can you believe it? After everything, here we are—practically carrying a piece of history across town."

Sadie grinned back. "I know! I feel like we've stepped right into one of those legends we grew up hearing. But this one's ours."

Luke chuckled, steadying the cart over a rough patch in the path. "Better than any tall tale I've ever heard, that's for sure."

Just as they reached the Town Hall steps, Emma suddenly stopped, clapping a hand to her forehead. "Oh, wait, the baby shower! It's tonight!"

A collective groan rose from the group, a mix of amusement and mild frustration.

"Of course, life keeps going," Sadie said, laughing softly. "And here we thought we'd get straight into uncovering the town's biggest secret."

Emma gave a sympathetic shrug. "I know, I know! I'm just as excited as you all, but my mom and Linda are already setting things up. They'll be expecting us in our Sunday best."

Gabe, a bit disappointed but trying to stay upbeat, looked at the others. "Guess that's our cue to let this sit for a bit longer. Besides, we don't want to rush the reveal."

Emma took charge, gesturing toward the heavy wooden door of the empty room in Town Hall with the impenetrable wall they'd cleared days before. "Let's lock it in here. This room is secure, and no one will bother it. We'll keep the key close."

One by one, they filed into the room, setting the chest down with a mixture of pride and reverence. Mr. Jenkins locked the door with a satisfied click.

Sadie let out a long breath, shaking her head in amazement. "It'll be hard to focus on anything else tonight."

Emma patted her arm with a grin. "We'll just have to be patient for a little while longer. Besides, tonight's special too—for Emma and Luke and the whole town."

The group exchanged determined nods, knowing that the next day would bring them right back to this room. But for now, they'd celebrate the future, knowing the past was safe and waiting, ready to reveal its secrets in due time.

***

As they secured the locked room, the group took a collective breath, stepping back to gaze one last time at the door that concealed the long-awaited treasure chest. Their excitement buzzed just below the surface, each one eager for the day they could finally open it and uncover the mystery within. But for now, another celebration called.

Emma turned to the group, her eyes alight with joy. "Alright, treasure hunters, we've got a big night ahead of us. Let's go get ready for the baby shower!"

Luke chuckled, clapping Gabe on the shoulder. "Tonight, we celebrate Emma and Sarah. Tomorrow, we dive back into history."

Sadie linked her arm through Hannah's, smiling. "I think we could all use a good evening with friends and family. Besides, it's not every day you get to celebrate the arrival of a new little one in Carter's Creek."

"Agreed," Mr. Jenkins said, his usual jovial tone tempered by a sense of respect for both the upcoming event and the chest they'd just secured. "A treasure waiting here, and a new life to welcome there. Just how it should be."

They each shared a look of contentment, excitement, and a hint of impatience. The thrill of the baby shower mingled with the promise of the treasure hunt, giving the evening a unique warmth and sense of adventure.

"Alright, let's split up and clean up," Emma said with a laugh, nodding toward Gabe's dirt-smudged sleeves and Sadie's dust-speckled cheeks. "If we show up looking like this, Linda's going to scold us all."

They all laughed, nodding in agreement as they filed out of Town Hall, the autumn afternoon casting a warm glow over the square. Each of them was buzzing with anticipation for the night's festivities, but the thought of the treasure chest waited just behind it, a steady promise of tomorrow's adventure.

With a final smile, Emma turned to the group. "See you all tonight! Let's make this a celebration to remember."

They each left, carrying the day's discoveries in their hearts and the promise of the evening ahead.

Chapter Twenty-Three
A Joyous Arrival

THE CHURCH HALL WAS transformed, bathed in the soft glow of pink and white decorations, twinkling lights, and an abundance of fresh flowers that filled the air with a gentle, floral fragrance. Handmade banners reading "Welcome, Baby Sarah" and delicate garlands of roses and eucalyptus lined the walls, each detail showcasing Linda's meticulous planning. Friends and family filled the space, their laughter and chatter adding warmth to the already inviting scene.

Emma moved through the crowd, her cheeks glowing as she greeted each guest. Every smile and hug reminded her how lucky she was to be surrounded by this community, one that had been there for her and Luke through every joy and every challenge. Luke stayed close by her side, one arm around her shoulder, his eyes shining with pride as they received endless congratulations and well-wishes.

Linda, who had been a whirlwind of activity all afternoon, finally took a moment to catch her breath, watching as guests mingled and chatted around the game tables she had set up. The games ranged from "Guess the Baby Traits" to writing heartfelt messages on little cards to place in a keepsake box for Sarah. Hannah had everyone in stitches, narrating each game with her signature humor, calling out with a grin, "Alright, everyone! Who thinks Sarah's going to have Luke's mischievous smile?"

In one corner, Mary and Pastor Daniel were proudly holding court, sharing stories of Emma as a child to anyone who would listen. "She's always been the caretaker," Mary was saying, her voice filled with love. "Sarah's one lucky little girl."

Nearby, Gabe, Sadie, and the rest of their friends gathered around the dessert table, sampling Sadie's treats with obvious delight. Gabe leaned over to Sadie, grinning as he bit into a cupcake. "You've outdone yourself, Sadie. I don't think anyone's going home without a sugar high."

Sadie chuckled, nudging him. "I'll take that as a compliment."

In the center of the room, Linda lifted her glass of pink lemonade and tapped a spoon against it, calling for everyone's attention. "Alright, everyone, can we raise a glass to Emma, Luke, and baby Sarah? May she grow up surrounded by love, laughter, and all of you—the best family anyone could hope for."

Everyone raised their glasses, voices blending in a heartfelt toast, "To Baby Sarah!"

As the evening continued, guests shared their advice for Emma and Luke. Ms. Beatrice stepped forward, a fond smile on her face. "Patience," she said, raising a finger. "It'll take you far as a parent—and just as far as a married couple."

Tommy chimed in next, grinning. "Make sure Sarah knows how to bait a fishing hook by age five. It's tradition."

The crowd laughed, and Luke pulled Emma close, whispering something in her ear that made her laugh and nod. She looked around, her heart full as she took in the faces of friends and family who had come together to celebrate their little girl before she was even born.

A JOYOUS ARRIVAL

Just then, Linda returned with a small, beautifully wrapped box. "Emma," she said softly, "this is from all of us—something for Sarah's future."

Emma carefully unwrapped the box, revealing a delicate silver locket with the initials "S.H." engraved on it. Her eyes filled with tears as she looked up at her friends and family. "Thank you," she whispered, touched beyond words.

The hall filled with applause, everyone clapping for the love that bound this small town together. As the night wore on, Emma and Luke basked in the joy, the room filled with the warmth of community, love, and the shared promise that Carter's Creek would always be home for them—and now for Sarah, too.

***

Emma was in the middle of laughing at one of Tommy's fishing stories when she felt a sudden, unmistakable shift. A warmth spread around her, catching her off guard. Her eyes widened as she realized what had just happened.

"Oh... oh my gosh," she whispered, looking down in surprise. Then, with a nervous laugh, she placed a hand on her belly and looked at Luke, her voice unsteady. "Luke, I think my water just broke."

The laughter in the room faded as those nearby heard her words. Gasps rippled through the crowd, and the hall fell into a hush as friends and family registered what was happening. Luke's face shifted from surprise to determination in a heartbeat.

"Everyone," he said, raising his voice with a hint of awe and excitement. "Looks like we're heading to the hospital. Baby Sarah's ready to make her grand entrance!"

The room erupted in cheers, and friends rushed to gather around Emma and Luke. Mary was at her daughter's side instantly, a reassuring hand on Emma's shoulder as she helped her sit down for a moment.

"Don't you worry, sweetheart," Mary said softly, her face brimming with calm confidence. "You're going to be just fine."

Linda, ever the organized one, immediately took charge. "Alright, everyone, let's get Emma and Luke to the car. Hannah, grab Emma's bag—they left it by the gift table. Gabe, make sure Luke has everything he needs."

As Hannah dashed off and Gabe checked Luke's pockets for car keys, Mr. Jenkins clapped his hands and cleared his throat. "And the rest of us? We'll take care of everything here, Luke. You just get Emma to the hospital safely. We'll secure all these gifts and clean up the hall. Don't you worry about a thing."

Emma looked around, overwhelmed with gratitude as friends handed Luke her bag, helped her steady herself, and guided her toward the door. The whole room had come together in an instant, all focused on supporting her and Luke at this unexpected moment.

Linda, her eyes filled with emotion, gave Emma a tight hug. "Go welcome that baby girl, Emma. We'll be waiting here, ready to celebrate with you all over again."

Emma managed a teary smile, squeezing Linda's hand. "Thank you all... for everything. We'll keep you posted!"

With one last look at the gathering of friends and family, Emma allowed Luke to lead her to the car. She took a deep breath, feeling a powerful wave of gratitude and love. Surrounded by her loved ones and the warmth of Carter's Creek, she felt ready to welcome her daughter into the world.

A JOYOUS ARRIVAL 261

As the car pulled away, the guests watched, waving and cheering, their hearts with Emma and Luke. Mr. Jenkins turned back to the group, clapping his hands once more.

"Alright, everyone—let's make this place sparkle. Baby Sarah's going to have a welcome like no other when they get back!"

***

The hospital waiting room buzzed with energy and anticipation as Emma's friends and family filled the space, each person trying to stay calm despite the excitement. Mary and Daniel sat close together, hands clasped tightly, while Tom paced back and forth, his usual confidence replaced by anxious restlessness.

Gabe leaned over to Sadie, murmuring, "I think Tom's done enough laps to wear down the floor."

Sadie chuckled softly. "Well, he's waited a lifetime to be a grandpa. I think he's entitled to a few laps."

Tommy, catching the exchange, leaned in with a grin. "I'd wager he's got a speech prepared already—bet it's a real tear-jerker."

Mary smiled, her gaze soft as she watched her husband, Daniel. With a deep breath, she gave his hand a gentle squeeze. "Daniel, maybe you could help everyone focus on the bigger picture with a prayer?"

Daniel nodded, his expression solemn as he stood. "I'd be honored."

The group grew quiet as Daniel bowed his head. The bustling energy of the waiting room softened as he began to speak. "Heavenly Father, we ask for your blessing tonight. Please keep Emma and Baby Sarah safe as they bring new life into the world. Give Luke strength, calm Emma's heart, and grant our family the courage to support them every step of the way. We're so grateful to be here together, waiting for this precious child."

As he finished, a soft chorus of "Amen" filled the room, the words laced with hope and gratitude.

Gabe cleared his throat, glancing around the room with a smile. "Well, I don't know about the rest of you, but Emma's always been like a sister to me. She's been there for all of us in one way or another, right? I think we're all here because she makes everyone feel like family."

Sadie nodded, leaning her head on Gabe's shoulder. "Absolutely. Emma's heart is as big as this town. Baby Sarah's going to be one lucky girl."

Tommy jumped in, unable to contain his grin. "And I can't wait to be the 'cool uncle.' I've already got her first fishing rod picked out." He winked at Tom, who was still pacing nearby. "I figure she'll be learning from the best."

Tom stopped his pacing and chuckled, giving Tommy a playful glare. "You'll have to take a number, Tommy. I've been waiting a lot longer than you for this moment."

Hannah laughed, shaking her head. "Between you two, Sarah's going to have quite the adventurous childhood."

They all fell into easy conversation, sharing stories about Emma, recounting her kindness, her humor, and the countless ways she had brought them together. Each story brought laughter and comfort, helping to ease the tension of waiting. As time ticked on, their anticipation grew, each person feeling the weight and joy of the moment as they supported one another.

Mary's eyes glistened as she spoke softly, "Emma's always had such a light. Even as a little girl, she had this way of bringing people together. And now she's bringing all of us together here, waiting for her little one."

Daniel nodded, putting an arm around his wife. "And we're blessed to witness it. Emma and Luke... they've found so much love here in this town, and tonight, they're bringing that love forward into a new life."

The room fell quiet again as everyone absorbed his words. Just then, a nurse entered the waiting room, a warm smile on her face. "Family of Emma Hunter?"

They all perked up, hearts racing.

"She's doing wonderfully, and it won't be long now. I'll be back soon with an update."

The nurse's words reignited the energy in the room. They exchanged hopeful glances, each person feeling the weight of this beautiful, life-changing moment. The wait was almost over, and they would soon welcome the newest member of their Carter's Creek family.

***

As dawn broke over the quiet hospital, casting a soft, golden light through the waiting room windows, the weary but hopeful faces of Emma and Luke's family and friends began to stir. Just as they were about to gather more coffee for another round of waiting, a nurse stepped into the room, her face lit with a joyful smile.

"Family of Emma Hunter?" she announced, her voice gentle but carrying a thrill of excitement.

Everyone looked up, barely daring to breathe.

"She's here," the nurse said, beaming. "Baby Sarah has arrived, healthy and beautiful."

A ripple of joy passed through the group, and they immediately rose to their feet, exchanging smiles, laughter, and a few misty-eyed glances. Mary's hand flew to her mouth, her eyes filling with tears of joy as Daniel wrapped an arm around her shoulders, giving her a comforting squeeze. Tom blinked quickly, clearing his throat as he ran a hand over his eyes, while Gabe, Sadie, and the others exchanged elated glances, each overcome with happiness.

After a moment, the nurse led them down the hall to Emma's room, everyone's footsteps slowed. Luke stepped out of the room, turning to the group, his face a mixture of joy and exhaustion.

"Emma and I want the grandparents to meet her first," he said gently, looking from Mary and Daniel to Tom, whose eyes brightened as he realized what this meant.

With silent nods and tear-filled smiles, Mary, Daniel, and Tom entered the room together, leaving the others waiting in a quiet line just outside. Gabe, Sadie, Hannah, and Tommy exchanged glances, sharing an unspoken understanding of this special moment.

Inside, the grandparents gathered around Emma's bed, where she held their new granddaughter in her arms. The baby's face was soft and peaceful, and each grandparent seemed to take a breath as they leaned in closer.

Mary's hand trembled as she reached out, gently touching Sarah's tiny hand. "Emma, she's... oh, she's an angel," Mary whispered, her voice breaking as she gazed down at her granddaughter. Her eyes filled with light tears, the joy too much to contain.

Daniel moved beside her, wrapping an arm around Mary's shoulders as he looked down at Sarah, a proud, soft smile gracing his face. "Emma, she's a gift," he said softly. He reached over, gently touching the top of Sarah's head, brushing a kiss to his daughter's forehead. "A true blessing to us all."

A JOYOUS ARRIVAL

Tom stood on the other side, visibly emotional as he looked down at his son, daughter-in-law, and granddaughter. "Luke, Emma... thank you for this," he murmured, his voice thick with pride and love. He leaned down, his hand cupping Sarah's tiny head. "And little one, you'll be spoiled, you have my word on that."

Emma and Luke shared a tearful smile as their parents lingered, each taking in the precious sight of Baby Sarah for the first time. Then, sensing it was time, they all shared a quick hug before stepping out to let the others in.

In the hallway, Mary wiped her eyes, giving the waiting friends a warm, emotional smile. "They want you all to come in now," she said, her voice thick with tears of joy. "Go on in, meet your girl."

Gabe, Sadie, Hannah, and Tommy walked into the room, their faces filled with excitement and awe as they moved closer to Emma, who smiled at them, her eyes shining.

"Everyone, meet Sarah," Emma said, her voice soft, yet brimming with pride and love.

They gathered around, each quietly marveling at this tiny, perfect addition to their lives, the love they all felt radiating through the room as they welcomed Baby Sarah into the heart of Carter's Creek.

Chapter Twenty-Four
Legacies Unveiled

Back in the familiar warmth of Sadie's Sweet Rolls, Gabe and Sadie settled down at one of the small tables near the window, both exhausted but buoyed by the joy of the night. The bakery was quiet, a soft morning light streaming through the windows, casting a peaceful glow over the room.

Gabe leaned back in his chair, stretching with a groan. "I don't know about you, but I feel like I could sleep for a week."

Sadie laughed softly, stirring her tea. "I'm right there with you. But... wasn't it just perfect? Baby Sarah is so beautiful, and seeing Emma and Luke like that—I don't know, it makes you feel...closer to everyone."

Gabe nodded, his face softened by the memory. "Yeah, it really does. It's like a reminder of why we're all here, why we stay in this little town and put up with each other's quirks." He grinned, reaching for her hand across the table. "And why I wouldn't want to be anywhere else."

They sat in a comfortable silence for a moment, fingers intertwined, both savoring the rare stillness. Sadie's gaze drifted to the shelves lined with flour and sugar canisters, but her mind was clearly elsewhere.

Eventually, she let out a soft chuckle, her eyes lighting up as she looked at Gabe.

"You know, I was just thinking about the chest we found," she said, a hint of mischief in her voice. "With everything that's happened, it feels like it's been a year since we dug it up. But now I'm wondering... do you think the key we found at the Masonic Lodge might actually fit?"

Gabe's eyes lit up, a spark of excitement breaking through his fatigue. "The key," he murmured, almost to himself, as if the thought had been hiding just out of reach. "Sadie, I think you might be onto something."

She nodded, her voice growing more animated. "It just makes sense, doesn't it? We've come this far—through journals, riddles, maps, and all of it leading us to that exact spot. What if the chest is the final piece?"

Gabe sat forward, his expression turning thoughtful as he considered the possibility. "You're right. All those clues, all those connections. And it would make sense that Captain Morgan would've left a key hidden somewhere equally meaningful, like the Masonic Lodge."

They shared a look, the thrill of the treasure hunt rekindled between them. "So, what do you say?" Sadie asked, barely able to hide her grin. "Shall we go see if this key unlocks one last part of the story?"

Gabe's grin mirrored hers. "I say it's time. Let's give this treasure chest a go and see what Captain Morgan left for us."

Just as Sadie and Gabe started to leave, Sadie paused, glancing at the empty display cases lining the bakery counter. In the excitement and whirlwind of the past few days, she'd completely lost track of her usual baking schedule. She gave Gabe an apologetic look, then a sheepish chuckle.

"Oh no... I just realized I haven't baked a single thing for today." She ran her hand over the counter, the absence of her usual array of sweet rolls and muffins feeling oddly out of place. "I guess I'll have to put up a 'Closed' sign. First time in a long time, but for a good reason this time."

Gabe put a reassuring hand on her shoulder, his eyes warm with understanding. "It's okay. Everyone's probably too busy talking about Baby Sarah and Emma to even notice. And honestly, Sadie, you deserve a day off now and then."

Sadie nodded, though she bit her lip, glancing around the quiet bakery. "I know. I guess it just feels strange—this place has never taken a day off." She gave a small, rueful smile, reaching for the little 'Closed' sign tucked behind the counter. "But if there's ever been a good reason, it's today. Let's go see what's inside that chest."

As she hung the sign on the door, they exchanged a look of excitement and anticipation, the mystery of the chest pulling them forward. Sadie took one last glance at the quiet bakery, then nodded to Gabe. "Alright, let's do this."

Together, they left the bakery, closing the door behind them, ready to finally unlock the secrets waiting for them.

***

As they headed out the door, Gabe pulled out his phone and quickly dialed Mr. Jenkins. After a single ring, the seasoned voice of Carter's Creek's keeper of secrets answered.

"Gabe! What's got you up so early?"

"Mr. Jenkins, Sadie and I...well, we want to try something. We found this key at the Masonic Lodge a while back, and it hasn't worked on anything else so far. We thought we might as well try it on the chest lock—just to see," Gabe explained, feeling the weight of his words and a surge of hope that he tried to keep in check.

There was a pause, then a warm chuckle. "Well now, that sounds promising! I'll meet you two there in five."

When they arrived at Town Hall, Mr. Jenkins was already waiting at the steps, keys in hand, wearing a look of anticipation mixed with curiosity.

"Come on in, you two," he said, leading them through the quiet, echoing halls of Town Hall. He unlocked the door to the storage room with a knowing smile. "I'll leave you to it—but I'll be right outside if you need anything."

Gabe and Sadie walked over to the center of the room, where the chest waited, its dark wood sturdy but softened with age. Sadie knelt down beside it, fingers running over the old metal bands, and Gabe reached into his pocket for the key, feeling its familiar weight.

"Alright," Gabe murmured, almost to himself. "Let's give this a try."

Sadie watched with bated breath as he slid the key into the lock, and to their amazement, it turned smoothly. With a soft, satisfying click, the lock released. They glanced at each other, wide-eyed, and Gabe carefully lifted the lid.

Inside, nestled within faded velvet, lay a pair of simple, elegant wedding rings, worn yet beautiful. A deep reverence settled over them both, and Sadie's hand flew to her mouth.

"These must have belonged to Captain Morgan and Eleanor," she whispered. "He kept them safe...for her."

Gabe's expression softened as he took in the rings. "His legacy—left for her, and for us to find. It's like a promise, Sadie. One that's lasted beyond a lifetime."

Just then, Sadie shifted a small cloth at the base of the chest, revealing another key, even more intricately carved than the first. Gabe picked it up, marveling at its detailed design.

"Do you think this might be…the one for the door in Town Hall?" Sadie asked, her voice filled with wonder.

Gabe looked at her, nodding slowly. "I think we're closer than ever, Sadie. We're just one step away."

The sense of discovery and the deep legacy they had uncovered hung in the air, a reminder of the love and history they were now a part of.

***

The thrill of their discovery lingered in the room as Gabe and Sadie took in the weight of what they'd found, but they both knew this moment belonged to more than just the two of them.

Gabe glanced at Sadie, already reaching for his phone. "We need to call the others. They've been with us every step of the way."

Sadie nodded, her smile growing. "Absolutely. This moment wouldn't be the same without them."

Gabe and Sadie exchanged a quick glance, and Gabe pulled out his phone to call their friends, the reality of what they'd found settling in. They needed everyone here to share in this moment.

First, he dialed Tommy, who picked up after the first ring. "Gabe, what's up?"

"Tommy," Gabe said, trying to keep his voice steady, "we opened the chest. We found something...something big. You'll want to get here."

Tommy's excitement was palpable. "On my way! Calling the girls, too!"

Gabe hung up, glancing at Mr. Jenkins, who nodded in approval as Gabe continued to make the calls. Next, Gabe dialed Emma and Luke. Luke answered, his voice a mix of fatigue and curiosity.

"Gabe, everything alright?" Luke asked.

"We did it, Luke," Gabe said, his voice full of excitement. "The chest is open. We found something we think might lead to the final step—another key, possibly for the hidden door."

There was a brief pause before Luke chuckled, his joy clear. "You're serious? This is incredible! Emma's gonna be thrilled to hear it, but...you'll have to save the details for us. We're staying put here with Baby Sarah, but we're with you in spirit."

"We'll give you the full story, I promise," Sadie chimed in, smiling. "You just focus on your girls."

As Gabe ended the call, he looked at Sadie, his excitement mirroring hers. Within minutes, Tommy, Hannah, Lily, and Maya arrived, breathless from their rush. They stepped into the room and took in the sight of the open chest, their eyes widening as they spotted the rings and the ornate key.

Tommy's grin spread wide. "Well, well. You actually did it! Captain Morgan's rings—and a key. This is next-level, Gabe."

Hannah took a step closer, eyes shining. "These rings...they must have been his promise to Eleanor."

Lily nodded, her voice full of wonder. "It's like we've uncovered a love story, not just treasure. And this key...there's only one place left it could fit, isn't there?"

They all looked toward the ornate key lying beside the rings, each of them feeling the weight of this final clue.

As Gabe and Sadie looked around the room at their friends, the excitement was undeniable. Gabe's voice was steady, but his eyes sparkled with anticipation.

"Alright," he said, gripping the ornate key tightly. "Who's ready to see if this key fits that door—right now?"

The group exchanged a glance, and a resounding murmur of agreement filled the room. Tommy clapped Gabe on the back with a grin. "You don't have to ask twice, man. Let's go open that door!"

As they approached the ornate door and wall, Gabe could feel his heart racing, the weight of the past and the mystery they'd followed pressing down on him.

Sadie, standing beside him, nodded encouragingly. "This is it, Gabe. Let's see what Captain Morgan left behind."

Gabe looked back at his friends, a smile spreading across his face. "Let's do this."

***

With everyone gathered in the dimly lit basement, Gabe took a steadying breath, the ornate key cool and weighty in his hand. Sadie stood beside him, her presence grounding him as they prepared to unlock the final mystery of Carter's Creek.

"Alright, everyone," Gabe said, turning to face the team, his voice a mixture of excitement and reverence. "This is it."

Sadie squeezed his hand before he moved forward, a silent show of support. Each step felt monumental as he approached the door, and as he raised the key, the entire group seemed to hold their breath.

In one smooth motion, Gabe inserted the key into the lock. A brief hesitation, then a soft *click* sounded, and the door swung open with a quiet, reverent creak.

A wave of awe swept over them all as they took in the hidden room. Shelves lined the walls, filled with journals, letters, artifacts, and photographs, each item a fragment of Carter's Creek's past. Lily's voice broke the silence, barely more than a whisper. "This is...incredible."

Maya nodded, her eyes wide as she took in the treasures. "It's like a window into the lives of everyone who came before us."

Mr. Jenkins stood in respectful silence, visibly moved by the legacy preserved before them. His eyes shone as he whispered, "This is history brought to life."

Sadie, her gaze sweeping over the room, felt Gabe's presence beside her more than she saw the artifacts surrounding them. The journey, the discovery, and the shared purpose had brought them to this moment. As they stood there, surrounded by the whispers of the past, she and Gabe turned to each other, both realizing the significance of what they'd found together.

Gabe gently pulled her into a warm embrace, his voice low. "Thank you, Sadie... for every step of this."

Sadie smiled, holding him close. "We did this together, Gabe. This is our story too."

As they held each other, surrounded by the legacy they had uncovered, the group around them shared in the quiet, profound sense of connection to Carter's Creek and the history they'd finally brought to light.

Chapter Twenty-Five
Love's Hidden Treasure

News of the hidden treasure's discovery and Baby Sarah's arrival spread quickly throughout Carter's Creek, igniting excitement among the townsfolk. By midday, the town square was transformed into a festive scene, brimming with vibrant fall decorations—pumpkins of all shapes and sizes nestled among bales of hay, and warm autumn leaves adorned every corner, creating a welcoming atmosphere.

Families began to arrive, each carrying dishes for a grand potluck, filling the long tables with an array of homemade casseroles, pies, salads, and other delights. The scent of warm food wafted through the air, mingling with the crisp autumn breeze.

Emma and Luke took their place near the great Oak Tree, where a soft blanket lay beneath the massive branches. Baby Sarah, wrapped snugly in a cozy blanket, slept peacefully in Emma's arms, blissfully unaware of the joyful chaos around her.

"Look at this place," Luke said, his eyes scanning the bustling crowd. "Everyone's here to celebrate."

Emma smiled, feeling her heart swell with gratitude. "I can't believe how much love there is in this town. It feels like everyone is part of our family today."

Just then, Ms. Beatrice approached, her warm smile lighting up her face. "Oh, Emma! She's absolutely precious," she said, leaning closer to admire the sleeping baby. "Just look at those little hands!"

Emma chuckled softly, gently brushing a stray hair from Sarah's forehead. "Thank you, Ms. Beatrice. She's already so loved by everyone."

Mr. Jenkins walked over next, his demeanor cheerful as he surveyed the lively scene. "This town really knows how to throw a celebration, doesn't it?" he chuckled. "And with the discovery in Town Hall, I reckon we'll be talking about this day for generations."

Mary and Daniel joined them, both beaming with pride. "Emma, you've brought so much joy into our lives," Mary said, her eyes glistening with tears of happiness. "And to think, all of this has happened in one week! A new baby and a piece of our history uncovered!"

As they spoke, townsfolk gathered around, drawn by the warmth of camaraderie and the soft coos coming from Baby Sarah. Each person took turns stepping forward, eager to congratulate Emma and Luke, offering warm hugs and heartfelt wishes.

The atmosphere was electric with excitement, laughter echoing through the square. Emma's friends and neighbors filled the space with stories, sharing memories of their own childhoods and hopes for Baby Sarah's future.

"Do you think she'll love pumpkin spice like her mom?" Luke joked, drawing laughter from the crowd.

"Of course! And maybe she'll inherit her dad's love for fishing," Mary replied, winking at Daniel.

Just then, Lily and Maya entered the square, glancing around in search of their brother. "Have you seen Ethan?" Lily asked, her brows furrowed in concern.

"No, why? Is he back in town?" Emma replied, frowning slightly.

Maya shook her head. "He heard on the news about the treasure being uncovered. He was frustrated about not being part of the discovery. He seemed genuinely upset when we spoke earlier, said he would be arriving shortly."

As if on cue, Ethan appeared at the edge of the crowd, looking perplexed and slightly out of place. His eyes darted around, landing on his sisters. They waved him over, and as he approached, the buzz of celebration fell momentarily silent, all eyes on him.

"Ethan!" Lily exclaimed, rushing forward. "You're here! You missed the big excitement!"

"How could that happen?" Ethan replied, crossing his arms defensively, a hint of irritation in his voice.

"Sadie and Gabe found the treasure!" Maya exclaimed, her excitement palpable. "And Emma and Luke welcomed Baby Sarah today!"

Ethan's expression shifted as he processed the information. "I don't understand, I was following clues! How could this happen? It was mine to find."

"Yeah, well," Lily said, her tone softer now, "it's not just about the treasure, Ethan. This is about the town and the people we care about. We're celebrating our family and community."

Ethan looked at his sisters, seeing the joy in their eyes and the love surrounding them. "I just wanted to be part of something important," he said, his voice lower, a hint of vulnerability breaking through.

"Then join us," Maya encouraged, placing a reassuring hand on his shoulder. "This is still our family. You can be part of this celebration. Let's put the past behind us and celebrate together."

Just then, the joyful laughter and chatter resumed, and Emma smiled at Ethan, who stood there, caught between his frustration and the warmth of family. "We'd love for you to celebrate with us, Ethan. There's always a place for you here."

As the crowd began to cheer and gather around, Ethan's face softened, the tension melting away. Perhaps he could let go of his frustrations for today. The warmth of the community washed over him, a gentle reminder that, while the treasure might have slipped from his grasp, the true wealth lay in the love surrounding him.

And as the afternoon sun dipped lower in the sky, the golden light cast a warm glow over the town square, illuminating the faces of family and friends united in joy, ready to welcome Baby Sarah into a life filled with love and support.

***

Sadie and Hannah busily set up a table in the town square, overflowing with an array of delectable treats from Sadie's Sweet Rolls. Mini pumpkin pies, golden-brown cinnamon rolls, and shiny caramel apples filled the table, each item more inviting than the last. The sweet aromas wafted through the air, drawing the attention of passersby who couldn't resist stealing glances at the colorful spread.

As Sadie arranged the last of the pastries, she couldn't help but glance around, searching for a familiar face. "I thought Gabe would be here by now," she murmured, her brow furrowed with worry. "He's meeting with his parents and the town attorney, but I don't really understand why. What's going on that requires all of them to talk?"

Hannah, busy tying colorful ribbons around the caramel apples, glanced up, sensing Sadie's unease. "Maybe he's planning something big for you! You know how he is when he gets an idea in his head."

Sadie rolled her eyes but couldn't entirely brush off the thought. "It just doesn't feel right. The town attorney? That seems a bit... serious.

What could they possibly need to discuss?" She glanced down the street again, her heart racing a little faster with each passing moment.

"Sadie, you're worrying too much," Hannah said, her voice reassuring. "He could be discussing something totally mundane, like town regulations or the treasure findings. And you know how Gabe is—he'll be here as soon as he can."

Sadie took a deep breath, trying to calm the storm of thoughts swirling in her mind. "I know, but I just wish I understood what's happening. What if it's something bad? What if they need to make some big decisions about the treasure or the town?"

"Just think," Hannah countered, winking as she placed the last caramel apple on the table. "He could be out there right now, plotting a grand gesture, like... a surprise date under the stars or something equally romantic."

Sadie chuckled, though it felt more like a nervous laugh. "You've been reading too many romance novels, Hannah. But a surprise wouldn't be the worst thing."

As they stood back to admire their work, the table now a masterpiece of sweet indulgence, the sounds of laughter and chatter filled the square. Sadie couldn't help but feel a rush of excitement for the celebration, even as her mind lingered on Gabe's absence.

"You know, whatever he's up to, it's probably good," Hannah reassured her, brushing a stray hair behind her ear. "He loves you, and he's probably just making sure everything is perfect for today."

Sadie smiled at her friend but couldn't shake the feeling of unease. "I just hope he makes it back soon. I want him to be here for all this."

Just then, a group of children ran past, their faces lit up with excitement as they darted toward the games set up around the square. Sadie watched them for a moment, the joy in the air contagious. She turned back to Hannah, feeling her spirits lift slightly.

"Okay, let's make sure everything is ready for when he gets here," Sadie said, her voice filled with determination, though a hint of concern remained. "No matter what he's planning, we've got a celebration to enjoy."

Hannah nodded, and they both dove back into their tasks, setting out plates and napkins while keeping an eye on the bustling crowd. With each passing moment, Sadie felt a sense of hope mingling with her worry, her heart swelling with the knowledge that, no matter what happened today, they would share it together—an unbreakable bond forged by love and the promise of new beginnings.

***

Gabe finally arrived at the bustling town square, his heart racing as he scanned the crowd for Sadie. He spotted her standing by the sweet table, surrounded by treats and laughter, but his gaze zeroed in on her. A smile broke across his face as their eyes met. She lit up at the sight of him, but before she could say a word, he gently took her hand and led her away from the festivities toward the gazebo.

The gazebo stood proudly in the center of the square, its wooden beams weathered by time and etched with the initials of Luke and Emma—a testament to love that had blossomed long before. As they stepped inside, a sense of calm enveloped them, muffling the sounds of laughter and celebration just beyond the wooden slats.

"Gabe, what's going on?" Sadie asked, a mix of excitement and confusion swirling in her chest.

He took a deep breath, glancing around to make sure they were alone, and then turned to face her, his expression serious yet tender. "Sadie, I've been thinking about this for a while now. With everything that's happened, especially with the treasure and the town's history... it's made me realize how important you are to me."

Sadie felt her heart skip a beat, her breath hitching in her throat as she watched him reach into his pocket. The world outside faded away, leaving just the two of them in their own moment.

Gabe pulled out a small velvet box, his hands trembling slightly as he opened it to reveal a stunning ring nestled inside. "This ring belonged to Captain Morgan. It was meant to symbolize a great love," he said softly, his voice barely above a whisper.

Sadie stared at the ring, feeling the weight of history in her hands. "I don't think these are ours," she whispered, uncertainty creeping into her voice.

"Wait," Gabe urged, shaking his head gently. "The town attorney confirmed that these rings were private property of the Morgan family. My parents agreed it was time for this ring to find its home—with you." He stepped closer, his gaze locked onto hers. "I want you to be part of my family, Sadie. You're the one I want to share my life with."

With trembling hands, he slid the ring onto her finger, his heart pounding as he did so. It fit perfectly, glinting in the soft light of the gazebo.

Sadie's breath caught in her throat, her eyes shimmering with emotion. "Gabe... this is so unexpected," she murmured, overwhelmed by the significance of the moment and the weight of the ring on her finger.

Gabe smiled, his expression a mix of hope and certainty. "I know it's a lot to take in, but I'm sure of this. You make me a better person, and I can't imagine my life without you in it. Will you marry me?"

Tears welled in Sadie's eyes as she looked down at the ring, then back up at Gabe. "Yes, yes! A thousand times yes!" she exclaimed, her heart soaring as she embraced him tightly.

They stood wrapped in each other's arms, the world around them fading away. In that moment, amidst the joy and celebration of the town, they had found their own piece of happiness—a promise of a future intertwined with love, history, and the enduring legacy of Carter's Creek.

***

As Sadie and Gabe rejoined the celebration, their hands entwined, Sadie's ring sparkled brilliantly in the autumn sunlight, catching the eyes of everyone around. The joy radiating from their beaming faces spread like wildfire through the crowd. Whispers turned into cheers, and soon friends and family began to gather around them, enveloping the couple in a warm embrace of congratulations.

"Did you really just get engaged?" Lily exclaimed, her eyes wide with excitement as she rushed forward to hug Sadie tightly.

"Congratulations, you two!" Maya added, her face lit with a huge smile. "You were just meant to be!"

Sadie laughed, her heart swelling with happiness. "Thank you! I can't believe this is happening!"

As they basked in the warmth of their friends' joy, they wondered over to tell Emma and Luke. They found them, sitting side by side, with Baby Sarah cradled in Emma's arms. The little one was blissfully asleep, completely unaware of the celebration unfolding around her.

"We heard the news!" Emma said, her voice filled with affection as she reached out to hug Sadie. "I'm so happy for you both!"

"Thank you! I wasn't expecting this, but ... Gabe, this couldn't have been more perfect! You keep surprising me!" Sadie replied, her eyes glistening with emotion.

As the sun dipped lower in the sky, casting a golden hue over Carter's Creek, the atmosphere buzzed with excitement and love. Friends joined together, raising their glasses in a toast to the newly engaged couple.

"To Sadie and Gabe! May your love be as strong as the roots of this town!" Mr. Jenkins called out, his voice carrying over the laughter and chatter.

The crowd echoed the sentiment, cheers erupting as they clinked their glasses together. Sadie and Gabe exchanged glances, feeling the weight of their community's support wrapping around them like a warm blanket.

As twilight settled in, the soft glow of fairy lights illuminated the town square, where a dance floor had been set up. The music began to play, and the townsfolk joined in, swaying to the rhythm of joyful melodies. Sadie and Gabe stepped onto the dance floor, and as they held each other close, they felt a deep connection to not only each other but to everyone around them—their friends, their families, and their beloved town.

"Can you believe how perfect this is?" Gabe murmured as he twirled Sadie beneath the warm lights.

"It really is magical," she replied, her heart full. "Everything feels right in this moment."

As the evening progressed, laughter and dancing filled the air, and everyone joined in the celebration of love, friendship, and the promise of new beginnings. The community danced together, the bonds of their shared history uniting them as they celebrated the joys of life and the milestones that marked their journey together.

With the sun setting behind the Oak Tree, casting long shadows across the town, Sadie and Gabe, Emma and Luke, and the rest of Carter's Creek found themselves filled with gratitude and joy. They were ready to embrace the future together, hand in hand, heart to heart, knowing that their stories were just beginning.

As the last notes of the music faded into the night, the people of Carter's Creek felt an undeniable connection—not just to each other, but to the history they cherished, the love that surrounded them, and the promise of a brighter tomorrow.

About the Author

For several decades, Judy has lovingly nurtured her family, raising two amazing kids, and now cherishes every moment as she spoils her two granddaughters with beach days and tropical adventures. A few years ago, she and her husband swapped the mainland hustle for the serene sands of Puerto Rico, creating a life filled with sunshine, adventure, and the closeness of a family that thrives together. And after 45 years of love and partnership, their story is still unfolding with as much excitement and heart as the day it began.

A love for reading was instilled in her by her mother, who took her and her two brothers to the library every week. Judy checked out the maximum number of books allowed, reading them all before it was time for their next weekly visit. As a child, Judy boldly declared, "I'm going to write books when I grow up!" And guess what? After all these years, she started writing books!

She began writing non-fiction self development books, because she knew the impact these books would have to change and better lives of others. Her first book was **Mastering Small Talk**, kicked off her *Mastering Life Series*, her second book was **Mastering Friendship**, Book 3 is all about **Mastering Personal Growth,** and Book 4 was**, Mastering Parenting Adult Kids** — continuing her journey to make not only her own dreams come true but to help others find their way to a lifestyle of continuous personal growth. Each of the books in this series can be read on their own, but if you enjoy one, you'll probably enjoy the others, too!

After successfully kicking off that non-fiction series, Judy turned to a genre she enjoys, romance novels, but wanted to write a good love story that could stand on it's own without the need for steamy sex scenes. That's exactly what's she's done with her first two books of the *Carter's Creek Love Story* series, **Love in Small Places**, and **Love's Hidden Treasures**.

Ready to reach for more? Judy's got you covered. Swing by **Judy Best.com** to dive deeper, grab a free companion workbook, and get the support you need to crush your goals. Judy is also available for coaching calls. Please follow Judy Best on Amazon, sign up for her newsletter at www.JudyBest.com to stay abreast of what's happening with the Best family!

Made in the USA
Columbia, SC
14 November 2024